*Sea Fever*

ANTONY TREW

# *Sea Fever*

ST. MARTIN'S PRESS
*New York*

Copyright © 1980 by Antony Trew
For information, write: St. Martin's Press,
175 Fifth Avenue, New York, N.Y. 10010
Manufactured in the United States of America

Library of Congress Cataloging in Publication Data

Trew, Antony, 1906-
   Sea fever.

   I.  Title.
PR9369.3.T7S4  1981    823    80-53083
ISBN 0-312-70813-0

For Nora, my wife, and John Guillaume,
owner-skipper of *New Melody*, both of whom
did so much to help

I must down to the seas again, to the
    lonely sea and the sky,
And all I ask is a tall ship and a star to
    steer her by,
And the wheel's kick and the wind's song
    and the white sail's shaking,
And a grey mist on the sea's face and grey
    dawn breaking.

John Masefield: *Sea Fever*

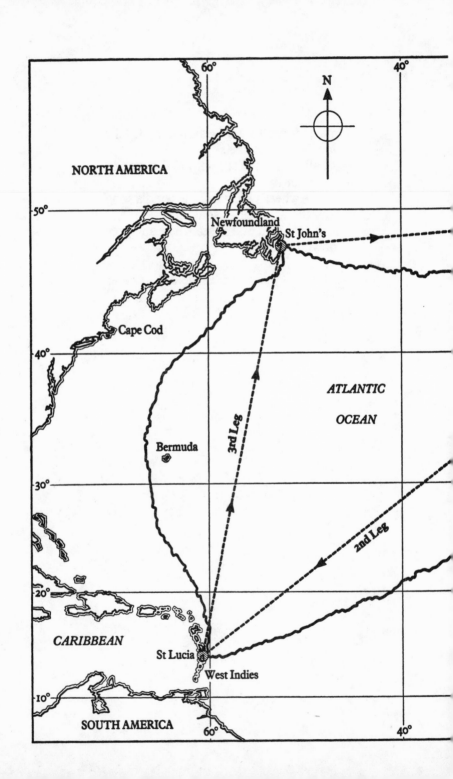

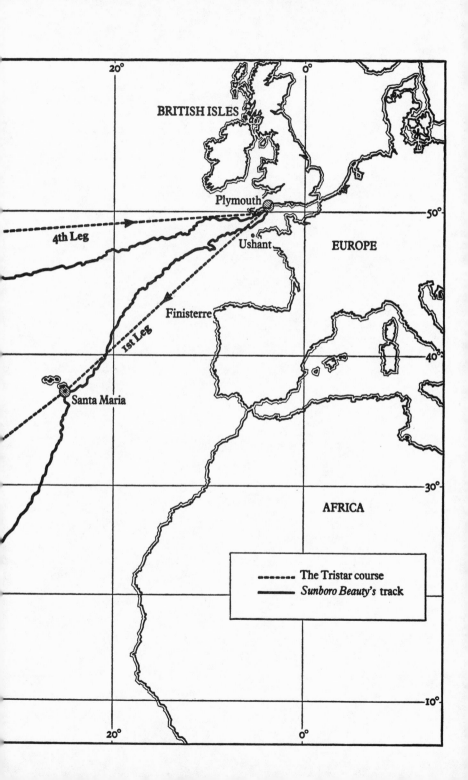

20°

BRITISH ISLES

Plymouth

4th Leg

Ushant

EUROPE

50°

Finisterre

1st Leg

40°

Santa Maria

30°

AFRICA

------- The Tristar course
——— *Sunboro Beauty's* track

10°

20°

0°

# CHAPTER ONE

It was a dark night of high wind and big seas which he could hear but not see, stinging spray, leeward rolls and lurches, water everywhere, the cockpit at times like a half-tide rock. The ketch had been broad-reaching under reefed mizzen and storm jib until midnight but as the barometer fell and the wind backed to the north-west it had blown harder and he had furled the mizzen, disengaged the self-steering, taken the wheel and run before the rising storm. Long ago he had learnt that it was wiser to reduce sail earlier rather than later. The falling barometer and the freshening wind, its gusts registering thirty-five to forty knots on the wind speed indicator, confirmed the gale warning broadcast earlier that night. They were, he estimated, about two hundred and twenty miles west-by-south of Ushant, clear of the main shipping lanes but for North Atlantic traffic bound to and from French ports. He was thinking about that when he heard the noise again – a muffled bang. Something adrift below, he decided. Probably a locker door. He would see to it when he went down.

By two-thirty that morning the wind had gone round to the west and was working up to a full gale. He set the wheel, crawled forward, using the safety harness as he went, and took in the storm jib. As a rule he didn't use the harness because it hampered his movements, but he was close to exhaustion now. The ketch's movements were so violent and unpredictable that he played safe, though it made taking in the sail a slower more cumbersome operation.

When he'd finished he went below and checked briefly that everything in the saloon was secure. He had not heard the noise again. Whatever it was must have settled itself. The ketch was lying a-hull now, beam on to the seas, and though she rolled heavily she gave to them so that the motion was

11

less violent than it had been and there was less noise. He set the alarm for thirty minutes, checked the setting on the cabin heater, removed his oilskins and seaboots, wedged himself into the bunk, secured the lee-cloth and tried to sleep.

Briefly he wondered about the other competitors, none of whom he had seen after the first day. Forty-seven yachts had crossed the starting line at Plymouth but it was the season of equinoctial gales and by nightfall the small fleet had scattered. He knew from their radio reports that a number of boats had already fallen out of the race because of weather damage. Some had been reporting their positions as he had done but others were silent, playing their cards close to their chests, he imagined. A few of these could have met with disaster – or perhaps it was no more than radio trouble. There were bound to be others in difficulty before it was all over. At least eight thousand miles of sailing ahead. He didn't care to think about that. All his energies, mental and physical, were concentrated on the first leg – the twelve hundred miles to Santa Maria in the Azores, the sailing distance closer to fourteen hundred. He thought *Sunboro Beauty* must be reasonably well placed because he'd spent most of the time at the wheel since Plymouth, leaving it only for sail changes, catnaps and essential chores. At those times he had set the wind vane and latched in the self-steering.

With strong easterly and north-easterly winds on the first two days the ketch had made excellent progress and he'd steered a better course than the self-steering could have. It had been an exhausting routine but he'd trained for it and knew it was worthwhile. Once clear of the gale and into an area of steady winds he would be able to make good use of self-steering and life would be easier.

His last thought before he fell asleep was what it almost always was on those occasions: the chances of being run down. It was one of the risks taken by single-handers and though the ketch had a radar reflector, and the deck lights on the spreaders were switched on, he knew from experience that merchant ships often kept a poor lookout, particularly when away from the land.

It was not the alarm which woke him but the banging noise he had heard earlier. Alerted, he listened. It came again, fainter this time. Somewhere in the after cabin: a locker door or WC lid? He groped his way past the chart-table and along the walkway beside the navigator's bunk to the cabin. A gurgling sound came from the heads. Christ, he thought, sea water getting in somewhere – plumbing failure? The ketch slid down the side of a big sea, heeling steeply to port. Wedged in the tiny space he waited, heard the heavy thud of water in the cockpit above him, felt the hull shudder and knew they had shipped the top of a broken sea. The ketch steadied for a moment before rolling to starboard to meet the slope of the next sea. He opened the door of the heads and saw a kneeling figure hunched over the WC bowl. For an instant he watched in shocked disbelief. Someone else on board? Impossible! It was a single-handed race. *Sunboro Beauty* had been at sea for almost forty hours.

The kneeling figure retched and the sweet-sour smell of vomit came to him.

'What in Christ's name are you doing here?' His angry shout drowned the sounds of the storm.

There was a shake of the head, another retching, a hand groping in the empty washbasin for the wet cloth which lay there. 'Oh, God. Can't you see?' came a broken voice.

For the first time he realized that the stowaway was a woman. The blue jeans, the thick woollen sweater – all his instincts about the intruder – had suggested a man.

The enormity of the offence enraged him. She had stowed away on his boat. He would be disqualified. This awful retching creature at his feet had disqualified him. He knew the rule by heart: *At no time between crossing the starting and finishing lines shall there be any person on board a competing yacht other than the entrant.*

Who would ever believe that he had not discovered her until the third day of the race? He seized a shoulder, pulled her backwards. 'You bloody bitch!' he shouted, almost incoherent with rage. 'You've disqualified me.' He realized as he said it that it was stupid, meaningless, a silly

13

understatement. She had done much more than disqualify him, she'd ruined him.

A wave hit the side with a dull thud, the ketch heeled sharply to port, the hull shivered and they shipped the top of another sea. The sprawling figure at his feet groaned, tried to sit up, slipped back and retched again; a dry retch which did no more than add froth to the rime round her mouth.

'Oh, God,' she croaked.

The absurdity of the situation returned him to his senses. There was no point in a harangue. She was a pitiful sight: lank hair tucked into the back of her jersey, the smudged face chalk-white with blue pouches under hollowed eyes; eyes as red as her dripping nose.

Do something to help her, his conscience prompted, but he resisted because it was monstrous that he should have to show sympathy of any sort. She deserved to be thrown into the sea. In the end conscience won and reluctantly he set about clearing the navigator's bunk. Before the race he had fitted battens along its inboard side to make a bin for stowing changes of dry clothing, spare sleeping bags and other soft gear. Working slowly because of the ketch's erratic movements and his own exhaustion, he took out the battens and shifted the gear and clothing to the after cabin where the starboard bunk had had built over it an extra bin for fairweather sails, and the port bunk had been converted into store lockers and racks. It was while doing this that he realized where she'd hidden. She'd evidently stretched out on top of the fairweather sail bin and covered herself with layers of Terylene which she'd unrolled from a spare bolt.

When he'd cleared the navigator's bunk he put a sleeping bag on it and went back to the heads. She was still on the floor crouched over the WC bowl. He saw that it had overflowed. She'd not used the pump. He dragged her out, pushed and pulled her along to the bunk. Her jersey was wet and smelt of vomit, but she was only half-conscious and there was nothing to be done about the jersey until the weather improved. He was wet, too, and so was a lot else. As always in bad weather there was water everywhere. Before getting her under a sleeping bag he made her eat biscuits and

14

wash down seasick pills with hot Bovril from a Thermos. He rigged a lee-cloth so that she couldn't roll out, gave her seasick bags and wedged an empty bucket on the sole beside the bunk. While doing these things with his hands, his mind tussled with the new problem. What would he do? What *could* he do? Report by radio that she was on board? That would be the end of the race for *Sunboro Beauty*. After all the sacrifices he had made, the work he'd put in? It was unthinkable. To go back now, to drop out of the race after only three days, would be humiliating. It would invite the ridicule of Tessa, of Derek Blandford and others in the office. He would look an absolute bloody fool having given up everything for nothing. It was something he couldn't contemplate. But had he any option? He was too tired and the ketch's movements were too fierce for him to answer that. He would decide during the coming day. All he wanted now was sleep. Odd snatches of thirty minutes would help. But before that he would have to mop up the mess she'd made in the heads and pump out the disposal tank.

He got more sleep than he'd expected, almost three hours in broken snatches of mostly thirty minutes. At daylight, refreshed by the rest and a mug of hot Bovril laced with brandy, he decided to go on deck. He slid open the hatch above the companionway, put his head and shoulders through and wedged himself. The sky was a dark mass of cloud racing with the storm, beneath it rolled huge grey seas streaked with lines of foam, the wind shrieking through the rigging, whipping the broken crests into flying spray.

A tangle of halyards and sheets lay around the masts and in the half-flooded cockpit. It was self-draining but there were limits to what the outlet ports could handle. Everything else looked reasonably ship-shape, including the self-steering gear which he'd always regarded as most vulnerable to heavy-weather damage. It was while congratulating himself on this that he loooked up to see a great sea racing towards him, its crest poised ominously. Before he could get down and slam shut the hatch the wave had broken on to *Sunboro Beauty*; a wall of water struck him and he clung on grimly. Seconds later he'd shut the hatch but a lot of water had gone below and was slushing about as the ketch rolled and gyrated to the pressures of the storm. Seawater was everywhere. Part of the deluge had landed on the chart-table and run off on to the girl in the navigator's bunk. She had popped her head from under the sleeping bag and called out in sudden alarm, 'What's happening?' He hadn't bothered to answer that and she'd returned to the misery of her nausea. For the rest of the morning he was busy squaring off, mopping up and pumping the bilge. It was during this time that he thought of what seemed at least the beginnings of a solution to his problem.

## CHAPTER TWO

On 10 November at noon a combination of dead reckoning and radio bearings put the ketch 260° from Ushant distant 130 miles; the drift before the south-westerly gale and the Biscay Current had evidently set them some forty miles to the east while lying a-hull. But he had little faith in DR and RDF under those conditions and treated the position as suspect.

By early afternoon the barometer was rising, the wind veering to west-nor-west, force five to six, the sea moderating with it. It was dark at four-thirty but before then he'd sorted out the tangle of sheets and halyards, exchanged the storm jib for a larger foresail, unreefed the mizzen and put the ketch on a south-westerly course. His battered spirits rose as *Sunboro Beauty* made way through the boisterous sea and once more became alive. An hour or so later he set a deep-reefed mainsail.

The girl had not left her bunk. He was relieved to be away from her and out of the saloon with its muggy wet stench. In spite of the biting wind it was good to be at the wheel again, the ketch gyrating, lurching and plunging as she fetched to windward. There was no escaping his problem, however, and the more he thought about the girl the more baffled he became. What had seemed a possible solution in the morning was by evening nothing more than a device to buy time. But he decided it was worth it if only for that.

When he'd cleared up the mess below that morning he had done some bilge pumping and drying out, and started the little Villiers two-stroke that charged the batteries. Later he got on with checking the radio. Fortunately the waterproof cover had been on when the sea flooded down the hatch and the set had not suffered. That night he called Portishead, the GPO station at Bristol which was the principal communications link for the race. In a deliberately subdued voice he reported water damage to the transmitter. While he spoke he jiggled the speak button on the handset, petering out his speech before switching off and hanging up. Portishead called him a number of times after that but he didn't reply. Next he went through the motions of working on the transmitter, though he did nothing more than remove an inspection panel and carry out a visual check. He replaced the panel, remarked in a loud voice, 'Bloody transmitter's on the blink.'

The girl stirred in her bunk, called out, 'What?' but though he'd intended his remark to be overheard he said nothing. His rage had gone but resentment was still strong and he felt for her now a cold anger which made communication difficult. When she followed up with, 'What did you say?' he again didn't answer but got on with warming up a stew, his first hot meal since Plymouth.

He was not happy about what he'd done to Portishead but at least it gave him time to think, and that was something he desperately needed. The radio station knew of the gale which he and other yachts had reported with their positions on the previous night. Portishead, having heard his feeble call peter out, would assume that the ketch's transmitter had finally thrown in its hand. They would know that he was left with nothing but the VHF radiotelephone with a range of about thirty miles. They would pass the news to Harry Billings who would be worried because reports from the ketch, regular news of her progress, of her difficulties and their surmounting, were the sponsor's dividends. Billings, PR man at Sunboro Beauty Products Ltd, had been a tremendous help and though his public relations bonhomie could be irritating, he was a capable warm-hearted man. Thinking about Billings took him back to early summer, to the very beginnings of what now seemed an ill-starred venture.

At first he had thought he wouldn't tell Tessa for a day or so but after they had finished the Chinese take-away and its accompanying bottle of wine, and made love on the settee in front of the gas-fire, he blurted it out. 'Told Derek Blandford I was packing up today. He was quite upset.'

'Packing up what, darling?' She snuggled up to him.

'The partnership. I'm leaving. Pulling out.'

She stiffened, lay still for a moment and he knew that she was bracing herself for the shock, wondering how it would affect her. 'I'm not surprised he was upset. Are you going on your own? Sure that's wise?'

'I'm going on my own, Tessa. But not in insurance broking.'

She sat up then, quite suddenly, and he remembered thinking how curiously the shape of her breasts altered when she did that.

'Going on your own, doing *what*?' There was disapproval in her voice and he knew his task was going to be difficult. He pulled her back, cradled her head in his arm. 'Listen, darling. It may sound crazy to you but it makes sense.'

She began to say something but he put his fingers over her mouth. 'Please, *please*, listen. Then tell me what you think.'

'I'll try. You know that sort of discussion doesn't work with me.'

He affected a noisy sigh. 'Please, Tessa. You want to know, don't you?'

'Of course I do.'

So he told her. Unfolded the story gently, reminded her how he had messed about in boats ever since he could remember, sketched the long period of graduation from dinghy racing to club racing in larger boats until in recent years he'd got into off-shore racing in big yachts. He emphasized that though he had been in insurance broking for years and done reasonably well, his real love was sailing.

'It doesn't provide a living, Martin,' she interrupted.

'It could do. I've never really tried except for odd delivery trips and some free-lance writing.'

'You mean those weekend and holiday trips, and the odd articles for yachting magazines? That's not real money, darling. You do it – them – because ...' She hesitated, and he knew she was choosing her words carefully, 'you love sailing and you like writing about it ... and it gives you some sort of status.' That last bit was Tessa point-scoring, but he took it because he didn't want a row and there was some truth in what she'd said. So he went on, spoke of what he regarded as his real achievements: crewing in the Fastnet, the Azores and Round Britain races. To her reproach that he had never been in a winning boat he pointed out that he'd always been in one which had finished reasonably well.

It was then that she pushed his cradling arm away. 'What's all this leading up to, Martin? What's it got to do with your leaving Blandford's?'

'Quite a lot.' Her challenging manner irritated him and his tone changed; if she wanted a row she'd get one. 'I'm entering for the TRISTAR.'

'The what?'

'The TRISTAR – it's an ocean race. British answer to the Route du Rhum. A hundred thousand pounds in prize money. Direct distance seven thousand four hundred miles. At least eight thousand miles of sailing. Upper limit fifty foot overall. T–R–I for three, S–T for saints: Santa Maria, St Lucia, St John's, turning points for the four legs. A–R for Atlantic Race. Got it?' He'd rehearsed that and was rather pleased with the result.

She said nothing, put on a wrap and went to the drinks cupboard where she fiddled among the glasses. Without

**19**

turning she said, 'Why does it mean you have to give up your job?'

'Because I'm going to enter my own boat.'

That made her turn round and stare, her face made ugly by her mood. 'You haven't got a boat.'

He looked away, nodded assent. 'I'm going to get one. That's why I'm leaving Blandford's. They'll have to buy me out. Part of the fund-raising scenario.'

'You must be mad!' She stared at him with hard, unblinking eyes, her face in what he called its bitch-witch mould. 'That will bring you ten thousand pounds, won't it? What will the boat cost?'

'Forty-five plus. It's not new but it's a bargain.'

'Forty-five thousand. My God! You *are* mad.'

'Not really. I'm going to sell this place, pay off the mortgage. That'll raise another twenty thousand. I'll borrow the rest against the security of the boat. And of course I'll try to find a sponsor.'

She looked worried then and suddenly older. 'You are quite definitely mad, Martin Savage. The only assets you've got are this place – on which you've borrowed a lot of money incidentally – and your share in the partnership. And you're going to flog all that to buy a boat?'

'That's right. As you say I've borrowed quite a lot of money on this place. A good bit of it has been spent on you, you know.' He regarded her quizzically.

For some time she stared at him in silence – he knew the symptoms – then it came in a choked voice. 'I've always known you were headstrong and ruthless, Martin, but my God I didn't think . . .' Without finishing the sentence she burst into tears and ran out of the room. He'd known that was coming too.

They had lived together for two years. It began as an arrangement of convenience. They met at a party and at once liked each other. She was newly arrived from Hampshire, had majored in English, worked as a secretary with publishers in the West End and was looking for somewhere to live. He had recently inherited the flat in Highgate, found domestic chores a bore and Tessa attractive, so he suggested she move in.

It was not long before they were sleeping together. At first this, too, was a matter of convenience; each continued to take for granted their own right to sexual freedom and no secret was made of other amorous adventures. But as time went on the relationship changed. Tessa became more possessive and he more dependent upon her. Neither wanted marriage but now other affairs were taboo. Their most powerful bond was the intensity of the sexual relationship. She was highly sexed, he average, but it worked well and more than compensated for the things they didn't share: his love of sailing which she disliked, and her's for ballet which bored him. Though his intellectual superior, she was easy to get on with, a willing aide, a cheerful companion and marvellous in bed. But all that was not enough to keep him away from what had become an obsession. In the past he'd always crewed for somebody else. Now he was determined to race his own boat, even at the risk of losing Tessa.

Thinking back it all seemed so long ago, yet it was part of the saga which had brought him to where he was at the wheel of *Sunboro Beauty*, his eyes on the sails, on the dark sky and the grey seas streaked with foam, his mind filled with images of Tessa so that he felt melancholy and alone, his conscience troubling him, telling him he had treated her badly. She had accused him of being headstrong and ruthless – so had step-mama; he was honest enough to accept that they might be right.

For the next two days the wind blew from the west at between twenty and twenty-five knots. Determined to make as much westing as possible he set more sail as the weather improved and the ketch beat steadily to windward. At noon on 12 November, his DR position put them 250 miles north-west of Cape Finisterre. In the afternoon the barometer began to rise, the wind veered to the north-west and he followed it round to a more westerly course. By using the opportunity of making to the west he was countering the Biscay Current and getting into position for the run down to the Azores when later the wind veered to the north-east as he expected it would with a rising glass.

The seas left by the gale had settled into a pattern which suited *Sunboro Beauty* and though the plunging and buffeting never ceased he had after some sail changing got her well balanced for the wind; much of the time now she was on self-steering and he managed to sleep in brief snatches. The problem the girl presented continued to baffle him. If he had found her within the first twenty-four hours he could have turned back to Plymouth, landed her and asked for permission to restart; but after forty-eight hours, plus the period spent lying a-hull, such a solution was impossible if he hoped to stay in the race. One thing was certain – he couldn't go on postponing a decision; yet he could not think of one which would enable him to remain in the race with even a remote chance of winning. So he continued to worry, to conduct a never-ending debate, while he played for time and hoped for a miracle to turn up.

The morning after the gale he had given her hot Bovril and dry biscuits and told her to get off her backside and do something unless she intended dying in her bunk. From his spare gear he had found her a second jersey, blue jeans, oilskins, neck towels and seaboots – all too big – and told her to get out of her wet clothing.

Later that morning he went below to work out a sunsight. The navigator's bunk was empty and the door of the after cabin shut, but he could hear her moving about inside. He was still working on the sunsight when she came back into the saloon. She had changed, cleaned her face, brushed back her long blonde hair and tied it with binding tape. For the first time he saw that she had good features, despite the pale, drawn face and blood-shot eyes.

'Can I go up?' She clung grimly to a companionway handrail, swaying to the movements of the ketch, regarding him with a questioning frown.

'Later.' He was deliberately brusque. 'You'd better do some explaining first.'

'Not now, *please*,' she implored. 'I'll be sick again if I stay.'

'Serves you bloody well right. What's your name?'

'Sarah Thompson. No use swearing at me. I'm here, aren't I?'

'You may not be for long.'

'Why not?'

'You could be lost overboard.'

'You wouldn't do that?' She shot him an apprehensive glance.

'The sea might.'

'You're not that sort of man.'

He ignored the remark, concentrated on the chart where he was plotting the ketch's position. Without looking up he said, 'Better explain how you came to be here.'

She made a noise halfway between a squeak and a moan, put her hand to her mouth and staggered back into the after cabin. He heard the sound of vomiting and hoped she'd reached the WC bowl in time.

'Christ!' he exploded. 'Won't someone take this bloody girl off my back?'

But in spite of the cry for help he suspected that somewhere deep in his subconscious, and in a sense without his consent, the decision had already been made. How otherwise could he explain that Plymouth was more than three hundred miles astern, with *Sunboro Beauty* still on course for the Azores.

The following day saw an improvement in the weather and once again she asked if she might go on deck.

Again he refused.

'Why?' Her voice was querulous.

'Still haven't had your explanation.'

'How could I explain? I've been too sick.'

'Right. Let's have it now.'

She told him then that she had been visiting Plymouth from London to see a boyfriend. They had gone to a disco the night before the race. She had a row with the boy friend. They left the disco and he drove her down to Millbay Docks. There the row continued. She got out of the car in a fit of rage and he'd driven off. She thought he would come back but he hadn't. She had nowhere to sleep that night and nothing but a shoulder bag. No money. She had lost her purse in the disco, Access card and all. She was exhausted, very upset, had to sleep somewhere. So she had decided on one of the yachts.

'Why mine?'

'I didn't know whose it was. It was just a yacht. A place to sleep. It was late, very dark. I saw a bearded man leave it and come up on the quay and when he'd gone I climbed down. It was lying inside another yacht where there were lights in the cabin and people's voices. I thought that would make it safer for me.'

'How d'you mean, safer?'

'Well, I didn't feel so alone sleeping by myself in this one.'

He watched her carefully before putting the next question. 'How did you get down below?'

'I opened the lid.' She indicated the emergency hatch on the after coachroof.

'It was secured on the inside.'

'No. It wasn't.'

'I wonder.' His tone implied disbelief. 'Forgetting to secure that hatch doesn't sound like Tim Baxter.'

Once on board, she went on, she had explored, decided on the after cabin because she could see it wasn't being used for sleeping and had its own WC. She had made herself as comfortable as she could on top of the sail bags, taken three Nembutal tablets and fallen asleep. 'Three knock you out, you know,' she explained.

What must have been a long time afterwards, thrown about by the violence of the motion, she woke up. She realized then that the yacht was at sea. She felt awful, dragged herself into the WC, was sick and after that took three more Nembutals. Much later – at least another day later, she thought – she'd been woken again by the ketch's plunging and bumping and the noises of the storm. Even Nembutals hadn't been proof against that. She finished her explanation with, 'You found me when I was being sick for about the fourth time. That's all.'

He looked at her with undisguised hostility, his eyes a

frozen blue, mouth set hard. She was very frightened, felt a pressing need to break the silence, to ask the obvious question. At length she did. 'What are you going to do?'

'I don't know,' he said. 'You're responsible for this. Any ideas?' Again the cold, steely look.

'Turn back,' she suggested. 'Or put me on a passing ship. One that's going back.'

'That would suit you, wouldn't it?'

She nodded. 'Yes. Of course. I didn't want to be here.'

There was a long pause after that before he said, 'Has it occurred to you to think of what you've done to *me*? What going back would mean for *me*?'

It seemed safer to say nothing, so she shook her head and looked miserable.

'It would mean abandoning the most important, exciting, worthwhile project of my life. I've sacrificed everything for this. My job, my house – other things.' He frowned. 'Christ! And you have the bloody nerve to suggest I give it all up to take you back.'

'Or put me on a passing ship.' She half whispered the reminder. He looked so furious then that she thought he was going to strike her but instead he said, 'And tell the world I've not been single-handed?' He moved closer, engaged in an absurd nose-to-nose confrontation. 'D'you really think I'd do that?'

She said nothing, shrank away.

He held her arms, shaking her. 'Answer my question.'

'I don't know what you'd do.' Her voice broke and she felt sick with anxiety. Trying not to show her fear she added, 'What will you do?'

He crossed to the other side of the cabin, leant on the chart-table, wedged himself there, head in hands. 'I don't know. I really don't know. Throw you over the side, I daresay. That's what you deserve.'

At that stage she burst into tears and he said, 'The drama bit won't help. Better forget it.'

It hadn't been an act. She was suffering from prolonged seasickness and the effects of too much Nembutal. She was weak, dehydrated and hungry.

After that he went on deck. He came down some time later and she again asked if she might go up to the cockpit. He gave her a calculating unsympathetic look. 'No. Not until you've got rid of that hair.'

'What d'you mean?'

'Cut it off.'

'No. Why should I?'

Grabbing her roughly by the shoulder, presumably to demonstrate his strength, he had given her the option of cutting it short herself or letting him do it. She could see he meant it.

## CHAPTER THREE

On 13 November he got the longitude with a sunsight in the morning, but at noon it was behind the clouds and he had to rely on dead reckoning for latitude. He entered the position in the logbook – Latitude 44°50'S, Longitude 16°30'W. After that he had a seawater shower and a shave – his first since leaving Plymouth – cooked himself a meal of tinned hamburgers, peas and potatoes, and listened to the BBC Overseas News while he ate. The washing up done, he went on deck and set about various repair and maintenance tasks which could no longer be put off. He had left the girl where she usually was; asleep, or pretending to be, in the navigator's bunk.

The barometer had continued its slow rise and before long the wind veered to the north. He took the last reef out of the mainsail, hoisted the big genoa, eased the sheets and put the ketch on a sou-sou-westerly course for the run down to the Azores; with a fresh wind blowing on the starboard quarter *Sunboro Beauty* was soon making seven knots through the water. It was warmer now and the sun shone between scattered clouds which sent dark shadows scurrying across the sea; the change in the weather, the deep silence of the ocean broken only by the hiss and slap of the sea, induced a feeling of well-being which for the time allayed his fears.

Far astern the superstructure of a northbound tanker still showed faintly above the horizon. It had passed within two miles and though he'd heard it asking him by VHF who he was he made no effort to reply. He imagined she was from the Caribbean, bound for the English Channel. They were well clear of the busy shipping lanes and it was the only ship they had sighted for some time. He had not seen any other yachts in the race since passing the Lizard on the first day, and he was reminded how soon the great spaces of the ocean could swallow forty to fifty yachts. It would be possible, he knew, to complete the TRISTAR without seeing any other competitor after that first day. While busy with these thoughts he was from long habit checking the set of the sails, easing the sheets as the wind veered further north, and comparing the readings on the windspeed and direction indicators with what his seaman's eye told him.

At noon he made the distance to Santa Maria 602 miles. They had already completed almost half the first leg, but they would soon be entering the Horse Latitudes where the winds were variable and headwinds not unlikely. He knew from their radio reports that a number of competing yachts were ahead of him, and he assumed there were others who for one reason or another were not reporting. But he was happy with *Sunboro Beauty*'s progress. His race strategy had paid off. The time spent before the start researching winds, currents and climatic conditions had been worthwhile. He had learnt from radio reports that competitors who'd not got as far to the west as he had in the earlier stages of the race were already lagging behind. The current was now with *Sunboro Beauty* and if the winds remained favourable her time to the Azores should be good.

On the mainsail high above him the black figures of the ketch's race numbers – 27 – were curiously distorted by the camber of the sails. Always superstitious, he wondered if the number had any special significance? At least it was good that a seven was there. His lucky number. The girl's voice broke into his thoughts. 'Can I come up now?' Her head and shoulders were framed in the hatchway.

He looked round the horizon. There was nothing in sight but the distant tanker. He said a reluctant, 'Yes.'

She came awkwardly through the hatchway, clutching at handrails and the cockpit coaming, slumping into a corner on the lee side.

'Get on to the other side.' He spoke sharply, pointing to windward.

She glared at him, moved over, wedged herself in the corner on the weather side and sat there looking defiantly out to sea.

There was still spray about and she was wearing the foul-weather clothing, safety harness, seaboots and blue woollen cap he had given her. But colour had returned to her cheeks and he thought she was beginning to look more wholesome. The long blonde hair had gone; now only its shorn ends jutted out beneath the cap. His brief impersonal glance concealed the satisfaction that gave him.

In the ten minutes she had been in the cockpit they'd not spoken to each other. If he wants silence he can have it, she thought – he's a swine of a man. She would never have done it if she'd known what it was going to be like. The awful discomfort, the misery of bad weather and his impossible behaviour, like the forced cutting of her hair, his refusal to let her help with the cooking – or in any other way – the veiled threats: 'If you show yourself on deck without my permission I'll throw you over the side. You'd better believe that!' He was a sadist and a bully. Monumental chip on his shoulder. Trying to compensate for some inadequacy by the exercise of authority. A bit like Carlos when things went wrong in the office.

He found her presence in the cockpit intensely irritating. It was a single-handed race and there were two people on deck. The fact that she was there emphasized the absurdity of the situation. It was just plain bloody provocative. If she hadn't been so completely insensitive she would have jumped over the side long ago. He thought he had done enough to make that a possibility though not, he assured himself, with that intention. It was simply his natural reaction to an intolerable state of affairs. After a few days on board she had asked if she could cook or do anything else to help. He had said 'no' as emphatically as he could. 'You've no right to be here,' he added. 'In fact you haven't any rights. You're a stowaway.'

At the time he'd been working on the radio, again going through the motions of trying to repair it. 'This yacht,' he continued, 'is competing in a single-handed ocean race and it's going to be sailed single-handed. I want no help from you. That includes deckwork, cooking, the lot. As far as I'm concerned you don't exist. Fend for yourself, and the less I see or hear of you the better.'

'Can I cook for myself?' She gave him a look, searching and uncertain.

'No. You're not to touch the stove. Or any of the food stores. If you do it'll be at your own risk.' He had not known quite what that warning meant, but it was intended to frighten her. From her expression he thought it had.

'So I'm to starve,' she said defiantly.

'You haven't starved yet, have you?'

'I'm very hungry. You don't leave enough on your plate.'

'This boat is provisioned for one person for three months. The voyage could last that long if we get the wrong winds and weather. So we've enough food and fresh water for one crew for ninety days. Any ideas?'

She looked worried then. 'Catch fish?'

'Ever tried fishing from a yacht racing on the high seas? Sounds good in books, doesn't work in practice.'

She had given up, made a gesture of helplessness, and gone back to the navigator's bunk.

Well, yes, he had been brutal. Surely that was the least she could expect after what she had done to him. Of course he wouldn't let her starve. He had a heavy work load, she had none, so she didn't need as much food as he did. The boat was generously provisioned, Billings had seen to that. But with two crew the diet would have to be a lean one. Water

29

wasn't a problem. There'd be plenty of rain before the race was finished.

The phone rang and a paunchy, bearded man watching television called out, 'You take it, Dolly. Probably one of your bridge friends.'

A woman answered from the kitchen. 'Oh, blast the damn thing.' She reached the hall, picked up the phone. 'Dorothy Brownson speaking.'

A girl's voice said, 'Oh, Mrs Brownson. This is Dinah.'

Mrs Brownson liked Dinah Ferrars, who shared a bachelor flat with her daughter Victoria in the Cromwell Road. 'Hullo, Dinah, how are you?'

'Is Vikki there?'

'Victoria here? No, dear. Why?' ... Mrs Brownson, who disliked diminutives, steadfastly refused to call her daughter Vikki.

'She left about ten days ago. Said she was going down to Plymouth.'

'To Plymouth?'

'Yes. But her things are still here. I don't think she had much money with her either. I'm beginning to be just a little bit worried, Mrs Brownson.'

'Oh, God! I hope she's all right. But why Plymouth? Did she say? What about her job?'

'She left her job a few days before.'

'Left it? But Victoria loved working there. Said advertising was marvellous. Exciting.'

'I know but ... it's a long story, Mrs Brownson.'

Mrs Brownson, sensing the girl's hesitation but determined to get the story quickly, said, 'Look, Dinah, can't I come over and see you?'

'What, now?'

'Yes, dear. This is very worrying.'

'Of course. One moment.' There was a pause. She could just hear Dinah speaking to someone, and the muffled voice of a man answering. Then Dinah came back on the line. 'Yes. Do come over, Mrs Brownson. I'll have coffee ready.'

'That's very kind of you. I'll come over right away.' Mrs

Brownson hung up the phone, put on a coat and found her car keys. She looked into the living room on the way out. 'That was Dinah. Victoria has left her job and gone to Plymouth. Days ago. Left all her things with Dinah. I'm very worried, it's most peculiar.'

'I shouldn't worry, Dolly. Girls do that sort of thing nowadays. You know she's inclined to act on impulse and . . .'

Mrs Brownson didn't stop to listen. She knew that Joseph Brownson disliked his stepdaughter. They didn't get on. It was the cause of great distress to Mrs Brownson.

'Now, Dinah, tell me. What's all this about. Why did she?'

'Did you know Vikki was . . .' Dinah hesitated, 'in love with a married man?'

'You mean Carlos Flenterman?'

'Yes, so you know.'

'I gather they've been together quite a lot lately. But he's left his wife, hasn't he?'

'She left him. Now she's come back. That's the trouble. Carlos told Vikki he was terribly sorry and upset, but . . .' Dinah spread her hands and shrugged her shoulders. 'You know – the usual story. Had to think of the children. The importance of keeping the family together.'

'So he dropped Victoria,' said Mrs Brownson.

'Yes. She was shattered. Very unhappy and depressed. That was a few days before she left the job. She was his secretary, you know. It was an impossible situation. She adored him.'

'What swine men are.' Mrs Brownson spoke feelingly. 'They're always doing that.'

'I think he was very fond of her. You know these advertising men. Emotional and unreliable. Get carried away by their own copy.'

With the fingers of one hand Mrs Brownson beat an impatient tattoo on the coffee table. 'Why did she go to Plymouth of all places?'

'She said she must get away from London to think things over. We were in a pub the night before she left – we'd had a

31

few drinks by then of course – and I said why Plymouth? Just like you have. Vikki said she had an old boy friend there. Wanted to look him up.'

'Did she say who he was?'

'No. I asked her but she brushed the question aside, changed the subject. Told me that a big yacht race was due to start from Plymouth in a few days. She said, jokingly, "Be fun to be a stowaway in one of those yachts. Have a gorgeous man to oneself for weeks on end".'

'Stowaway? Victoria would never do a thing like that. She's much too level-headed.'

Dinah paused, looked doubtful: she knew Vikki to be a headstrong, determined girl. But there was no point in adding to Mrs B's worries, so she went on to explain that because they'd had a fair number of drinks and it was late at night she had treated the whole thing as a joke. They'd gone back to the Cromwell Road flat and next morning she went off to work leaving Vikki in bed. Before leaving she asked about the Plymouth trip. Vikki said she hadn't made any plans about Plymouth or anywhere else. She just couldn't make up her mind what to do. Felt terribly unsettled.

That, said Dinah, was the last she had seen or heard of her. She'd left no note, no message of any sort. 'Must've gone off more or less in the things she was wearing. Jeans, T-shirt, jersey and a shoulder bag. She took a few face things, hair and toothbrush, perhaps a spare T-shirt and panties, nothing else.'

'Do you think she's gone back to that Carlos man, Dinah?' Mrs Brownson's voice was husky; she was close to tears.

'No. I phoned yesterday. He hadn't a clue where she was. Said he was sorry and put the phone down.'

'Beast,' said Mrs Brownson.

'Typical man,' said Dinah.

The discussion went on for some time and finally they agreed that Mrs Brownson should report her daughter's disappearance to the police. Just in case all was not well.

# CHAPTER FOUR

The barometer continued to rise and the wind to veer until the morning of 15 November when it steadied, blowing force five to six. *Sunboro Beauty* ran before it with the wind almost dead astern, the big genoa and the mizzen boomed out to starboard and the mainsail to port. Under those conditions she was comfortable, lifting and dipping to the following seas with the unique motion of a ship under sail, logging between seven and eight knots for hours on end under a sky patchworked in white and blue.

The weather was much warmer now and they had at last been able to discard their foul-weather gear. Wearing nothing but shorts he stood braced at the wheel, around him the sleeping bags, blankets, pillows, jerseys, oilskins and other gear which had been laid out to dry.

The girl was wedged in a corner near him reading a paperback which she put down at times to look out to sea. Her T-shirt was tucked into blue jeans rolled to the knees and for the first time he was conscious of her figure. Grudgingly, he admitted to himself that it was not at all bad. Good legs and thighs, the bra-less breasts firm, round and slightly upturned in the manner of the Capitoline Venus.

He had a curious feeling that he'd seen her somewhere before. The face was faintly familiar; or was it simply that she looked like someone he'd met a long time ago and couldn't place? He gave up. While his eyes were on the sails, the compass and the sea, his mind was busy with a soliloquy: another instalment of the endless struggle with his conscience. Why have you stayed in the race, not reported that she's on board? he asked himself.

I'm playing for time—

How will time help you?—

Don't know really. I suppose I'm waiting for a miracle—
What sort of miracle?—
Difficult to say—
Haven't you at the back of your mind a hazy idea of what
that miracle might be?—
Well, I suppose one that meant she wasn't here—
How would she have gone?—
I don't know. It would just be that I'd wake up in the
morning and find she had gone—
But how?—
I don't know—
I think you do but you don't want to admit it. At the back
of your mind you see her falling overboard at night when
you're asleep, don't you? Perhaps the worrying thing about
that is that you would have to report it? Or would you? After
all, nobody knows she's on board—

Determined to get away from such thoughts, disliking
himself because of them, he set the windvane, engaged self-
steering and went below to work on the battery charger.

But the thoughts wouldn't go away. They hung about like
a bad smell; something unpleasant which he couldn't
pretend was not there. When he'd finished the adjustments
to the charger he went back to the cockpit and took the
wheel. The girl had gone forward and was standing on the
weather side abreast the mainmast, holding on to a shroud,
swaying as the ketch lurched and plunged.

He shouted to her to get down and come aft. She nodded,
made her way towards him, crouching, crawling, moving
awkwardly, holding on to the coachroof grab-rail with one
hand and a guard-rail with the other. At last she got back to
the cockpit and wedged herself in a corner. For a moment he
regarded her in glowering silence. 'I've told you to stay in the
cockpit or down below,' he said.

'I wanted to see what it was like there.' She threw out an
arm towards the foredeck. 'It was great.'

'Don't be bloody stupid. You haven't got your sea legs.'
He spoke with parental anger. 'You don't know how to
move about in these conditions. You must never stand up
like that. Always keep down. Next thing you know you'll be

over the side. And you're not wearing safety harness or a lifejacket.'

'Nor are you.' She was suddenly aggressive. 'Anyway I'm feeling fine now.'

'That's not the point,' he said harshly. 'While you're on board you obey my orders. Do you understand?'

She replied with a reluctant long drawn 'yes', adding with a frown, 'I'm surprised you worry about my falling overboard.'

He ignored the remark but in a strange way he was pleased she had made it. His reaction to her foolhardiness had been genuine and somehow answered his earlier attacks of conscience. She half turned her back on him, picked up the paperback and began reading. He saw that it was Clare Francis's *Come Hell or High Water* and remembered what Tessa had said.

For some time after he'd broken the news about the TRISTAR, Tessa had resolutely refused to discuss it or for that matter anything else. Suddenly cold and withdrawn, she kept him at a distance. It was when he came home from the office that Friday night, tired and worried, that she had with chilly disapproval handed him the letter from the Hamble boatyard, dropping it on the table in front of him as if it were contaminated.

When he'd read it he said, 'Good. Tim Baxter wants me to go down for a sailing trial on Sunday. She's ready.'

'*She* being the boat?' Tessa was sitting up very straight in a hardback chair, her hands clenched on her lap, her face white and strained.

'Yes. It's a month late but we've still got two months left for fitting out and tuning. That should do, though I suppose it'll be a bloody rush at the end. Always is.'

There was a short silence after which she said, 'When are you leaving Blandford and Co?'

'At the end of the month.'

'I see. And then?'

'I'll move down to the Hamble. Find digs. Tim will help. You come down and join me two weeks later when the new

35

people move in here.' He waited for her reaction, but there was none, so he went on. 'No problem getting a job there. Good secretaries are in short supply everywhere, I'm told.'

'You've got it all worked out, haven't you, Martin?'

'Somebody has to,' he said defensively, sensing the coming onslaught. 'See any snags?'

'Of course I do.' Her voice was suddenly strident. 'Don't be so stupidly insensitive.'

'I'm not insensitive. What are the snags?'

'For a start I'm not leaving London. I'll find somewhere else to live.'

It had never occurred to him that she wouldn't go down to the Hamble with him. 'You can't mean it. D'you realize we'll see just about nothing of each other if you stay in London?'

'Pity you didn't think of that before you made up your mind. Surprising though it may sound, Martin, I too have a life to lead. I'm not chucking up my job and moving to the coast just because you've gone mad.'

'I haven't gone mad.'

'Haven't you? What are your chances of winning the TRISTAR?'

'As good as most people's, I suppose.'

She laughed derisively. 'Including the superstars? The British, the French, the Americans?'

He could see that Tessa was getting into her stride; she could be devastatingly eloquent on these occasions. 'Wake up, Martin,' she went on. 'Stop dreaming. What will you use for money when the TRISTAR is over?'

Tessa being snide again, he decided. Keep calm. She's looking for a row. 'For a start,' he said, 'the yacht will be a pretty useful asset whether or not I get a place. I can earn good money with it doing charters. Apart from that I can do delivery trips, tuning and fitting out. And I'll go on writing, free-lancing – and of course there'll be the book.'

Tessa had been looking bored but that brought her back to the attack. 'What book?'

'I'm going to write a book about the TRISTAR. About my experiences in it.'

With a gesture of contempt she pushed away an invisible

36

barrier. 'Oh God, not that,' she said. 'Books about single-handers have been hopelessly overdone. The greats have all done it – Chichester, Robin Knox-Johnston, Chay Blythe, Clare Francis, Naomi James, Bernard Moitessier – plus a lot of not-so-greats. Who's going to publish a book, let alone buy one, by an unknown single-hander in yet another ocean race? Not even a round-the-worlder at that. My dear man, you should grow up.'

That finally triggered the resentment which had been building up while she delivered her lecture. 'Look, Tessa,' he said, 'your job as secretary, or whatever you call it, to an editor in a publishing house doesn't make you an authority on publishing. What you don't realize . . .' There was no point in completing the sentence because she'd gone into the kitchen, slamming the door behind her.

What she didn't realize, he'd been about to say, was that a couple of million people were keen on sailing, it was a growth industry. These were the potential readers. Single-handed ocean races over great distances were among the few remaining challenges left to man on his own against the elements.

His thoughts were interrupted by the girl's voice. 'Isn't that a ship there?'

He looked in the direction of her outstretched arm. Fine on the starboard bow the upperworks of a ship were just visible on the horizon. She has damn good eyesight, he conceded privately. 'Yes,' he said. 'You'd better go below.'

'I'd love to see it pass. Can't I stay here? So stuffy below.'

'No. You can't. Get below.'

'Why can't I ever see ships pass?'

His manner became suddenly fierce. 'Don't argue. Do as I bloody well tell you.'

She glared at him in silence before moving into the hatchway. As she went down the companion-ladder he heard her muttered, 'Christ, what a bastard.'

Not long afterwards the sound of music came up from below. Crystal Gayle singing *I'll Get Over You*. Second time she'd played it that day. What was the message? Whatever it might have been he was reminded that she was a threat to any chance he might have had of writing a book about the TRISTAR.

Or was she?

In a moment of intuition he wondered if there wasn't room for another sort of book about a single-hander in an ocean race? One with a stowaway on board?

Crystal Gayle finished her defiant melody as he focused his binoculars on the ship ahead. It had come a good deal closer now. From its lines it was a cruise ship. It called him by radiophone and lamp but he made no reply, went below and did not go back on deck again until it was well clear.

The phone on Thorold's desk rang. He picked it up. It was his secretary, Mrs Grieves.

'Detective Inspector Mitchell is here, Mr Thorold,' she said.

'Right. Show him in, please.' He looked at the wall clock: 10.20 a.m. Mitchell was punctual.

Mrs Grieves ushered in a heavily-built man whose thick, dark hair, bushy eyebrows and ample moustache dominated a rubicund face in which were set two small, surprisingly dark eyes.

Robert Thorold, senior partner in a well known firm of solicitors, and Andrew Mitchell of the Plymouth CID, had met on a number of occasions in connection with court work. They greeted each other and exchanged uncomplimentary remarks about the weather, whereafter Thorold pointed to a chair. 'Please sit down.'

'This is a semi-official call,' began the Inspector. 'I'm seeing you in your capacity as Chairman of the TRISTAR Committee.'

'So you said on the phone. I'm intrigued, Inspector. What's the problem?'

'It's not really a problem. We've had a missing-persons inquiry referred to us by Scotland Yard. Routine matter but for one aspect with which we thought you might be able to help.'

Thorold laughed. 'Gets more intriguing by the minute.

Who's the missing person?'

'It's a young woman, Victoria Brownson, unmarried, aged twenty-three, works and lives in London. Reported missing by her mother two days ago. She's been missing for close on two weeks.'

Mitchell went on to sketch in the background based on the information given by Mrs Brownson and Dinah Ferrars, both of whom had been questioned by Scotland Yard. 'We've made the usual inquiries. There's no evidence to confirm that she came to Plymouth,' said Mitchell. 'All we've got to go on is the girl's chat with her flatmate in a pub on the night before she left. She could be anywhere. British Isles, Europe, America – God knows where. Hundreds of girls pull out of London each week without letting their parents or anyone else know what they're up to or where they're going.'

'I think the stowaway angle is most unlikely,' said Thorold. 'Competing yachts are heavily stored and most of them are pretty small – nothing over fifty foot in the race. Very difficult for anyone to conceal themselves for more than a few hours, I'd say. Incidentally, each yacht is thoroughly inspected by race committee officials – and a Certificate of Acceptance is issued – before the boat is eligible to start.'

'How long before the race begins does that happen?' asked Mitchell.

'The TRISTAR inspection took place during the five days before the start. A number of boats were done each day.'

'So it would be possible for a stowaway to get on board a boat *after* the inspection?

'Yes, in theory, I suppose so,' Thorold agreed reluctantly. 'But most unlikely that she'd go undetected. We know all the competitors. They're people well established in offshore and ocean racing. If any of them had found a stowaway on board it would have been reported long ago. The rules are quite clear. A competitor who found he had someone on board would know he was disqualified simply by that fact.'

'What could he do, knowing that?' interrupted Mitchell.

'Report by radio what had happened, return to the starting line and hand over the stowaway. If he asked the Race Committee for permission to re-start it would be granted if we were satisfied with his story.'

Mitchell ran a tentative tongue along the underside of his moustache. 'If the competitor didn't discover the stowaway for a day or so he wouldn't have much chance on a re-start, would he?'

'No, he wouldn't. His alternatives then would be to accept the forlorn chance offered by a re-start or abandon the race.' Thorold fiddled with a paperknife. 'The girl has probably gone off to France in a non-competing boat. Yachtsmen are human. An attractive young woman could be a welcome addition to crew.' He smiled. 'Is your Victoria what's-her-name attractive?'

'They say she is,' the Inspector spoke casually, looking through a window at the grey wintry scene across the Sound to Drake's Island. 'Any point in sending a signal to competitors saying that a girl stowaway may be in one of the competing yachts?'

'If a competitor has her on board and has failed so far to report it, he's not going to react to that sort of signal now.' Thorold's tone was quietly emphatic. 'All you're working on is a joke remark by a half-stoned girl in a London pub. A girl who's apparently gone footloose after a broken love affair. I don't think we should take that too seriously.'

Mitchell nodded in agreement. 'As I said, it's no more than a routine inquiry but it was necessary to discuss it with you.'

'Yes, indeed. And I'm grateful.'

'Is each boat inspected at the end of the race?'

'Not every boat,' said Thorold. 'There's no handicapping. The six boats first over the line will be boarded by race officials who will carry out inspections. There are only three prizes but we inspect six boats in case any of the first three are disqualified for one reason or another. In view of what you've told me I'll see that our people carry out a particularly thorough check on this occasion. I can assure

40

you if that girl were on board she'd be detected.'

'What about the other boats?' Mitchell probed. 'The boats your officials don't board?'

'We don't inspect them,' said Thorold. 'But you could tip off Customs and Excise. They're supposed to check each boat. Pretty nominal of course.' He grinned. 'Difficult to pick up contraband during a non-stop ocean race.'

'Good idea,' said Mitchell. 'I may do that if she hasn't been traced by then. When d'you say the finish is likely to be?'

'Can't be exact, but I'd say in another sixty to seventy days.'

'Well, I'd better be getting along.' The Inspector got up. 'Fine view you have over the Sound.'

'It is good, isn't it?' Thorold left his chair, went with Mitchell to the door. 'I imagine the girl will have turned up long before that,' he said. 'A final point, Inspector. I hope this matter will be handled confidentially. In other words, may we keep it to ourselves? I'm prepared to accept responsibility for that on our side. Shan't even tell my Committee. I'd much appreciate the same undertaking from you. It would be disastrous if the media got hold of this. A great deal of money is involved in this race. Something we very much regret. We'd much rather have kept that sort of thing out of it. But the French started it last year and, well to ...' Thorold held out open hands. 'The pressure on us built up and eventually we had to give in. . . .'

Mitchell nodded sympathetically. 'There's no way of keeping money out of sport these days. Too many vested interests.'

Thorold returned to the subject. 'As I was saying, it would be disastrous if the media got hold of this story. The Race hasn't been staged for that sort of journalistic romp. It would put every competitor under suspicion. Most unpleasant. Spoil the whole thing. No one wants that. Least of all the sponsors.'

'Quite so,' Mitchell looked at him speculatively. 'She was listed in the Yard's missing-persons press notice last week as "believed to be in the Plymouth area". That's enough for the media, I'd say. I'll see that we treat it as confidential.'

Thorold opened the door, held out his hand. 'Well, thank you for consulting me about this, Inspector. Should I hear anything relevant you may be sure I'll let you know.'

## CHAPTER FIVE

During the night the wind veered to the east and dropped to no more than a gentle breeze, the ketch ghosting, barely making headway in a lumpy sea. Self-steering was of little use in such conditions so he remained at the wheel; both for that reason and because he did not want to reduce sail although he feared a squall. He was tired, his morale at a low ebb, his mood sombre. *Sunboro Beauty* had experienced such good winds, made such excellent progress, that to all but lose the wind so near the end of the first leg was doubly frustrating.

The girl was sulking below. It had all started because she'd opened a can of bully beef without his permission and there had been a row. When he'd pushed her away from the stove she had fallen, hitting her head against the saloon table. She had burst into tears, but still angry he'd said, 'Oh, for Christ's sake dry up.' Later he saw that she had a bruise on her forehead and in a moment of guilt he apologized and was sympathetic.

'I don't want your sympathy,' she flared. 'You're a sadistic bully. I just want to get out of here. Somehow. Anyhow. If we were near land I'd swim for it.'

At that his anger returned. 'You'll have to wait,' he said thickly. 'Quite a long time, I think.'

The look she gave him was so full of venom that he had turned away, shaken his head and gone on deck.

In the early hours of morning the squall came. Earlier he had twice dozed off in the cockpit and, sensing the danger that posed, he'd reduced sail to a reefed mizzen and a staysail; it had been hard work getting in the big genoa which he'd handled carelessly because he was so tired; things had gone badly wrong and a good deal of the sail had fallen into the sea before he'd finished. But in the end he had got it safely stowed.

He must have dozed off again. His first knowledge of the squall was the lash of rain in his face and the wailing and shrieking of the wind through the rigging. It came with raw fury, flattening the sea, driving rain and spray before it, heeling *Sunboro Beauty* over sharply to leeward. He let the sheets fly and brought her head to wind, the sails flogging and cracking with sounds like gunshots. Within minutes the squall passed, the wind fell away again and for many hours they lay becalmed and he slept fitfully until daylight to an accompaniment of slatting sails and other noises inseparable from a calm. At midday it began to blow afresh, the wind switching from quarter to quarter, more or less boxing the compass until it settled in the north. A busy time sail changing had followed but with the ketch now settled on a south-westerly course he was able to engage self-steering, set the course alarm and go below to prepare a hot meal.

It was a fine morning of blue sky with occasional banks of cumulus and an indigo sea on which the crests of small waves turned to white horses under the brush of the north-east Trades. *Sunboro Beauty* was broad reaching with the wind abaft the beam, her best point of sailing. She was under full sail: genoa, main, mizzen staysail, mizzen and a spinnaker hoisted for the first time since leaving Plymouth.

The abundance of seabirds – a sure sign that land was not far away – and a school of dolphins leaping and diving made the ocean seem a less lonely place than it had in the days before.

He was busy about the deck checking the rigging, repairing a jib clew, and seeing to other tasks, the number and variety of which seemed endless. It was decidedly warm and he was grateful when it was time to check for a landfall. Searching ahead with binoculars he picked up a faint blue smudge on the starboard bow and knew it was Pico Alto, the highest point on the island of Santa Maria, the most southerly of the Azores. It had been good to see the peak show up at about the time he had estimated, for though they had already passed the tiny islet of Formigas and the dangerous Dollabarat Shoal to the east of it, they had not sighted the islet.

The Race Briefing Notes instructed competitors to round Punta do Castello, the southernmost point of Santa Maria, before making for the anchorage at Vila do Porto where the TRISTAR launch would come out on request.

He decided that he would not call Vila do Porto by VHF to give them an expected time of arrival until he had dealt with the girl.

He was focusing binoculars on the distant peak when she joined him on the foredeck.

'What are you looking at?' she asked, holding on to a shroud, the wind ruffling her hair, a frown puckering her forehead.

'Pico Alto.'

'What's that?'

'A mountain peak. Nearly two thousand feet. Highest point on Santa Maria.'

The fix he'd got by starsights that morning had been good, it was a fine day, the sun was shining, and he'd given himself a breakfast of eggs, bacon and chips. One way and another he was in high spirits and for the first time reasonably well-disposed to the girl in spite of the last row and her tell-tale bruise.

'You mean you can see land?' She looked at him uncertainly and her smile, something he'd not seen before, transformed her face. 'But oh, that's marvellous,' she said. 'After all these days at sea.' Once again he had the strange feeling that he had seen her somewhere before.

Better do it now, he thought, while there's still plenty of

time. We're about twelve miles off. That's at least an hour and a half if the wind holds.

He passed her the binoculars. 'Care to look?'

'Oh, please.' She sat on the coachroof, back to the mainmast, while he showed her how to focus. It took her a long time to find the distant peak. 'It's tiny,' she said. 'Just a little blue lump on the horizon.'

'We're about twelve miles from it.'

'Are we?' She looked at him curiously and he imagined she was wondering why for the first time he was so friendly.

'Must have a look at the chart,' he said and went below, leaving her on the foredeck. Shortly afterwards he shouted up through the hatchway, 'Bring down the binoculars, Sarah.'

She came down the companionway backwards, gingerly, the binoculars in their leather case slung over her shoulder. As she reached the bottom step he slipped the rope noose over her shoulders and in one quick movement drew it tight, threw his arms about her and after a brief struggle forced her face downwards on to the sole. It was not all that easy. She was surprisingly strong and she fought hard, kicking, scratching and writhing.

After her first startled scream nothing had come from her but gasps and groans. When he finally got her down and sat astride her in the narrow space between the saloon table and the starboard bunk she was silent but for her distressed breathing.

'Not going to hurt you.' His exertions made him gasp. 'Don't struggle. I have to do this. I'll untie you in a few hours. Things will be back to normal then.'

She struggled anew for a moment, tried once more to dislodge him. 'Why are you . . .?' she shrilled. 'Why this . . .?' She went suddenly limp and lay still, her body shaken by small sobs like those of a tired child. The terror in her eyes was very real and he hated himself for what he was doing as he tied her wrists behind her back, bound her arms to her sides and roped her legs together. That done he knelt beside her, put a pillow under her head. 'Sorry. Some time I'll

45

explain. Not now. You'll have to stay like this for a few hours.'

She looked up at him, her frightened eyes wet with tears. 'Please,' she implored. 'Don't do this to me. Please don't.'

He got to his feet, shook his head sadly and climbed the steps of the companionway. What else could he do? He was too far committed now. Within hours the first leg would be completed – and *Sunboro Beauty* was doing well.

Rape was her instinctive thought when the rope went over her shoulders and she was grabbed from behind. His sudden friendliness on the foredeck had caused her a mixture of surprise and relief. Was the awful period of sullen silence, of rows and abuse, coming to an end? She had hoped so because she felt she couldn't endure much more. At times she wondered if he wasn't mad. The swift eruptions into violence, the threats, the studied gloom. It was understandable in the beginning because of what she had done, but surely it could not go on indefinitely?

Once she realized that the purpose of the attack was not some sort of sexual assault, it was even more frightening. What on earth was he up to? What was it all about, she kept asking herself as she lay bound hand and foot, shivering with fear? He probably *was* mad. He had said 'for some hours'. They were approaching land, he'd not said for what purpose; just as he had not told her anything about what the ketch was supposed to be doing except that it was in a single-handed race – and *that* only when he'd found her on board and gone into his first frenzy.

He had never mentioned the race again, never answered her questions about it. She didn't know where they were going or for how long. Day after day he ignored her. When he prepared food he would leave a small portion for her. If he had a snack, and she was awake, he would leave some of it. But he would say nothing on these occasions. It was always done in silence. Early on he had shown her how to flush and pump out the WC, and on the fifth day when the weather improved he'd shown her how to wash her clothes in seawater with special soap. But his instruction had always been given in an unyielding way with never a trace of friendliness or humour.

It was her fault. She'd been crazy to get involved. It had begun that Thursday, two days before the start of the race, when she had seen him for the first time.

The November day had broken cold and grey to match the misery of her mood. With nothing to do after a few days in Plymouth, and nearing the end of her mental and material resources, she had gone for a walk. Without any definite plan she made for the harbour which she had seen from the windows of her hotel room perched high above Millbay.

As she walked she thought how disastrous the Plymouth visit had been. She should not have left London. Soon after arrival she had phoned Patrick, only to be told by his mother that he'd gone abroad on business a day or so earlier. The abruptness of his mother's voice, the cold message it conveyed, told its own story. He probably wasn't abroad. She shouldn't have written that silly note, or even thought of seeing him again.

The traffic on Union Street was heavy and she waited to cross. A maroon Jaguar approached and for an absurd moment she thought it was Carlos, but the man in it turned out to be old and bald. Stupid of her. Carlos was in London. And anyway it was all over: 'You don't realize, Vikki, that unless one's completely brutal one can't just walk out.' A hesitation, a brushing back of the dark lock of hair so carefully trained to fall over his forehead. 'I may be square, Vikki, but for me there's a certain sanctity about the family unit. It's, well – something one can't just shrug off. . .'

No, but you can shrug me off, can't you, Carlos, she thought. Nothing insensitive or brutal about that, even if you have used me and my body for three years . . .

'Oh rubbish,' she murmured to herself. 'Stop thinking about the wretched man. You're just as much to blame. Takes two to make an affair.'

The traffic paused and she crossed into Phoenix Street. A cat, thin and bedraggled, crouched in the doorway of a disused building. It looked at her for a moment with hostile yellow eyes. Like me, she thought; deserted, afraid, unwanted.

She wandered on, reached the Millbay Road, followed along the high perimeter wall, passed a garage, came to the docks entrance and made for the East Quay. She was not alone. There were numbers of people about; some onlookers, others going to and from the yachts which lay below the high walls of the quay. She remembered having read about an ocean race which was shortly to start from Plymouth and she wondered if those yachts were taking part in it. It was a busy scene, the crews working on their boats, engrossed in tasks she didn't understand, and over it all the hum of voices broken by occasional shouts and laughter. There were French, German and other ensigns and sometimes snatches of foreign languages.

She knew nothing about yachts but she thought they were beautiful; the sweeping lines of their hulls, the slender masts, incredibly tall; the cockpits with their wheels and instruments so suggestive of action yet to come; the glass ports and windows hiding the mystery of what was inside. Cabins, bunks, somewhere to eat, a cooker? She'd no idea, but whatever it was would be snug and comfortable, of that she was sure. The crews looked interesting, unusual people, purposeful and happy. How marvellous to be one of them, going off all those thousands of miles to faraway places in the sun.

She spent some time walking round the North and East Quays, moving slowly, stopping now and then, unwilling to leave the scene. Eventually she found a bollard on the edge of a quay wall where she could sit. From it she had a view of what was going on. Below her two yachts lay side by side. One of them she found particularly interesting, not only for its fine lines and attractive colours, a mixture of white and Cambridge blue, but because of its strange name: *Sunboro Beauty*. She had used a sun-tan lotion with that name and she wondered about the connection, recalling the slogan: 'Borrow the Sun with Sunboro'. Carlos had once said it was a great slogan. Wished his firm had the Sunboro account.

For some time she watched the bearded man at work in the cockpit. He was kneeling, intently busy, working with an electric power drill. At one stage he called over his shoulder to someone out of sight, 'Martin. That rubber insert on the chart-table. Bring it up, will you?'

There was an answering voice from below. 'Okay. Coming.'

Soon afterwards a man came up through the hatchway. He was lean and brown with sun-bleached hair and a weathered complexion. His voice was deep. Very masculine, a man's man, she decided. The bearded man said something she couldn't hear. The newcomer laughed, his face crinkling, and she had an impression of blue eyes and strong white teeth. What a gorgeous man, she thought.

That was the first time she had seen him.

After she left the Millbay Docks that Thursday she made for Royal Parade without any idea of what to do with the rest of the day. Somehow time had slipped by: a cheese salad at a counter in a café, endless walking and window shopping, an hour in the library with *Cosmopolitan* and *Harpers*, back to the hotel, resting in her room, thinking, her mood one of confused uncertainty. What should she do? Return to London, find another job? No point in hanging about Plymouth with Patrick either abroad or in hiding. That had been a crazy idea. No sort of substitute for what she'd lost. Never could be. And why had she run away? She couldn't or wouldn't accept that she'd not see Carlos again. So what was the point? If she were in London, somehow, somewhere, they'd get together. She knew his habits, his haunts, the timing of his daily routine. It would not be difficult to arrange a chance meeting.

That great resolve of his was phoney. He would come to heel, put on the usual act of contrition, take her to lunch and all would be well again. In part she despised Carlos, but she needed him and wasn't going to give him up without a fight.

Later that night in The Futtock and Shroud she joined up with Dieter and Ludwig, two young seamen from a German

49

trawler. She'd been picked up by them the night before. They had made the usual passes, accepted her refusal cheerfully but insisted that she remain with them – 'for good friendship you know'. It had been fun. They were easy to get on with, interesting because theirs was another world, they were madly generous and possessed of a robust good humour.

She told them of her morning in Millbay Docks, enthused about the yachts preparing for the big race; but they were not interested and soon changed the subject. She felt momentarily sad and deflated. After that they drank a lot, talked a lot and laughed a lot, and she forgot her troubles and enjoyed herself. When the pub closed they took her back to the hotel in a taxi.

'You like us put you to bed?' asked Dieter as they disembarked.

'Quite safe,' assured Ludwig brightly. 'The two of us, you understand.'

'Can't imagine anything more dangerous.' She laughed gaily, went towards the hotel entrance, weaving slightly. There she turned and waved. ''bye Dieter. 'bye Ludwig.'

There was a hoarse shout, ''bye-bye, Sarah. We see you tomorrow,' and the taxi moved off.

Before falling asleep that night she indulged in a brief fantasy about *Sunboro Beauty* and the gorgeous man. They were together in the yacht, anchored in a palm-fringed lagoon across which the moon laid a silvery path. It was a warm humid night. She was in a bikini, he in shorts, his chest bare. They were on deck, on a Li-lo, listening to distant music; a steel band playing a haunting melody somewhere along the beach. The gorgeous man whispered something in her ear, kissed her passionately. When she was able to draw breath she said, 'But darling, of course I want you.'

That reminded her of Carlos and ended the fantasy. Her last act before falling asleep was to decide on the immediate future; she would spend the next day in Plymouth, phone Carlos in the morning – why wait for a chance meeting? – take the Inter-City back to London on Saturday. With those reassuring thoughts she fell asleep.

50

# CHAPTER SIX

The sun rose higher in the sky and shone with increasing vigour, its strong light reflected on the ketch's sails and the crests of white-capped seas. To starboard Pico Alto had changed from blue to green, a soaring volcanic peak, dominating the thirty-five square miles that made up the island.

The lighthouse perched high above Punta do Castello, the most southerly point, showed up clearly in his binoculars. When he estimated its distance to be five miles he set the self-steering and went down to the saloon.

The girl was lying on her side, knees drawn up, wedged between the base of the table and the lockers under the starboard bunk, her frightened eyes turned towards him. Bracing himself for what he had to do, he took cotton-wool, a reel of plaster and scissors from the medicine locker and made a wad from the cotton-wool. He knelt beside her. 'I'm sorry, I have to do this. It's not for long. Don't struggle or you'll choke. Keep calm, breathe through your nose, and you'll be fine.'

She shook her head with frightened emphasis, her eyes wild. 'No. Please don't. I promise I won't make a sound. I truly promise. On my honour.' The pleadings came in broken, staccato sentences.

'Sorry, I have no option.' He spoke with a brusqueness he did not feel, forced the wad into her mouth and sealed it with strips of plaster.

For a few minutes he stayed with her, checking her breathing, patting her arm, reassuring her. 'There you are,' he said. 'Not too bad, is it? And it won't be for long.' Her shoulders shook and he felt guilty and ashamed as he moved across to the chart-table, picked up the handset and called

51

Vila do Porto. There was some delay before the Portuguese operator replied. 'We reading you, *Sunboro Beauty*' – he pronounced it 'Sshandbro Booty' – 'Pass your message.'

'Please inform the TRISTAR official that I expect to arrive off your port at fourteen hundred this afternoon,' he said.

The operator acknowledged and he replaced the handset.

Once round Punta do Castello he kept well to seaward, afraid that in the lee of the rocky peaks and cliffs of the island the wind, gusting down from the valleys, would oblige him to reduce sail.

He was brooding over the prospects of this when he saw a fast moving motorboat coming out from the land, its bows throwing up clouds of spray. Turning the ketch downwind and away from the island, he settled it once more on a south-westerly course.

Before long the motorboat – a large cabin cruiser – had all but overtaken *Sunboro Beauty*; closing gradually, it took station some thirty feet away on the ketch's port beam. From the stub-mast over the wheelhouse it flew the TRISTAR burgee, a pink star on a sea-blue ground.

Two men came out on deck. One of them looked vaguely familiar. Yes, my God, it's him, he thought. And it was. Harry Billings himself, aiming a camera, waving excitedly and shouting: 'Bloody good show, old dear. Only six ahead of you.'

'Hullo, Harry. What the hell are you doing here?' he shouted back, turning the wheel and keeping his eyes on the sails, determined that the ketch should stay on course.

'Flew into Fayal on Saturday. Got a lift by chopper to Sao Miguel on Sunday. Crossed over here by boat the same day. Brought you a spare radio from the UK. Didn't you get our message via Portishead?'

'No. Must have been asleep.' He had been slack about the listening schedule. With the transmitter 'officially' out of order, there hadn't been much point in being otherwise. 'How did you know where I was?'

'Ship reported seeing you a few days ago. We reckoned

you'd be here last night or this morning. Said you didn't answer his VHF call.'

'Too busy, I expect.' The cruise ship, he realized. It had passed close enough for the ketch's race number and name to be read with binoculars. While his mind worked overtime on the problem of what to do about the spare radio set, he kept the shouted conversation going. 'Marvellous of you, Harry. But I've just got the transmitter on beam again after a hell of a struggle. Had to dry out various bits and pieces, then re-assemble them. Not been easy in the weather we've had. Tested it out half an hour ago. It's okay.'

'Listen, old dear. You'd better take the spare set. You've a long way to go.'

'Not necessary, Harry. Anyway, we can't transfer it out here. Rules don't permit. And even if they did this weather's no good for that sort of thing. Don't relish being stove in by your flaming cabin cruiser.'

'Juan Fernandez here,' Billings pointed to the man next to him, 'is the local TRISTAR commissar – says follow us inshore. There's calm water in the anchorage at Vila do Porto.'

'Hang on a moment, Harry, I'll go below and look at the chart. Keep well clear. I'm going to put her on self-steering.' He set the wheel, adjusted the wind vane, engaged the self-steering and went below. It was a wonderful opportunity. He'd already had a good look at the plan of Vila do Porto on the Admiralty chart, but he needed time to think – and to see if the girl was all right.

She was lying on her side in the position he had left her, eyes closed. He knelt down. She was breathing regularly. He went to the chart, measured the distance to Vila do Porto. Six miles. After that he read what the Admiralty Sailing Directions had to say about Santa Maria. He had done that the day before, but doing it again spun out the time.

Five minutes later he was back at the wheel. He waved to the cabin cruiser and it moved in.

'No good, Harry,' he shouted through the loud-hailer. 'Six miles to Vila do Porto. At least a couple of hours' sailing to get there. Probably more. Calms and gusts in the lee of the island. Sail changing, transferring the set, regaining position would take another three to four hours. Just can't afford the time. Sorry – after all the sweat you've put into it.'

'Nonsense, old dear. Take the set. Why worry about a few hours? You've another eight weeks or so ahead of you. Play safe.'

'No way, Harry. I'm not chucking away seven or eight hours. There's a lot of boats on my tail. But it's marvellous of you to have tried.'

He looked at the set of the sails, the wind burgee at the top of the mainmast, and the sea, checking what he saw against the cockpit dials. The ketch was still logging around six to seven knots. He thanked his stars they were not in a flat calm or even a light breeze.

Over in the cabin cruiser he could see Harry Billings taking more photographs. Fernandez had the loud-hailer. 'Ees everyteeng okay, Meester Savaarge? No troubles?'

'Everything's okay, thanks. Who's ahead of me?'

'*Tornado Four* – *Grande Rapide* – *Mercedes Express* – *Sweet Ribena* – *Wilson's Savoury* – and *Omega Challenger* has reported in that arrangement. *Tornado Four* ees nearly one day in front of the rest. *Omega Challenger* ees five hours in front you.'

For some time after that the cabin cruiser remained in company, Billings firing a steady stream of questions about weather, conditions on board, sails and rigging, food, water, the need for action photos and a lot else; for good measure he added items of news about the other competitors, their successes, failures and disasters. Martin shouted monosyllabic replies, got the camera from below – he'd forgotten all about it – photographed Billings and the cabin cruiser.

'Thanks, Harry, for all your trouble. No photos yet. Too much to do. Sorry to have been a problem. I'll be able to report from now on. Will hand over photos for posting at St Lucia and St John's. 'Bye now.' He waved, turned the wheel, steadied the ketch on SSW. The distance between them widened. Billings was waving. 'Look after yourself, old sport,' came faintly across the water as the cabin cruiser turned away and made for Vila do Porto. Later, when they were well out of sight of each other, they had a brief chat by VHF – there was no shutting up Harry Billings.

It was not the discomfort, the awful dryness of the cotton-wool pad, which made her heart pound. It was the knowledge that she couldn't call for help if she were seasick. She had a ghastly mental picture of choking to death in her own vomit. Not that she was feeling sick but she was terrified. Anything might happen.

The man was mad. She was sure of that now. No sane human being could be as unpredictable and brutal as he was. What on earth was he up to? What was he going to do with her? Desperately, bitterly, she thought of the difference between the man she now knew and her fantasies about him before she'd sneaked on board that night in the Millbay Docks.

Her thoughts were interrupted by his shouting. Who was he shouting at? Who was the 'Harry' he was evidently so surprised to see? She'd heard a man's voice in the distance shouting in reply but couldn't make out what he said – only picked up odd words that didn't make sense. She was overcome by an overwhelming sense of her own helpless-ness. The motion had not changed and she was now sufficiently familiar with *Sunboro Beauty*'s behaviour at sea to know that they were still on more or less the same course, sailing quite fast. She realized there must be another boat close too, going in the same direction. The shouting stranger surely couldn't be another maniac? If only she could let him know, she was certain he would help. But the maniac in the ketch had made sure that couldn't happen.

At first she thought the binding and gagging was because he had decided to go in to Santa Maria. Now she knew that wasn't it, they weren't stopping. She tried to concentrate on the shouted exchanges still taking place on deck, listening with taut nerves, believing that somehow her life depended on what was being said.

What was that about having got the transmitter going? He was lying. She knew he hadn't tested the transmitter 'half an hour ago', nor had he dried out any 'bits and pieces'. She'd have seen him doing that if he had.

There was more shouting. She heard him say he was going below to look at the chart. Shortly afterwards he came down the companionway. She shut her eyes and although her heart beat faster she managed to affect the deep breathing of sleep. Next he was bending over her, his breath on her cheek, the warm smell of his body in her nostrils. It needed all her self-control to keep up the pretence of sleep. He went over to the chart table and was doing something there; she could hear him turning the pages of a book. A few minutes later he went up on deck. The shouted messages which followed were about time and distance to somewhere on the island and he was telling Harry he couldn't afford the time. What time? And to do what? She couldn't understand. Then he was asking who was ahead of him? That must mean in the race, she supposed. The stranger's reply was indistinct, incomprehensible. For some time after that the shouted exchanges continued. At last she heard Martin saying goodbye and promising regular reports in future. The other boat was going, taking with it the stranger who might have helped her if he had known.

So Martin Savage was hiding her away because he was determined to stay in the race. She had begun to suspect that some time ago. The Santa Maria incident confirmed it. He would have to finish it single-handed. Sooner or later he would get rid of her. How and when? She was terrified. Her eyes filled with tears and she wept quietly.

After the cabin cruiser had gone he was left with a lot to think about. To be confronted at Santa Maria by Harry Billings and the spare transmitter was something he had not bargained for. It was a situation he'd had no opportunity of rehearsing. Taking on board a spare transmitter would have been disastrous. Once in Vila do Porto, the race rules would have permitted Billings to come on board to assist in installing the spare. Billings knew that. Fortunately the rules prohibited the transfer of equipment and boarding by any person while the yacht was at sea.

56

So he'd done the only thing he could – claimed that he'd repaired the transmitter. That meant he could no longer maintain radio silence. He would have to report *Sunboro Beauty*'s position from time to time and pass Billings morsels of news for what the PR man had referred to as 'the action and drama scenario, old sport'. Well, there was plenty of drama so far, he reflected, but not the sort Harry wanted.

It had been exciting to hear that *Sunboro Beauty* was seventh to report at Santa Maria. From their radio messages he had already known about four of the six, but *Grande Rapide* and *Mercedes Express* had made no reports that he'd heard. Pierre Fougeux and Kurt Grosse playing their cards close to their chests, he decided. Before Fernandez's news he thought there would be several more ahead who had not radioed their position. To find that he was in fact seventh was far better than he had expected. Of the six ahead three were multihulls: *Grande Rapide, Sweet Ribena* and *Mercedes Express.* That Gary Maddox was leading in *Tornado Four* was no surprise. The American's fifty-foot cutter was known to be the fastest boat in the race and Maddox one of the most experienced competitors. A nice chap but a bit too frank and self-assured. Nor was it surprising that there weren't more multihulls ahead. The monohulls had been favoured by bad weather at the start and their ability to sail to windward. It was this ability, particularly in heavy weather, that had persuaded him to buy *Sunboro Beauty*.

So that was how the race stood. What then was his position? Billings and the race officials still believed him to be in it. Obviously they didn't know the girl was on board. But *he* knew she was on board, and *he* knew he was disqualified.

What should he do?

What, in fact, was he doing?

Haven't a bloody clue, he told himself, shaking his head and knowing that he hadn't. But of one thing he was certain – he was going to press on.

What about the book? It had better be that. Of course it was that. There'd be some explaining to do when the time came. He would say that he'd known he was disqualified

57

when he found her on board, but the failure of his radio had made communication impossible, and distance and weather had made it too late for a re-start. So he had decided to plod on – for the challenge it presented and the experience and, above all, because he'd decided to write a book about the race. A book with an unusual angle. He had kept the girl's presence on board a secret so that at the end, when he disclosed it, the element of dramatic surprise would heighten interest in the book. Wrong of Martin Savage, he could hear people say, but nevertheless understandable and after all no harm was done.

It was not a brilliant solution, he conceded, but it was workable and it would have to do unless a better one presented itself. He skimmed over that, preferring not to delve too deeply into his mind on such a sensitive point.

As for the sponsors – well, it was surely better that the yacht bearing their name should carry on, giving Sunboro Beauty Products a run for their money, rather than the dead loss of early withdrawal from the race. The object of the investment was to keep their name in the public eye. That, he assured himself, would be done; when the secret of the stowaway was revealed at the end of the race there'd be more publicity for *Sunboro Beauty* than any other competing yacht – except, perhaps, the winning boat.

The knowledge that this could not be his, provoked a moment of intense anger. *Sunboro Beauty* was lying seventh with three-quarters of the race still to go and the bloody girl had disqualified him. For Christ's sake what can I do? he kept asking himself. But it proved to be an anger he could not sustain. A change of mood made him think about the fear, humiliation, loneliness and discomfort she must have suffered, and he was left with a nagging sense of guilt. After all, was it really her fault? She'd not known that *Sunboro Beauty* was sailing in the TRISTAR next morning.

He looked at the time and was surprised. Nearly an hour had gone since he'd waved goodbye to Billings. Must go down to the girl, he told himself. He engaged self-steering and made for the companionway.

# CHAPTER SEVEN

After Santa Maria she remained below, deeply upset emotionally, her wrists, arms and thighs chafed and painful from the ropes which had bound her, the mucous membranes in her mouth inflamed by the gag, her appetite gone. Sleep was the only escape and she spent hours in her bunk, using some of the precious Nembutal to deaden the misery of consciousness. He had done his best to get her on deck, cajoling, threatening and pleading, but convinced that she would be disposed of in the course of a voyage which was proving intolerable, she refused to move.

In spite of the apologies and explanations he'd offered when he untied the ropes and took out the gag, she didn't believe his story. He'd admitted having behaved atrociously but what, he said, did she expect when she'd confronted him with such an impossible situation? He'd continued in the race after finding her, he said, because he'd been quite unable at first to accept what had happened. It was after the Biscay gale that the idea of the book, the new angle, had taken shape. For that reason he'd had to keep her presence on board a secret. He'd not told her of his plans because he didn't want to make the final decision until Santa Maria. There, had he changed his mind, he would have been able to put her ashore.

'Now,' he'd said, 'Santa Maria's behind us. I've made the decision and I want you to be in the picture, to enjoy the adventure. There are all sorts of ways in which you can help. I'll teach you to sail and steer. We can share various tasks. From now on I'll be making notes for the book.' He'd given one of his rare grins, touched her shoulder but she drew away. 'I'd like you to do the same. The voyage from the point of view of the stowaway.'

59

She had said nothing, stared at him blankly. It had been too sudden a change. She didn't believe him. Sooner or later he would get rid of her. Waiting for an answer, he'd said, 'Think it over. Make life on board more fun for you.' With that he'd gone on deck.

*Fun*, she thought, . . . *enjoy the adventure*. You stupid, insensitive beast. I wonder if you realize what you've done to me?

On the second day he tried again to get her up on deck, brought as a peace-offering a bottle of sun-tan lotion and a tube of protective face cream. She showed no interest in these though she was faintly amused to see that they'd been manufactured by Sunboro Beauty Products Ltd. When giving her the lotion and cream he warned that it would be hot on deck – would she care to borrow a pair of his shorts or underpants? She shook her head. 'Much too big.'

'Not these.' He held up a small blue garment. 'They stretch like mad. Fit any size really.'

Against her better judgement she refused, pushed them away. She wasn't on those terms.

On the third day the stuffiness of the saloon, her hunger and boredom, forced a change of mind. She accepted the food he prepared, washed herself down with seawater in the shower cubicle, combed and brushed her hair, cleaned her teeth and went on deck. Wedged in a corner of the cockpit, breathing in the freshness of the day, she felt a lot better. Above her scattered clouds rode across a blue sky, the wind crumpling the tops of waves into lace-like frills, white and sparkling, the ketch heeling to leeward as it plunged and surged on its long journey to the south. The weather was exhilarating and, refreshed mentally and physically, she thought again about his offer. The chances of survival would surely be better if she accepted? She was in no position to fight; that could only make her situation worse. From now on she must concentrate on survival; try to develop a worthwhile relationship, to win his sympathy, make herself somehow important to him.

In the four frightening hours she'd spent tied up in the saloon she had thought up a plan. She would say that before leaving Plymouth she had posted a letter to her London solicitors; a letter containing a sealed envelope to be opened if they did not hear from her within three months. The envelope, she would tell him, had in it a message informing them that she had sailed in *Sunboro Beauty* with the connivance of its owner, Martin Savage. The message would also record that a friend of hers, Dinah Ferrars, had driven her down to Millbay Docks that night and seen her go on board.

There was, however, a flaw. The story wouldn't accord with what she had already told him of how she came to be on board. Her thoughts went back to that last day in Plymouth and she sighed sadly.

The wailing of an ambulance siren woke her. She saw the time, almost nine o'clock, got out of bed, went to the window and pulled the curtains. The morning was as bleak as the others had been; wet and grey and miserable, matching her mood until she remembered she was to phone Carlos at eleven-fifteen. That raised her spirits. Just after eleven he would return to his office from the regular Friday report-back meeting at the end of the passage. She didn't know who had taken over from her as his secretary, but whoever she was she'd be a captive audience, listening to an account of how heavy the meeting had been and, by innuendo, how effectively he'd handled it.

'But God,' she could hear him saying as he brushed back the dark lock of hair, 'why do *I* have to think up the creative stuff? We employ some of the best men in the industry for that. Pay them a bomb. I just don't know.' Then, shaking his head and half smiling in that sexy way, the tips of his ivory teeth moist beneath the pelmet of the dark moustache, he would repeat, 'I just don't know.'

To which the new girl would be expected to say something like, 'But that's what it's all about, isn't it? I mean, that's why you're managing-director', and he would shrug his shoulders modestly. That was Carlos the humbug. She knew many other Carloses.

After she'd had a bath, done her face and hair, she took a T-shirt from the bathroom radiator where it had been drying, jeans from the towel-rail, went into the bedroom and dressed. Downstairs she had coffee and a biscuit and looked through the morning paper. On page two there was a photograph of the yachts in Millbay Docks, beneath it a list of the TRISTAR competitors. She felt a slight thrill, as if she were personally involved, when halfway down the list she read, *Sunboro Beauty – M. Savage*. She had just begun to read the story of the race when a husky voice on public address announced, 'Will Miss Thompson please come to the desk.' That was the name she'd registered under. Must be Dieter or Ludwig, she thought – no one else knows I'm here. She hurried to the desk only to find it was 'Mrs Thompson' who was wanted. When she got back to the table the newspaper had gone.


'Flenterman, McCallum,' announced the switchboard operator.

'Vikki here, Joan. Put me through to Mr Flenterman please.'

'Hullo, Vikki. You all right, love?'

'Yes. Fine. You, Joan?'

'Madly busy. One moment. I'll put you through.'

'Mr Flenterman's office.' It was a strange voice; the new secretary; bound to be good looking.

'Put me through to Mr Flenterman, please.' Keep calm, she cautioned herself, your heart's beating like mad.

'Who shall I say it is?'

'Miss Brownson.'

'Oh.' It was long-drawn, a mixture of surprise and caution. 'Just one minute.'

One minute turned out to be several. Eventually the strange voice came back. 'I'm sorry but he's left his office. Is there a message?'

She took a deep breath. 'Yes. Please tell him I phoned. I'll do so again at five o'clock.'

She put the phone down, went back into the lounge. It was

almost certainly a brush-off. He'd not wanted to speak to her. Or was it genuine? Had he left his office by the side door and gone somewhere else in the building?

Upstairs in her room she took three Disprin. There was an awful buzzing in her head as if it were about to burst. Crying wouldn't help. Screaming might. That was what she really wanted to do. Just scream and scream. But that would bring people running. There was only one thing for it, get out and do something. Do what she'd done the day before – go down to Millbay Docks.

There was the same bustle of people, the same going and coming, the men in the yachts, and sometimes girls, working, talking, laughing.

Sitting on the same bollard, looking down on *Sunboro Beauty*, she forgot about Carlos and London. At first the gorgeous man was not there but later he came on deck and looked up and she felt curiously shy and looked away. For some time after that she watched him working on a sail with a sewing machine, but he didn't look up again and she doubted if he'd noticed her. The bearded man came up at one stage and they talked together for a few minutes before he went below.

The gorgeous man looked more interesting than ever, his sun-bleached hair careless and disarranged, the deeply tanned face stronger and more purposeful than it had seemed the day before. Not that he was good looking. It was just that it was a rugged, attractive face; his voice, too. Deep, on the edge of harshness, but essentially masculine; the thick woollen sweater and oilskin trousers very much the clothes for the man.

How marvellous, she thought, to sail away with him, to spend weeks alone together at sea. So different to the clandestine meetings with Carlos outside the office; lunch in the sort of restaurants clients didn't use; or love made in hotel rooms, the occasion always dominated by time, Carlos's eyes never far from his wristwatch even at the most intimate moments. He once called it 'the split second timing of a commando raid' and laughed, preening himself on the phrase, until she spoilt it all by saying she'd read the same article in the *Observer* a few days before.

She looked at the yacht and its owner with admiring, longing eyes. It would be so different with this man, cruising to faraway places.

It began to rain, a thin persistent drizzle. That and the dark sky persuaded her to return to the hotel. On the way, acting on impulse, she stopped at Woolworths and did some minor but essential shopping.

The five o'clock call to Carlos had been a repetition of the first.

Mr Flenterman is not available. He's in conference. Yes, he was told that you would phone at five o'clock. No. He did not leave any message for you.

On the way back to the hotel her mood bordered on hysteria. The new secretary, so evidently briefed by Carlos, had spoken in a tone curt to the point of rudeness. Typically, Carlos had delegated his dirty work to an underling. To be dropped by him had been awful; to have it done in this callous, insulting way confronted her with a situation she couldn't accept emotionally. The outlet for her frustration lay in hysteria, and to this she gave way in her room, throwing herself on the bed and burying her head in the pillows.

It was some time before she pulled herself together, cleaned and tidied, and went down to the office. There she announced that she was leaving first thing in the morning and paid her bill.

In The Futtock and Shroud that night Dieter had put a hand on her shoulder, frowned. 'What's wrong, Vikki? You do not laugh so much tonight.'

She shook her head, smiled thinly. 'Nothing's wrong, Dieter. Headache. That's all.'

'I get some aspirins, hey?' suggested Ludwig. He went to the end of the room and spoke to a large peroxided barmaid.

He came back with a glass of water and the tablets. 'No aspirin. Only Panadol. But that is good.'

'Sweet of you, Ludwig.' She swallowed them, drank the water, coughed and blew her nose. After that she tried to shake off her misery, working hard but unsuccessfully at matching the cheerfulness of the Germans. It was some time later, during a lull in the general hubbub, that she became aware of a voice, deep, resonant, vaguely familiar. She looked across to the far side of the horseshoe bar and saw the gorgeous man. His companion was an older, swarthy individual with a grey streaked beard and a bony face; the black beret, red scarf and blue denim jacket shouted Frenchman even if he hadn't at that moment thrown his head back, his arms in the air and roared, '*Merde, mon vieux. Mais c'est impossible.*'

Those near them were silent for a moment, looking at the Frenchman in the way people in a street look at a motorist who has hooted unnecessarily.

While Dieter and Ludwig ordered more drinks and talked and joked and laughed, her attention kept wandering to the two men opposite. A time came when the gorgeous man turned and their eyes met. Her stomach churned and her cheeks burnt as she experienced that curious moment of recognition: a man and woman seeing each other across a crowded room for the first time, strangers without commitment, yet aware of sudden intimacy. It had ended when she smiled and looked away.

The clock on the far wall showed ten minutes to ten. 'I must go now,' she said to the Germans with sudden resolve. 'I have to make an early start for London tomorrow.'

They protested, urged her to have a final drink, but she was adamant. Ludwig went in search of a taxi. He returned with it and they offered to escort her to the hotel. She rejected that in a very positive way. They looked at each other uncertainly, shrugged their shoulders. Ludwig said, 'Right. You take the taxi, we go to drink some more.'

At the hotel she told the driver to wait, ran up to her room, threw the few things she had into a shoulder bag and hurried back. She was trembling with excitement, her heart pounding. The drinks and the Panadol, she thought, controlling a desire to burst into tears or laughter as she climbed into the taxi.

'East Quay, inner basin, Millbay Docks.' She realized that her voice was pitched too high.

The taxi came to a stop, she got out, paid the fare and it rumbled off through the rain towards the dock gates.

The dimly-lit quay was deserted but there were lights in the yachts and sometimes the low hum of voices, music and occasional laughter. She walked purposefully along the quay, hoping that anyone who saw her would think she belonged to a yacht. When she reached the familiar bollard she stopped. For a minute or so she stood still, a wary eye on *Sunboro Beauty*'s lighted windows. To her alarm she saw a blur of movement in the saloon. Uncertain what to do, she took up a position behind a stack of crates. From there she could watch the quayside, though she could see nothing of the ketch but its masts.

She had almost decided to give up when the tall masts moved slightly. Someone was coming up the rope ladder. Head and shoulders appeared. It was the bearded man. He climbed on to the quay and stopped for a minute to light a cigarette before walking towards the car-park near the gates. She lost sight of him but heard a car start and later saw its headlights as it drove away. Leaving the crates, she returned to the bollard and looked over the side. The rope ladder was there. She went down it gingerly, facing the quay wall the way she'd seen other people do. There were lights in the yacht lying on the far side of *Sunboro Beauty*, and she could hear voices coming from its cabin. Very quietly she landed on the ketch's deck and moved into the cockpit. She tried the sliding top of the hatchway but it was locked. Perplexed, she looked around. There was a half-open hatch in the stern coachroof. Lights shone from the windows of the cabin beneath it. She crept up to the hatch, first listened, then looked down; there was no sound or other sign of life. With some difficulty she opened the hatch fully, lowered herself into the space below and returned the hatch to its original position.

That, she reflected, had been the beginning of an awful experience.

## CHAPTER EIGHT

The north-east Trades had lived up to their reputation, blowing steadily at between fifteen and seventeen knots for days on end, rolling before them endless ranks of foam-topped seas, the spray sparkling and glistening in strong sunlight. These were ideal conditions for the ketch which for most of the time had been running on a course of sou-sou-west, the wind fine on the port quarter.

At noon on 21 November he made the position 29°55′N: 27°30′W, and the day's run 168 miles. 'Super,' he said to himself. 'She's averaged close on seven knots since Santa Maria.'

Telling the girl to keep her weather eye open and let him know if she sighted anything, he went below. She looked pleased at that and he was surprised, because it was the first time she'd shown any sign of co-operating. She was without sailing experience but at least she could keep a lookout; not that there was much likelihood of seeing anything for they were well clear of the shipping lanes.

For some time he was busy at the chart-table making a summary of the ketch's progress. The race had started from Plymouth on 7 November and they had reported at Santa Maria shortly before noon on the 17th; the direct distance from Plymouth was 1180 miles and it had been made good in ten days, though the ketch's route had entailed another 200 miles of sailing. It had been accomplished notwithstanding the Biscay gale, the long beat to windward against the westerlies, and the time becalmed after the squalls north of Santa Maria. He consulted the race notes for the second leg: Santa Maria to St Lucia, West Indies. The direct distance was approximately 2360 miles, twice that of the first leg but considerably less than the southerly route taken by sailing ships in the past – the route he intended to follow which was between three and four hundred miles longer. With any luck *Sunboro Beauty* would have the wind with her most of the way; that, aided by the North Equatorial Current, promised a reasonably good passage. But he had no illusions. St Lucia was in Latitude 14°N and before they got that far south they might well experience variable winds and tropical storms.

The night before he had, as usual, heard a number of competitors reporting their positions. Of the six yachts ahead of him at Santa Maria, all had reported but for *Grande Rapide* and *Mercedes Express*; these two were evidently still determined not to show their hands. The order of the others was unchanged, *Tornado Four* still leading the field.

Of those astern only one appeared to have gained on him. *Caspar's Folly*, a trimaran owned by John Caspar, an old sailing friend, was now less than sixty miles behind. Under prevailing conditions it would certainly be gaining on the ketch.

The race rules did not make reporting compulsory but competitors had been reminded in the briefing notes that it was in their own interests to do so. A competitor in serious trouble stood a better chance of rescue if his position were known.

He had reported *Sunboro Beauty*'s position on the previous night. It was the second time he'd spoken to Portishead since leaving Santa Maria. On the first occasion, the night following the ketch's meeting with the race launch, the duty operator had congratulated him on getting the transmitter to function again. In reply he had stressed that the transmissions would be limited because of the need to conserve battery power. Understanding the problem, the operator had been sympathetic.

The off-course alarm sounded seconds before the ketch heeled over sharply from starboard to port. He winced as he heard the clatter of booms and sails crashing over in a gybe, followed by a high scream. Christ, he thought, she's gone overboard. He raced up the companionway to find her lying on the cockpit grating, eyes wide open, evidently much alive. The spinnaker was flogging noisily, the outboard end of its pole hard up against the forestay. He hard-sheeted the main and mizzen, grabbed the wheel, over-rode the self-steering and brought the ketch slowly round. Easing the sheets to the wind as the stern slewed from starboard to port he settled her back on course, set the wind vane and re-engaged self-steering. The spinnaker was still flogging, its guy having carried away from the outboard end of the pole. He went forward, got the huge sail down and lashed it along the guard-rail after a long and tiring struggle. Back in the cockpit the girl had got up from the grating and wedged herself in the after-weather corner.

'You all right?' he asked.

'Yes. Sorry. I got an awful fright. The sails and everything suddenly banged across without any warning. Right across from one side to the other,' she repeated. 'And we went over the wrong way. I thought we were going to capsize.' For a moment he looked at her with frowning concern, then he smiled; blue eyes friendly, teeth white against the sunburnt face. 'Your first gybe. Can be frightening. We're lucky. No serious damage as far as I can see. The guy came adrift. Shouldn't have happened. Wasn't properly secured. My fault. No wonder the Bosun couldn't cope.'

She looked puzzled. 'Who's he?'

'The self-steering. My name for it.'

After that she wanted to know what a gybe was. He explained, told her what had caused it. 'Sooner I teach you some of the rudiments of sailing the better,' he said. 'First lesson tomorrow forenoon. Okay?'

'Yes. That'll be super. I'm useless at the moment.' A

deprecatory half-smile showed fleetingly.

What a difference that makes, he thought. How good she looks when she does that.

In the south-west the setting sun laid a glittering path of light across the sea, splashing banks of cumulus with apricot and salmon.

'Light's going,' he said. 'Sun'll be below the horizon in about fifteen minutes.'

'It's lovely,' she said. 'More beautiful than I could have imagined.'

Before dark he hoisted a genoa in place of the spinnaker. Even if the guy hadn't come adrift he'd have done that. The spinnaker was too big and unhandy a sail to risk with self-steering at night.

It was dark by the time he got the ketch properly balanced again and was able to set the wind vane and self-steering and go below.

The girl was sitting on the forward end of her bunk, her elbows on the chart-table.

'Checking the navigation?' he asked.

'No. Just looking. We've a long way to go, haven't we?'

'Yes. More than six thousand miles before we're back in Plymouth.'

'How many days?'

'About sixty to seventy if we're lucky.' He heard her catch her breath. 'Cheer up,' he said. 'It'll go quickly once you're busy.'

'I suppose so.' She looked at him doubtfully.

'How would you like to cook up something for tonight?'

She turned from the chart. 'Of course. But I'm not much good.'

'I'll show you how to get the better of the stove. It's rather a special technique in a sea-way. Like cooking on a roller-coaster.'

She smiled. 'I'll do my best. I've watched you doing it.'

Between vacating the Highgate apartment and the start of

the TRISTAR he had seen little of Tessa. For those six weeks he'd been down on the Hamble – and later at Lymington – fitting out, tuning and sailing *Sunboro Beauty* with Tim Baxter.

Tessa, now sharing a flat with a girl friend in Camden had refused to come down to the Hampshire coast. 'No. Why should I? Everything you do, Martin, is based on what suits *you*. What *you*. want. Well it doesn't happen to be what *I* want.If you want to see me you can come up here. What about this weekend?'

It was a phone conversation and that always inhibited him. Difficult to sort things out if you couldn't see the person you were talking to. 'Can't this weekend, Tessa. I'd love to but we're battling against time. I've arranged with Tim that we'll do a thrash towards the Scillies this weekend. We're hoping for bad weather. Want to test her windward sailing.'

There was a longish silence after that. 'Well, I hope you enjoy it,' she said eventually and rang off. That was how most of their phone calls now ended.

The week of the race he phoned her at work and suggested she come to Plymouth for the farewell party. It was to be given by the yacht club the night before the start. She was non-committal. It might be difficult but of course she'd come if she could.

In the event she hadn't turned up and for him the party had fallen miserably flat. That she'd not thought it worthwhile was a bitter disappointment. After all, they were not going to see each other for some time, and he *was* embarking on a fairly hazardous undertaking.

Pierre Fougeux, a misogynist who disliked parties, had suggested leaving the yacht club early. 'We go to The Futtock and Shroud, *mon vieux*. They 'ave absinthe and we need it. *N'est ce pas?*'

'I don't,' said Martin. 'Whisky will do.'

So they went and he and Pierre made a night of it. At some stage or other he was hazily aware of a girl smiling at him from the far side of the bar. In no mood for that sort of adventure he ignored her.

At closing time they set off on foot for Millbay Docks. A policeman stopped them, suggested that their rendering of the *Marseillaise* was unnecessarily loud; might be regarded as creating a disturbance, he added darkly.

Pierre Fougeux told him in dockland French to piss off. Looking puzzled and displeased, the policeman asked Martin to translate.

'He says we are extremely sorry,' said Martin.

Fougeux lifted his beret and bowed, whereupon the policeman told them to get along and watch it unless they were looking for trouble.

So they'd got along, found their yachts and returned on board in the early hours of morning, a good deal the worse for wear but marvellously happy.

On the Saturday morning he began casting off at ten o'clock in order to get the ketch to the starting line in good time. In the middle of this operation there was a shout from the quay. He looked up. A postman was waving a small package.

Marked 'Special delivery', the handwriting on it and on the note inside was familiar: *Sorry I couldn't make it, Martin. Quite impossible. Hope all goes well. Best of luck. Love Tessa.*

It had been wrapped round a cassette: Crystal Gayle's *I'll Get Over You.*

How like Tessa. She never could resist turning the knife.

The girl shouted to him up the companionway. 'Supper's ready.'

He joined her below. 'Smells good.'

'I expect it'll be awful.' She turned her head from the stove and smiled and in a moment of vivid recollection he knew where he had seen her before.

'Ever been in The Futtock and Shroud?'

'The pub, you mean?' She looked at him with questioning eyes.

'Yes. Saw you there the night before the race. With two chaps. Right?'

'Yes.' She seemed surprised. 'I didn't see you.'

'You smiled at me.'

'Did I? Couldn't have been *at* you. Dieter and Ludwig must have said something funny.'

'Was one of them the boy friend who deserted you in Millbay Docks?'

She hesitated. 'Yes. The dark one.' Turning back to the stove she spoke to him over her shoulder. 'Hey. This will spoil. Come and help yourself.'


# CHAPTER NINE


Day after day *Sunboro Beauty* ran before the north-east Trades, the wind blowing a steady force four to five under a cloud scattered sky, the ketch lifting to the following seas, surging forward with sudden vigour and settling gently as they passed. The only sounds were the hiss and slap of the sea against the hull, the flap of the sails as they lifted and filled, and occasionally the murmur of voices.

Each day he would take a sight in the morning – stars or sun, depending on cloud – a meridian altitude at noon, and another sight for longitude in the afternoon or late evening. At least once a day he would get an azimuth for compass correction and check the chronometer by radio time signal. There was the usual daily round of checking water in the bilges, maintenance and repair work on deck and below, on sails and rigging, battery charging, writing up the log and voyage notes and other tasks. They listened regularly to the BBC World Service and at times to cassette music. Their tastes were widely different: he liked classical music, she country singing.

They now shared certain of the routine tasks. To compensate for his work load she had taken over the

73

preparation of meals and cooking and as she became more proficient under his instruction she was doing spells on the wheel by day – but not yet at night unless he was with her.

Because she was doing more work, food was no longer shared disproportionately. He insisted, however, that she consult him each day about what they should eat, and she could use only the quantities he stipulated. This meant a fairly strict regime, but he believed it was adequate and that it ensured their supplies would last out the voyage. 'On the last leg we'll be able to lash out a bit,' he told her. 'It'll be cold then. High winds and big seas. That's when we'll really need the food.'

Since Santa Maria he had kept the spreader deck lights on at night, and each morning they found a few flying fish on deck which helped supplement their diet. Two days from the island there had been a heavy rainstorm and they'd collected four gallons in buckets lashed to the main and mizzen goosenecks.

As the ketch drove south the sun got steadily hotter and by day he seldom wore more than shorts or bathing trunks so that his body, leaner and harder than ever, was burned a deep brown. The brown of her face, arms and legs almost matched his, but the rest of her body was white; she disliked the patchwork and worried about it.

Some days after Santa Maria he was explaining sail rigs for different types of weather when she burst out with, 'Wish *I* had a different rig. It's terribly hot. These are quite hopeless.' She looked down, fingered the rolled up jeans and the T-shirt which she now wore outside them.

'So what?' He was looking over his shoulder at a following sea, spinning the wheel to check a yaw. 'You refused my underpants.'

'Wish I had a bikini.'

'What's wrong with knickers. Wear them, don't you?'

'Of course I do. They're not a bikini. Anyway, I haven't got a bra to go with them.'

'I've noticed that. Go topless – or bottomless for that matter. Won't worry me.'

She looked at him speculatively, as if trying to read his thoughts. 'I don't think that's a very good idea.'

'What's the trouble? Afraid of rape?'

'Not particularly.'

'What's it then?'

She ignored the question. 'Actually I could make a bikini out of one of those gingham tea towels. Mind if I cut one up?'

'Go ahead if you feel the urge for modesty.' He smiled caustically. 'We've lived for more than two weeks within a couple of feet of each other and without privacy. I'd have thought there wasn't much room left for inhibitions of that sort.'

She didn't bother to answer. Later that day she began to make the bikini.

On 24 November the noon position was 24°10′N: 33°15′W, and the distance to St Lucia 1680 miles.

That night he called up Portishead at the scheduled time and reported the ketch's position. It was his custom now to do this every third day. As usual he listened to other competitors reporting. There appeared to be little change ahead, but astern things were different; *Caspar's Folly* was now only thirty miles away though some distance to the north of *Sunboro Beauty*'s track. For the first time he heard the Australian trimaran *Karamagee* reporting. It was 45 miles astern of *Sunboro Beauty*, but rather further to the south. Nick Farran who was sailing her was a newcomer to European waters though well known in offshore racing in Australia; a likeable man from Sydney whom he had met several times in Plymouth but didn't know well.

The multihulls were, as he'd expected, showing their paces running before the wind in good weather. The real test for them was still to come. On the third leg, St Lucia – St John's, there would be adverse winds and seas with the weather deteriorating as they beat north: the fourth leg, St John's – Plymouth, would be bitterly cold – and gale-ridden.

*

75

Keen, intelligent and physically strong she was quick to learn and rewarding to instruct, and that pleased him and made the effort worthwhile. She could steer a compass course, handle sheets and halyards, engage and disengage self-steering and use the self-tailing winches. She knew how to trim the sails to the wind, the meaning of in-irons, close-hauled, reaching, broad reaching and running; she was aware of the need to keep an eye on the wind burgee and the run of the sea, to anticipate yaw and correct it in time; and he'd impressed upon her the importance of keeping a good lookout and a seaman's eye on things generally.

The instruction periods always ended with the emergency drill for a man overboard. 'It's not too difficult in reasonable weather in daylight,' he told her, 'but it's difficult to bloody impossible in bad weather, especially at night. Thing is, you've *got* to know the drill.' So she would repeat it to him again and again, miming the action of throwing the horseshoe buoy, its drogue and strobe light overboard – then turning on to the reciprocal of the course steered and making a wide sweep to leeward before coming up-wind to the man in the water. He explained how, if she lost sight of him, the recriprocal course should be criss-crossed by tacking at set intervals. 'If you know the drill there's a fair chance of picking him up.'

'Or her,' she suggested tentatively, a swift probing look in her eyes.

'Of course,' he said. 'Man embraces woman.'

'Why wouldn't we use the engine in an emergency like that?'

'No propeller. Under the race rules the shaft has to be sealed, or the propeller removed. We took it off. Reduces drag.'

'Isn't it dangerous without an engine? On a voyage like this, I mean?'

'A voyage like this is always dangerous,' he said with sudden sharpness. The subject was changed to the watches they were to keep: six-hour spells by day, three by night. 'I'll introduce you to it gradually,' he promised.

*

Some time after four in the morning of 26 November the slatting of the sails and the changed motion woke him from deep sleep. He jumped up, checked the barometer. It had fallen three millibars since last he'd looked. The girl appeared in the hatchway above him as he began to climb the companionway. 'I'm coming up,' he said.

When he reached the cockpit she said, 'I was just going to call you. The wind's gone. It's been falling away ever since I came on watch.'

'I know. It woke me. Calms always do.'

It was a dark night, a half-moon riding high, struggling through the clouds in the south. A swell came in from the west but the sea was already subsiding.

'Wheel amidships?'

'Yes.'

'Good. Better prepare for a blow. We'll take in the big stuff. Leave the mizzen set and bend on a working jib. Big genny in first, then the mainsail.'

Working together they had soon handed the sails, furled and lashed the genoa on deck and the mainsail on its boom, sheeted the mizzen hard-in and made the jib ready for hoisting. He opened the fore and aft emergency hatches to get more air into the boat before joining her in the cockpit.

'Makes a difference,' he said. 'Two crew instead of one.'

'Am I improving?' She asked with a note of uncertainty.

'Yes. You're good. For a beginner.'

There was silence after that but for the lap of water against the side, and the slatting of the mizzen as the ketch rolled to the long westerly swell.

Presently she said, 'Aren't you going back to sleep?'

'No. It's too hot down there and there's too much noise.' Later he said, 'How d'you like the night watches?'

She had come on at three o'clock that morning for her second night of watchkeeping. Not that she'd been altogether alone; he had come up at half-hour intervals to check that all was well.

'Super,' she said. 'Sailing at night is strange, isn't it? It's more what you hear and feel and see, really. The darkness is so isolating when the moon goes behind the clouds. We could be in another world.'

'In some ways we are. It's marvellous in good weather like these Trades. Can be grim in bad weather.'

Another silence followed before she said, 'You don't sleep much with that alarm waking you every half-hour, do you?'

'I'm used to it. Trained hard for it. You can keep going for a long time on short snatches. I can catnap in the cockpit unless the weather's really bad. Blondie Hasler crossed the Atlantic with fifteen-minute catnaps most of the way. I think he pioneered the technique.'

'Not my scene,' she said. 'I pass out when I sleep. Stay like that for hours.'

'So I've noticed. Won't need to do half-hour checks on you soon. That'll step up my sleep ration.'

'And help my ego.'

It was some time before he said, 'Things have been better lately, haven't they?'

'How d'you mean?'

'Between us.'

'Yes. I suppose they have.' There was a fleeting note of doubt. Little was said after that and at six o'clock she handed over and went below.

It was airless and humid in the saloon and, as he'd said, there was a good deal of noise from above. Still wearing what she'd been in while on watch, a T-shirt over her bikini, she lay on the sleeping bag and shut her eyes, but tired though she was sleep would not come.

She thought of what he'd said about things being better between them. Of course they were, superficially. Life was much more pleasant. Since leaving Santa Maria eight days earlier he had been a different man, kind and considerate, sometimes almost gentle. But she didn't trust him. The change was too sudden; it didn't ring true. Though things *were* different now, and at times she found herself unashamedly enjoying the voyage, it was never for long. She could not forget what he had done to her, and the gnawing uncertainty played on her mind.

Like when he had told her about *Caspar's Folly* and *Karamagee* gaining on them. Why, if he really was only continuing for the sake of the book, had he sounded so worried about that, as if it were some sort of disaster? She very much doubted if there was going to be a book although he'd been keeping what he called his voyage notes, and given her a ring-bound notebook and insisted that she do the same. She recalled the conversation.

'Don't know what to write,' she'd protested. 'It'll all be in the logbook and your notes anyway, and it's not easy to write with all this movement.'

'Easy enough if you try. Write about it from your point of view. You, the stowaway. How things strike you. Your reaction to what happens. From the start. Record what you've actually felt, your thoughts then and now – as the voyage goes on.'

She'd given him a long, searching look. 'You might not like to read what I actually thought then – or now. Bound to involve you. Thoughts are very private things.'

'I know they are. But if the book is worthwhile we've both got to be absolutely honest about our feelings. It must be a human document, not just another voyage narrative.' He put a hand on her shoulder, turned her towards him. 'Look – I promise you that until the voyage is over I'll not read your notes. And you mustn't read mine. You can keep your notebook locked up. I'll give you a key to a locker in the after cabin. And I'll keep mine under lock and key. Fair enough?'

So she had begun her voyage notes, but they were brief and for the most part uninteresting: her impressions of being in a gale; the misery of seasickness; the discomfort of being confined in a small space with violent movement; cooking in a small boat at sea; her clothing problems. Notes about the gybe and her fears at the time, the exhilaration of sailing in good weather, the instruction he was giving her, watch-keeping at night and other trivia – but never did she write a word of her real feelings about him, her private fears and misery. It was too dangerous. She didn't believe his promise never to read her notes. He probably had a duplicate key.

Then there was what she privately called the 'camera

conspiracy'. He had taken dozens of photographs, mostly of himself doing things on deck and below; but the camera was kept locked up when he was not using it. It had a clamp which he had used at first so that he could photograph himself, but recently he'd been getting her to take the photos.

'They're for Billings,' he explained. 'I'll hand them over for posting at St Lucia. The best of them will be for the book.'

'You never take *me*,' she said, trying to sound half-petulant, half-amused.

'Of course not.' The cold blue eyes stared into hers. 'Billings mustn't know you're on board.'

That had sent shivers of re-awakened fear down her spine. Deliberately casual, she said, 'Won't it seem odd? The exciting thing about the book is supposed to be the stowaway angle, but there'll be no photos of the stowaway.'

He looked past her, working his lips in the way she knew he did when he was thinking up an answer. 'We'll get pictures of you on the last leg. With the weather we're likely to get then they'll do for the Biscay gale as well as the Western Ocean. When those films go to Billings the secret will already be out. So it won't matter.'

But that didn't explain why he kept the camera under lock and key. She dared not ask him that, but she thought it must be to prevent her photographing herself when the opportunity arose.

Then there was the time when she asked him why he shaved at sea. Didn't single-handers always grow beards? Having asked that, she could have kicked herself. The words *single-hander* were to him what the bell was to Pavlov's dogs. The muscles in his cheeks flexed, his eyes narrowed. 'Unfortunately I'm not a single-hander. I shave for the same reason that I made you cut your hair.'

'What is that?' she asked, seeking confirmation of what she believed to be the answer.

But he said nothing, gave her a tight-lipped look and went below. She knew the symptoms of his mood changes. A difficult day would follow.

# CHAPTER TEN

Dawn came warm, humid and overcast, the smooth sea rising and falling to the passage of the swell, endless convolutions of grey water on which the ketch rolled with the monotony of a pendulum. There was no apparent wind but she was ghosting, barely making way through the water.

It was too hot for sleep, and though the girl had only come off watch at six she joined him as daylight grew stronger, bringing with her half-filled mugs of fruit juice. As if respecting some well-understood convention they were silent. She sat in the cockpit and he on the forward end of the coachroof, both looking out to sea, not far from each other yet separated by their silence; a silence imposed on the background noise of sails and the sea, a pattern now so familiar that it would be noticed only if it were not there.

Later she brought breakfast from below: eggs, bacon and chips, and mugs of hot coffee, and not until they had finished did either speak. 'What d'you think of the weather?' she asked at last, wondering what his mood was.

It was as if she'd woken him from sleep. He turned, blinked his eyes, and looked round the horizon before answering. 'Difficult to say. Barometer fell four millibars early this morning. Now it's gone up two. Can't seem to make up its mind. Radio Trinidad put out a tropical storm warning shortly before six. I reckon it must have passed to the south-west of us.'

'Are they bad to be in?'

He was slow to answer, frowning as if he disliked the question. 'Very bad,' he said and lapsed into silence. Much later and quite inconsequentially he said, 'D'you realize that but for you I'd have had two eggs on my plate?'

So it was going to be one of those days. She sighed with

resignation as she put the breakfast things into a bucket. How different he was to the gorgeous man of her fantasies.

The calm lasted throughout the morning.

After doing his usual rounds and chores he went below. When he came up she saw that he'd exchanged shorts for a bathing slip. She put down the T-shirt she was mending to watch him at work on the foredeck where he was making the end of a heaving line fast to a lifebuoy. She wondered uneasily what he was about when he came aft and threw the buoy over the pulpit rail with a great heave so that it fell well astern. He paid out the line and made fast its inboard end; then, from the after hatch he hauled up a rope ladder and hung it over the stern.

'Going to fish?' She meant to sound flippant.

The blue eyes, white teeth and brown face managed a grin which reminded her of the first time she'd seen him in Millbay Docks.

'No,' he said. 'Swim.'

'What's the rope for?'

'Lifeline. In case the wind comes.'

'Aren't you afraid of sharks?'

'Very.' He looked at her sideways, hesitated as if in contemplation of something unsaid.

'Don't forget the man overboard drill.' He dived in with a noisy splash. 'It's great,' he spluttered, treading water. After several circuits round the ketch he climbed the rope ladder, sat on the coachroof and began drying himself. Leaning forward, he put a large hand on her shoulder. 'Come on, Sarah, your turn. About time you christened the bikini.'

It was a situation she had visualized but the moment of confrontation, the impact of what he said, his cold blue eyes staring at her, were frightening. Of course she wasn't going to swim. Once she was in the water she'd never come out again. She was quite convinced he'd see to that. It was the first time he'd called her Sarah; an obvious confidence builder which only made her heart thump more violently. In a shaky voice she said what she'd rehearsed while he was in the water. 'Swimming's not for me. I'm scared stiff of sharks.

Anyway I can't swim properly.'

He looked at her in disbelief. 'You can't swim? Can't *remember*, you mean?'

'Can't remember what?'

'Oh, forget it. It's not important.' For a long time after that he didn't speak to her.

The wind came in the afternoon, weak and variable, at best no more than enough to stir the sails and ripple the sea. At times it would fall away and another calm would threaten. Then a light air would come from a different quarter and the sails would flap and fill.

It was a period of constant sail changing, of short beats on mostly unsatisfactory headings; but towards five o'clock, with the barometer rising, the wind blew freshly from the north-east and seemed settled there. Back on course for St Lucia, the ketch showed her paces, once more heeling to port, the wind on the starboard quarter.

'The Trade's with us again.' He smiled, handed her the wheel. 'We're making six knots.'

'Lovely to have the air through the boat,' she said. 'Not nearly so stuffy below now.'

In the late evening three warships steaming in company came up on the starboard beam. Steering a south-westerly course, they soon passed ahead.

'Soviet Navy.' He handed her the binoculars. 'I'll look at *Jane's*.' When he came back he took the binoculars again, focused on the ships. 'Yes. Two KRIVAK guided missile destroyers, escorting a LAMA-class missile cargo ship. Bound for Cuba, I daresay.'

'What for, I wonder?'

'Haven't a clue. Maybe on their way to replenish Soviet submarines at sea. That's what the LAMAS are for.'

'Awful thought, isn't it? The world getting ready to blow itself up.'

'That's a boring subject, Sarah. Let's do something interesting.'

She tried to read his expression. It was the second time

that day he'd called her Sarah. 'What's that?' She brushed loose strands of hair from her eyes.

'Have a jar, old sport, as Billings would say.'

'Super,' she said. 'I'm exhausted after all that sail changing.' She might as well have said 'after the fright you gave me this morning', for that was what she was thinking.

The heat of the afternoon sun beat down fiercely and it was really too hot to be on deck unless one had to be there. On watch until six in the evening and tempted to use the self-steering and go below, he had nevertheless decided against it. The ketch could do better with a helmsman and in fact he liked being on the wheel. It was possible to make the best of the wind, to react automatically to yawing and course wandering without having to concentrate. So he was able to think of other things and what he was thinking about now was the girl.

She had lied when she said she couldn't swim. When they'd had the row about the bully beef, and she'd bumped her head, she'd said, 'I just want to get out of here. Somehow, anyhow. If we were near land I'd swim for it.' That didn't sound like a non-swimmer. He was pretty sure he knew why she lied. It was fear. She was afraid that once in the water he'd leave her there. Christ! What a crazy thought. Didn't she realize that he could throw her over the side any time he chose? There was no need to wait for her to have a swim.

Her fear in the beginning was understandable but their relationship had changed; life on board was more pleasant now that both had accepted the situation. Of course there were times when he loathed her for what she'd done but they came at increasingly long intervals and were usually triggered by news of the race.

She was not only useful crew but a good companion. It was marvellous not to have to prepare meals – something she did much better than he could – and the shared watches meant he got more sleep. With someone on the wheel most of the time the ketch was making the best of the wind, and it was safer going. Crew on top keeping a look-out and an eye on things generally, meant less chance of disaster.

As the days passed he began to think of her in a more personal way. Living their lives as they did in a confined space with virtually no privacy, day after day, week after week, was having its affect. She was an attractive girl, physically and temperamentally, and the urge to make some sort of pass was strong. Certain things restrained him, however: fear of a rebuff – she hadn't given him the slightest encouragement – and a sort of residual loyalty to Tessa. That, he felt, was probably misplaced, as she hadn't even bothered to come down to see him off. But there was another reason and it weighed heavily; he knew that Sarah was not only afraid of him but helpless, and entirely dependent on his goodwill. If he made a pass she might feel he was trading on this and he didn't like the idea of forcing his attentions on an unwilling victim. So he resisted the temptation; at least for the time being, for it was one which seemed unlikely to go away.

Close to her in the darkness when she was at the wheel, the pressure of her body at times against his as the ketch lifted and dipped, he wondered about her love life. She must have had some experience, though she never discussed that sort of thing with him. He remembered their conversation the night before. It had been a serious one, about music, their likes and dislikes; they'd got on to country music and he said, 'You seem to be well and truly hooked on Crystal Gayle.'

'You mean *I'll Get Over You?*'

'Yes. You play it often enough. Unhappy love affair?'

It was dark in the cockpit so he couldn't see her expression when she said, 'Yes, I suppose so.'

Having explained to her that the cassette was a farewell gift, he changed the subject and they discussed other things. Half an hour later he took over the wheel.

Before going down below she said, 'The farewell gift. Was that an unhappy love affair?'

'Not sure – yet.'

'Poor you,' she said. 'I know how it feels.'

When he came off watch he brought the DR position up to date, entered the logbook and was about to tackle his voyage notes when he heard Portishead calling. He looked at the clock over the chart-table: 1915; they were in longitude 45°W so it would be 2215 in England. A personal call for *Sunboro Beauty*, said the operator. Would he take it? He said yes, and hoped it was Tessa. After some delay he heard the operator telling the caller to go ahead.

'How are you, old sport?' came through loud and clear. 'Gather you've dropped back a couple of places. Not that we're worried, of course. You're doing splendidly. Those multihulls are like bloody whippets downwind in good weather. But just you wait, me lad. The Western Ocean will sort them out. Don't forget to post the pics from St Lucia. And let's have some more drama, old dear.'

He answered Billings briefly, perhaps a little curtly, hanging up after remarking that the ketch's batteries couldn't support long telephone conversations, that he was sorry about the absence of drama, and that he trusted Billings would have a comfortable night.

An hour later he had almost finished writing up his voyage notes when he heard the warbling of the alarm on the main receiver. It was on 2182 kiloHertz: the international distress frequency. As he got down to the saloon the short-range VHF speaker crackled into life. It was *Karamagee* broadcasting a MAYDAY. On fire, out of control. Nick Farran, sounding cool, gave his position, said he was about to abandon the trimaran; fire, he added, had prevented use of the long-range transmitter.

He at once acknowledged, gave *Sunboro Beauty*'s position, told Farran he would make for the MAYDAY position. While he worked on the chart he left the receiver switched on, hoping to hear other acknowledgements but none came. Not that he was surprised. From the position reports he had heard at 2230 GMT that night, *Sunboro*

*Beauty* was the only competitor within VHF range. Just my bloody luck, he thought bitterly, as he plotted *Karamagee*'s position and up-dated his own, his mind busy with the implications of the new situation. It was still at least eleven days sail to St Lucia. If he picked up Farran now the story of the girl would be out, *Sunboro Beauty* would be disqualified, and the whole point of continuing in the race, of keeping her presence on board a secret until the finish, would be lost. 'The game's up,' he mumbled to himself. 'The whole flaming project's ripped wide open.' But there were no options. He couldn't desert Farran. That bloody girl was again the problem. But for her . . . he shook his head and his resentment switched momentarily to the Australian. Why did he have to have his goddam fire at a time when *Sunboro Beauty* was closer to him than anyone else? A day or so either way and it might have been different. He sighed, shook away the unproductive thoughts and concentrated on the chart. Farran was, he found, twenty-four miles to the south and west of *Sunboro Beauty*. Next he up-dated *Caspar's Folly*'s position; it was forty-seven miles to the north and west of the burning trimaran, well out of VHF range and twice the ketch's distance from where Farran was probably already drifting before the north-east Trades in an inflatable life-raft. Transmissions of the warbling note on 2182 kiloHertz had ceased. Presumably the fire was responsible for that.


CHAPTER ELEVEN


For what seemed interminably long minutes he ran through the courses of action open to him, considering each as if it were a computer read-out, discarding it and passing on hurriedly to the next, only to end in a state of confused anxiety. But he had to act quickly and the unavoidable thing was to alter course towards Farran. He stood in the companionway, shouted to the girl at the wheel. 'Ease the sheets and put her on two-two-five.' She repeated the order and he went back to listen for transmissions from Farran's emergency beacon. None came.

He switched on the main transmitter, relayed the MAYDAY on 2182 kiloHertz, gave *Sunboro Beauty*'s position and added that he was making for Farran's. He was deliberately circumspect about that, giving neither the course he was steering nor an estimate of the time at which he expected to reach it.

Acknowledgements came in quick succession: Trinidad, Barbados, the US Naval and Coast Guard Station at Portsmouth, Virginia, the Liberian tanker *Gratulana* – northward bound, ninety-six miles from the MAYDAY position and on course for it at seventeen knots – and two TRISTAR competitors, *Caspar's Folly* and *Wilson's Savoury*. John Caspar gave his position, said he was altering to a south-easterly course and hoped to reach Farran within six hours. *Wilson's Savoury*, reporting a position fifty-eight miles to the west of *Karamagee*, stressed that the north-east wind would involve him in a long beat to windward. He could not, he said, hope to reach Farran in under fifteen hours. Portsmouth, Virginia – call sign NMA – interrupted to say that it was now controlling the operation: the search was to be left to *Sunboro Beauty*, *Caspar's Folly* and the tanker *Gratulana* all of which should reach the scene within six hours. Station NMA added that certain US Navy units had been alerted.

It was evident that his action in relaying Farran's MAYDAY had paid off. The Australian would be getting a lot more help now than *Sunboro Beauty* alone could give, even if she were nearest to the scene of the disaster. It was a move towards the solution of his central problem – the impossibility of giving Farran a rational explanation of Sarah's presence on board if he picked him up.

In a misery of indecision, he checked the reading on the automatic log. Six point eight knots on the new course, the wind almost dead astern. Four to five hours allowing for the drift of the life-raft. The ketch should be somewhere near

88

Farran's position at around two in the morning. It would still be dark then and if the emergency beacon didn't function the search would be a long and difficult one; possibly hopeless in a force five wind and sea. It might have been a different story if the ketch's propeller had not been removed from its shaft.

It was dark under the overcast sky when he reached the cockpit, but he could see her face in the reflected light of the binnacle.

'Why have we altered course to the south?' she asked.

'A MAYDAY,' he said laconically. '*Karamagee*'s on fire. Nick Farran's abandoning her. We're going down there.'

'Oh God! Will he be all right?'

'Who can say? Can't hear his beacon bleeping. He's thirty or so miles south-west of us. Or was. The life-raft will be drifting.'

She repeated her question. 'D'you think he'll be all right?'

'Who the hell can say?' The reply was noisy, irritable. 'A life-raft's a small target on the open sea in this sort of weather.'

'How long before we reach him?'

'About six hours. If the position he gave was correct.' He was again deliberately circumspect. 'Then the real problem begins. The search. Pitch dark. Won't be easy. He must get that bleeper going.'

'Is anyone else looking for him?'

'Yes. John Caspar and a Liberian tanker.'

'*Caspar's Folly* is further away than we are, isn't she?'

'Yes.' It was a grudging admission. 'But Caspar and the tanker are both within about six hours of him.'

'Good. So we might get there first.' She said it with the enthusiasm of a schoolboy reviewing the prospects of a race.

He made no answer to that but a minute or so later came out with, 'Do you realize what this means?'

'In what way?'

He ignored that. 'I'm going below to listen for a bleeper signal.' Before she could repeat her question he had gone.

He was back a few minutes later.

'Any luck?'

'No. Nothing yet.'

'D'you think he's all right?'

'For Christ's sake stop asking that. How the hell do I know?'

A shower of rain swept over them, the noise of it drowning anything she might have said.

With the mizzen and main unreefed, booms well out port and starboard, and the big genoa holding a bellyful of wind to port, the ketch was running before the wind, surging and surfing, the seas hissing by.

The night was warm and his rain-soaked body, naked but for a bathing slip, glistened wetly in the binnacle light. Near him the girl was manning the wheel, her bikini clad body as wet with rain as his. Under other circumstances he would have found running like that exhilarating but his only emotion was anxiety and the stress of it was in his voice.

'Right. I'll take over now,' he said curtly.

'It's only ten,' she complained. 'I'm on till eleven.'

'Get some sleep. We'll be hard stretched when the search begins.'

'Don't feel like sleep.'

An edge of temper came into his voice. 'Do as I tell you.'

She said something he couldn't hear, handed over the wheel and went below. A few minutes after she'd gone he brought the ketch's head up from 225° to 240°, and adjusted the sheets until she was balanced on the new course, the wind now fine on the starboard quarter.

Though he would not allow himself to dwell on the possible consequences of what he'd done, he was aware that with the alteration of course he'd probably resolved a desperately difficult problem.

Half an hour after he'd ordered her below to get some sleep she was back in the cockpit, groping her way aft to where he was at the wheel.

'What d'you want?' he asked gruffly.

'Why have we altered course?'

90

He waited before answering, trying to comprehend the state of her mind. She must have felt the change in motion and looked at the compass in the saloon. 'I think you'd better leave the conduct of the search to me,' he said.

'You told me,' her voice was trembling, 'that the MAYDAY position was about thirty or so miles away – that it would take us about six hours to get there.'

'You're annoying me.' It was a warning growl.

'I've been looking at the chart. At what you plotted. The distance to Farran was only twenty-four miles when we received the MAYDAY. We've been – still are – logging almost seven knots. That's three and a half hours, not six.'

'Any more information you'd care to give?'

'Yes. On this course we'll pass about four miles north of him.'

'You know,' he observed coldly. 'You should mind your own bloody business for a change.'

'It's everybody's business.' Her voice had risen. 'Nick Farran's somewhere down there in a tiny life-raft and you're *deliberately* deserting him, aren't you?'

Mustn't lose my temper, he told himself, must keep calm. 'I don't owe you of all people any explanation. But for your information, I'm doing what I believe to be best.'

'No you're not,' she contradicted. 'You're putting your own interests first as usual. The race, or the alleged book, or whatever. It's you, you, you – and your decision can cost him his life.'

With the girl ranting at him in that hysterical high-pitched voice, his mind torn with worry, he felt like throwing her overboard and having done once and for all with that problem. But it was a wild thought and he suppressed it. 'You have the bloody nerve to say *my* decision may cost Farran his life. Can't you see, you silly goddam bitch, that it's your decision? If you'd not decided to stow away in my boat the problem wouldn't have arisen. I wouldn't have had to worry about how to explain your being on board if I picked him up. It's an impossible thing to explain. It's your bloody stupidity that's responsible for all this. Like it has

91

been for disqualifying me and everything else.' He waved an arm at her, his voice choking with anger. 'For Christ's sake go away before I really lose my temper and . . .' He didn't finish the sentence.

'You wicked bastard,' she said quietly, staring at him with a contempt which the darkness disguised. He said nothing and she went below.

She took off the bikini, dried herself with a towel, put on a T-shirt and a pair of his underpants and lay on the bunk, curled up, knees against the side, back to the lee-cloth. She was too upset for sleep. What he was doing appalled her. She couldn't rid her mind of a picture of Nick Farran somewhere out there in the darkness in the life-raft, aware that failure of the emergency beacon had diminished his chances of rescue, but believing that *Sunboro Beauty* would soon be there searching for him.

She felt nothing but revulsion for Martin Savage. How *could* he behave as he had? His obsession with the race was sick, absolutely obscene. If he was prepared to desert Nick Farran like that he'd do anything. Nothing would be allowed to stand in his way. He could say what he liked about the book, she was convinced he believed he still had a chance in the race. She had no illusions about what that meant for her.

She had expected him to react violently when she told him what she thought of him. Instead he'd said nothing and she found that even more terrifying because it was so unlike him. But she'd been too upset to care. Her feelings had burst out of her. Now, with time to think, fear returned. Just when their relationship was becoming tolerable this had to happen. She was back where she was on the night he discovered her; at the mercy of a man who was probably half insane. Such a strange mixture: kind, considerate, almost tender at times; yet capable of violence, even cruelty at others. And it was not always just a matter of mood. The desertion of Nick Farran was a calculated, cold-blooded thing.

A strangely unbalanced man, she decided, remembering

their conversation about music a night or so before. He had spoken of Handel's *Messiah*, how it had to be heard in the setting of a cathedral for all its beauty to be appreciated. She asked him then if he were religious and he said no, not in any formal sense but ...

'But what?' she probed, and he laughed in a small, deprecatory way. 'You wouldn't understand. It would sound peculiar to you.'

'What would?'

'My religion. It's my own thing. My prayers, my choir, my cathedral.'

'Your cathedral?'

'You wouldn't understand that either.'

Knowing that silence was more compelling than speech she waited until at last he said, 'The sea and the sky – the sublime setting for the music in a man's soul.' He finished with another nervous laugh which seemed out of place in one so rugged and strong. Anything she might have said after that would have sounded trivial, so she was silent and he changed the subject. But how could a man who believed things like that, and was able to express them so sensitively, behave as he did?

When she called him a wicked bastard and stood there in that threatening way his mind plunged and he had been as near to instinctive violence as he supposed it was possible to be. Anything might have happened, even murder.

Somehow he controlled himself, said nothing and he was now grateful for that. He had already suffered enough self-disgust without adding to the burden. But what struck him as grossly unfair was that the girl should attack him for a course of action which she had forced upon him. Once again he thought how incredibly insensitive she was, so quick to see herself as the innocent victim in a situation for which she alone was responsible. Not once since he'd found her on board had she apologized. She knew of the sacrifices he had made to get into the race, yet she'd never expressed sympathy or regret, or shown any awareness of the enormity of her offence.

Though he had never really come to terms with the consequences of what she'd done, he had tried to make the best of a wretched situation, to be reasonably considerate, even friendly – and this was his reward: screaming, insulting abuse from a hysterical young woman.

The trouble was, he told himself, he'd been too friendly, too considerate; kindness had undermined his authority. She wouldn't have dared speak to him like that earlier in the voyage. He ridiculed his earlier thought that they might make love. If he let that happen the situation would become even more difficult.

Baffled and resentful, his thoughts went back to Farran. It was his intention to take *Sunboro Beauty* some miles west of the MAYDAY position then, once past it, to go south, well downwind, before beating up on a wide zigzag covering the probable track of the dinghy's drift. He estimated that drift at about two knots; in four hours say as much as eight miles. By the time the ketch was sufficiently downwind, *Caspar's Folly* and the tanker should have arrived. The three of them could then carry out a systematic search. He had only one reservation – and it was this that had dictated the element of delay in his plan – under no circumstances was he prepared to take Farran on board. That would be for John Caspar or the tanker, even if *Sunboro Beauty* had to lead them to the life-raft.

As for the girl, he would see to it when the time came that she was out of sight.

# CHAPTER TWELVE

At 0138 GMT on 30 November, some three hours after *Karamagee*'s MAYDAY, the US Naval Coast Guard station at Portsmouth, Virginia, informed those concerned that, consequent upon the arrival in the search area of two United States Navy frigates with onboard helicopters, the services of *Sunboro Beauty, Caspar's Folly* and the tanker *Gratulana* would no longer be required.

*Sunboro Beauty* and *Caspar's Folly* were by then only eighteen miles apart and in touch with each other by VHF radio telephone. After a brief discussion their skippers agreed to abandon the search and resume course for St Lucia.

'If the US frigates and their choppers don't find Nick, nobody will,' said John Caspar.

Martin had agreed. 'No point in hanging around now that Portsmouth has told us we're not needed.'

So the two yachts headed once more for St Lucia, *Caspar's Folly* having lost a good deal more ground than *Sunboro Beauty*.

Shortly before noon on the following day Portsmouth, Virginia, reported that the frigates had recovered *Karamagee*'s life-raft twenty-three miles downwind of the MAYDAY position. There had been no one in it, nor had the radio beacon been switched on. It was assumed that Farran had failed to board the self-inflating raft after launching. The frigates had found the burnt-out remains of the trimaran afloat but without an occupant and had sunk it by gunfire.

He entered a summary of the Portsmouth, Virginia messages in the ketch's logbook but did not tell the girl about them. Determined that she should be punished, he had ignored her since the outburst the night before. That was why, when she came up to take over the watch at three o'clock the next morning, he told her peremptorily, 'I don't require your assistance.'

That night he spoke to Billings via Portishead, gave him the *Karamagee* story. Billings' 'Great – that's the sort of drama we need, old dear,' made him feel faintly sick and glad that he was far out at sea, isolated in a world of his own in which the sort of motivation which drove Billings didn't exist. Well, not quite his own – there was the girl. His resentment flared.

At midnight on 2 December – forty-eight hours after the *Karamagee* incident – the wind fell away and when daylight came, hot and humid, the surface of the sea, rising and falling to the long undulations of the northerly swell, was oil smooth.

He had spent most of the night on deck, either in the cockpit or sail changing. Indeed most of the last forty-eight hours had been spent there, both because he had refused to allow the girl to take over a watch and because he wished to avoid being below with her. On a number of occasions, probably to escape from the stuffiness of the saloon in hot weather, she had come up on deck but, in no mood to forgive, he continued to ignore her.

As always he enjoyed seeing the beginning of the new day, for him the best time at sea, the stars fading, the eastern sky growing lighter, slowly revealing the sea and the sky.

While *Sunboro Beauty* rolled gently to the swell, sails sheeted hard in, waiting for a wind which seemed never to come, he sat in the cockpit watching with an empty mind the scraps of weed which floated nearby. For days now they had seen these isolated tangles of mustard-coloured weed, and it was while speculating about the mythical Sargasso Sea that he saw the blur of a dark shape, immense in size, pass under the ketch from port to starboard. Apprehensive, astonished, he had decided it must be a submarine, when a plume of water shot into the air a hundred or so yards from the ketch and he heard the shrill whistle of a whale spouting.

Not long afterwards a school of porpoises came up from astern, breaking the surface into foaming white water as they swept by, leaping and diving in motions so graceful and joyous that he felt like shouting applause. Instead he did something a good deal more prosaic; went below to make a mug of coffee, found the girl already busy at the stove, ignored her restrained 'hullo', and returned to the cockpit frustrated and annoyed.

The coffee was something he had been looking forward to, but he just could not bring himself to talk to her or in any other way acknowledge her presence. Sitting in the cockpit, staring defiantly out to sea, he decided that even if it was stupid and self-defeating he was damned if he was going to give in. In the midst of these surly thoughts the girl came through the hatchway. She stood at the fore-end of the cockpit, hands on the coaming, facing the bows, her back to him. It was nut brown, like the rest of her body outside the bikini, and he confessed to himself that it looked rather good.

Without turning her head she said, 'I'm sorry. I owe you an apology. I've behaved so badly. Until I heard you talking to John Caspar – discussing the search with him on the radiophone, I mean – I honestly thought you were going to desert Nick Farran and I was terribly upset. Since then I've also seen what you wrote in the logbook – those Portsmouth messages about the USN frigates finding the life-raft but not poor Nick. And – well, you know. I can only say that I'm desperately sorry. It was beastly of me. Especially after all I've done to you.' Without waiting for an answer she went below again.

He was glad of that because he hadn't been ready for an apology; didn't quite know how to handle it. It was something he'd have to think about. Made things difficult really – but at least it was good that she'd apologized.

It was full daylight now and on the western horizon he saw the dark silhouette of a tanker. It was the first ship they'd seen since the Soviet warships had passed a few days earlier.

# CHAPTER THIRTEEN

On 3 December he entered the noon position in the deck log: 16°10′N, 52°50′W, distance to St Lucia 487 miles. Since leaving Santa Maria the ketch had made good 1873 miles, though she had logged 2157 miles of sailing along the southerly route. He was pleased with the progress made for it was a considerable improvement on her time from Plymouth to Santa Maria. Since the start from Plymouth on 7 November, *Sunboro Beauty* had made good 3051 miles in twenty-seven days, an average of 113 miles a day. Those ahead of him had obviously done better, but he was well satisfied.

With the ketch still becalmed he tackled various tasks during the forenoon; working on the starboard track to the genoa fairlead; checking locking wires on the rigging, repairing stitching on No. 2 jib, and dealing with a defective gland in the bilge pump. That was something he'd hoped to put off until the cooler weather but it wouldn't wait.

In the two days following the girl's apology their relationship had improved steadily and that, combined with the prospect of reaching St Lucia soon, had raised his morale – and, he supposed, hers for she seemed unusually cheerful.

While he worked on deck she sat in the cockpit machining a seam on the heavy-weather mainsail and they were able to keep up a running conversation. The subjects discussed ranged from the BBC news of the night before to *Sunboro Beauty*'s food stocks, notes for the book, the progress of the race and the whims of the weather. She asked him about St Lucia.

'Where do we report when we get there?'

'The race launch should be off Port Castries. That's St Lucia's main port. Round on the western side, in the lee of the island.'

She was thoughtful. 'Think you'll get any mail there?'

'Probably. Bound to be something from Harry Billings and my mother. A few reminders from my creditors, and hopefully newspapers.' He looked at her keenly, wondering if her questions were prompted by thoughts of escape at St Lucia.

'Lucky you,' she said. 'I won't get anything.'

'I imagine you won't.'

'Think you'll hear from . . .' she paused, looked up, half smiled. 'Crystal Gayle?'

'I don't know. Maybe. There was nothing from her at Santa Maria.'

She stopped machining. 'Do you still love her?' It was said lightly and might have been taken for a throw-away question had she not watched him so closely.

'Ready to swap confidences?'

'Up to a point – yes.'

'Well, I daresay I do. We lived together for nearly three years, you know. She's an attractive person. Intelligent, and amusing when she wants to be. Very much out for herself.'

'Aren't you?' She softened it with, 'I mean, aren't we all?'

'I suppose so.' He shrugged, then probed. 'What about you? Still love *him*?'

She looked towards the distant horizon. 'I used to think I was deeply in love. Looking back, thinking objectively about it now that I'm away from his influence, I realize that it was infatuation. We didn't live together. I was his secretary for nearly three years. In an advertising agency. He was the boss. Much older than me. Very kind and decent really, but terribly – I don't know – superficial, I suppose. And conceited. Yes, very conceited. I mean, I think he believed a lot of what he said but mostly he was acting a part. Pretending to be the sort of man he wanted you to believe he was.'

'Sounds rather a yawn. Did you sleep with him?'

'Of course. It was an affair. From what the girls in the

office said I was the latest in a longish line. I took it very seriously at first. Thought it might even mean marriage. But he ditched me. He had rather a nice wife, and of course she won. They almost always do, you know. The little women at home.'

'Doesn't that comfort you? You'll be a wife yourself one day.'

'Not particularly comforting. Especially if it means having a husband like Carlos.'

'That was his name, was it?'

'Yes. What's her name?'

'Tessa.'

'H'm, rather Thomas Hardyish.'

'She isn't like that at all. Much tougher. Have there been other men?'

She nodded without looking up. 'Two brief encounters, as Carlos would say. Both married men. They seem to be my weakness. Nothing else. I'm only twenty-three, you know. Carlos was the first real love affair. Barbara Cartland would say he'd had the best years of my life. Sob, sob.' Her smile betrayed her embarrassment. 'Have you had lots of women?'

'A few. I suppose about average for my age.'

'What's that? Your age I mean.'

'Ten years older than you.' He checked the last of the locking wires, straightened his back, looked round the horizon. 'The lonely sea and the sky,' he quoted sententiously. 'Now for the bloody bilge pump.'

They'd got on to dangerous ground, he decided, as he went down the companion-ladder; but it was stimulating, lent an edge to the relationship.

That night the wind came fitfully; first no more than light airs switching from one point of the compass to the other, but settling later in the north-east from which it blew gently for several hours. At two in the morning it veered to the south-east and towards dawn settled, perversely, in the west so that the best heading the ketch could make was well off her course.

All this entailed a hectic night of sail changing, of trying various headings, of one frustration after another and a good deal of bad language. The girl had stayed up most of the night sharing the work and providing a useful and cheerful help. By daylight the wind had gone and *Sunboro Beauty* lay becalmed once more, mainsail and mizzen sheeted hard in to reduce rolling and the noisy slatting of the sails.

Though tired from their exertions in the course of an almost sleepless night they managed a good breakfast. After it he went for a swim. As before she made her excuses for not joining him. Instead she drenched herself with several buckets of seawater and lay on the coachroof drying in the sun, wishing she could lie there naked instead of in the wet bikini.

While he swam round the ketch, kicking, splashing and occasionally shouting to her, she thought of the previous night. When reporting *Sunboro Beauty*'s position to Portishead he had as usual listened to other competitors giving theirs and afterwards, when he joined her in the cockpit, he said, 'We're lying eighth. Would have been ninth but for *Karamagee*.'

'Poor Nick,' she said. 'Who's leading?'

'Still *Tornado Four*. *Grande Rapide* and *Mercedes Express* are gaining on her, especially *Mercedes Express*.' He laughed in a dry unamused way, as if only to signal that what was to come should be regarded as funny. 'Pierre Fougeux won't like that. He can't stand the German. An old personal rivalry, I think. Actually Kurt Grosse isn't a bad sort. Bit arrogant, but he can't help that. It's in the blood, you know.'

'So Fougeux and Grosse are now reporting their positions?'

'That's right. I imagine because St Lucia's not far off. Doesn't matter if the route they're on is known at this stage. They've obviously plumped for the northerly route. It's shorter but you take a chance with the wind. It must have worked for them. *Omega Challenger* hasn't reported for a few days. No idea why. John Caspar has almost made up the distance he lost to *Wilson's Savoury.*'

He had rambled on, enthusing about *Sunboro Beauty's* performance, how the ketch would do even better once they got into the bad weather, and how he'd settled for a forty-five-foot monohull for that reason.

That had awakened in her the old fears. Martin Savage was so obviously absorbed in the race, fascinated by the prospect of finishing well, and oblivious, apparently, to the fact that he wasn't really in it at all.

She had no doubt that it was *she* who stood between him and his burning ambition; what would happen, she asked herself, if the ketch really came into the running later on?

St Lucia would, she believed, be a repetition of Santa Maria. There'd be no chance of escape there, although their relationship had mended and he was friendly and considerate again, even showing signs of interest in her. Surely then, she reasoned, her best protection was to strengthen the emotional ties between them, to make him need her not only as a help but as a woman. It wouldn't involve any sacrifice. When he was in a good humour he was an attractive man – at times almost the gorgeous man of her fantasies.

These thoughts were interrupted by his shout, 'You don't know what you're missing, Sarah.' Soon he was back in the cockpit, puffing, dripping, rubbing himself down with a rough towel. Watching him, thinking how marvellously brown and lean and muscular he was, she returned to the thoughts which he'd interrupted and delicate waves of anticipation, encouraged by fantasy, rippled through her body.

With the towel still in his hand he came and sat beside her where she lay on the coachroof. 'You really should swim on these hot calm days. There won't be many opportunities. It's great. Tremendously invigorating.'

She smiled apologetically. 'You know my problem. I can't swim.'

'Don't believe you. Something else, isn't it?'

'No, of course not. I'd say if it was.' She shied away from the subject. 'This sun is heaven. I'm almost Polynesian.'

His eyes followed hers. 'Polynesians are brown all over.

No bikini blight.' He slipped a strap off her shoulder, revealed a breast, touched it gently. 'Look. Spoils the effect – that white patch. Why bother about a bikini out here in the blue? It's absurd.'

'It's not,' she said unconvincingly, pushing at the hand on her breast, not very hard because hers was no more than a formal protest; and she rather liked what he was doing.

'You don't really enjoy covering up everything, do you? It's a sort of built-in feminine modesty carried to ridiculous lengths.'

He was closer now, leaning over her, gently dislodging the bikini bra. She continued a token resistance, felt his lips on hers and became mistily aware of a hand pulling away the lower part of the bikini.

She gasped. 'No. Not now. Please don't . . .' The words were lost as his mouth covered hers. It was then that she forgot her inhibitions and grasped him with fierce and sudden strength, her mind swimming.

Lying on the coachroof, her head on his arm, she turned sideways to look at him. 'You shouldn't have done that.' She frowned, regarded him with quizzical, disapproving eyes.

'You seemed to enjoy it.'

'I did. But you didn't ask me.'

'Of course not. You'd have said no.'

'Brute!' She laughed, got up suddenly, went to the stern, climbed the rail and dived over the side. When she'd swum some little distance away he shouted, 'Keep close alongside. Don't go far.'

Before long she was back on board, water streaming from her brown body, her eyes mischievous. 'Lend me your towel.' She thrust out an arm.

He passed it to her. 'Thought you couldn't swim?' The blue eyes wrinkled accusingly.

She ran a hand affectionately down his naked body, looked at him with a pretence of penitence. 'Sorry. Some time I'll tell you why.'

# CHAPTER FOURTEEN

It was three days before the wind came again from the northeast to break the long period of calms and light airs. In that time the ketch had made little progress through the water, though the drift of the North Equatorial Current had carried her slowly westwards. The smooth sea which had for so long mirrored the heat of the sun was by no means lonely for they had seen ships pass in the night, and each day dolphins and flying fish played about the surface with proprietorial assurance; once they saw a thresher shark attacking a shoal of fish, leaping high out of the water, falling with arched body, threshing the sea as it fell.

In some ways this was an idyllic period, for though he cursed the calm and prayed for wind, for her time stood still and fantasies came true. During the mornings they would work at various tasks until noon when he would fix the ketch's position while she prepared a snack lunch. Then they would swim, one of them always on board while the other was in the water. That done he would announce that, the sun being well over the yardarm, it was time for Calypso Cup – his rum punch – and they would sit on the coachroof drinking it to a background of cassette music. The punch finished – never more than one, he was strict about that – they would lunch, finding what shade they could under the windless sails. In the afternoons they would read, wash the few items of clothing they used, write up their voyage notes, sometimes sleep and often just talk, finding out what they could about each other's lives. On each of those becalmed days they made love beneath triangular white sails set against a blue sky, the affection and intensity of their love increasing as the days went by. It was a time so heady, so unbelievably right, that she feared its end – and end it did with the coming of the wind and a boisterous sea. Then the serious business of sailing took over again and left no time or energy for idylls.

There was little doubt in her mind that she was falling in love, beginning to think of him in a very different way. Inevitably, this led to comparisons with Carlos. The two men were so different: Martin she saw as a stronger, more determined character, less talkative but more assured; kind, affectionate now, but ruthless and brutal when it suited him. He would, she thought, be a much more dependable man in dangerous times. Unlike Carlos he was without conceit, never bragged directly or by innuendo. Indeed he seldom talked about himself. On balance probably the better man, though certainly more difficult and complex. She had always been able to manipulate Carlos; something she knew was not possible with Martin. She realized, too, that the comparison was in some ways unfair; for example, the circumstances under which they'd made love.

She remembered her excitement when Carlos first suggested lunch – a month after she'd become his secretary. 'I know rather a super little place in Soho. Doesn't look much, but the food – ah, su-pairb.' The phonetic exaggeration had been accompanied by the crooking of an index finger against a thumb, hand held before the eyes.

The super little place turned out to be a rather sleazy establishment with a strangely assorted clientele and unremarkable cooking. But at twenty, lunching with the handsome managing-director was an occasion so breathtaking that these shortcomings had passed her by. After coffee and liqueurs Carlos had frowned with almost hypnotic intensity. 'You do things to me, Vikki. Incredible things. I'm on fire inside.'

It was pure corn of course, but she fell for it and in an upstairs bedroom which matched downstairs in its sleaziness they made awkward and hurried love. The thought of it now made her wince. How marvellously different was the gorgeous man's love-making in *Sunboro Beauty*.

During twilight on 8 December he got a star-fix and checked

it with RDF bearings from Martinique and St Lucia; the plotted position put *Sunboro Beauty* forty-seven miles from Pointe du Cap, the northermost tip of the island. Course was set to pass two-and-a-half miles north of the point, outside the twenty-fathom line, and he estimated the time of arrival there to be 0445 if the wind continued to blow from east-north-east at about twelve knots. He hoped to be off Port Castries itself by 0615, the approximate time of sunrise.

The barometer was steady and it promised to be a fine night though hot – and dark because the moon had set. The ketch was logging four knots but making good five with the help of the Equatorial Current which set towards the Windward Islands. At 0200 the girl came up to take over the watch. They chatted quietly for a few minutes, he told her of the ETAs for Pointe du Cap and Port Castries, said he'd sighted nothing during his watch, gave her the course to steer, mentioned the set of the sails and handed over the wheel.

Having said that she was to call him an hour later – earlier if she sighted anything – he went below, wrote up the deck log and without removing his shorts – all that he wore – he lay down on his bunk. It was his first rest of the night and he was soon asleep.

The ringing of the course-alarm woke him. He jumped up, saw from the instruments over the chart-table that the time was 0240 and that the ketch was turning sharply to starboard. Above him the nagging noise of gear banging and sails flogging told him that *Sunboro Beauty* had come untidily into the wind.

He raced up on deck, saw with one eye that the ketch was in irons, and with the other what looked like Brighton Pier – brilliantly lit – crossing astern less than a quarter of a mile away.

'Christ!' he said. 'It's a cruise liner. How the hell did she get as close as that?'

'I don't know,' the girl shrilled. 'One minute she was miles away and the next almost on top of us, coming up fast on our

106

port bow. I didn't think she'd seen us, the bearing was steady, so I put the helm up and came into the wind.'

He took over and they sheeted in the sails, got the ketch under way and back on course, and eased the sheets. She handled the jib sheets and he the wheel and the main and mizzen, and it was soon done.

Only then did he say, 'Why wasn't I called when you first sighted that ship?'

'You'd not been down long and I knew you were short on sleep.'

'That has nothing to do with it. I told you to call me if you sighted *anything*. You know perfectly well that's a standing order.'

'Sorry, I knew I'd be calling you at three o'clock anyway. Thought it was important you should have at least an hour undisturbed.' She spoke quietly and apologetically. 'You've had hardly any sleep in the last twenty-four hours.'

'In future obey my orders and don't think up excuses for disobeying them.' It was blunt and brutal, he knew, but that was the way he'd learnt, and it was the only way she would. Safety was paramount at sea. There wasn't room for sentiment.

There was an uneasy silence after that until he said, 'You'd better go below.'

'May I ask you something first?'

'Yes. What is it?'

'When we get to Port Castries. Is it going to be the same as at Santa Maria?'

'Yes. I'm afraid so.'

'You won't gag and bind me again?' It was more a plea than a question.

'No option,' he said. 'I can't afford to take chances, too much at stake.'

'Why? Surely you can trust me now? Everything's different, isn't it? Since what's happened to us?'

'No. I can't trust you. Too much has been put into this project. I'm not prepared to risk it. You're a stranger. I don't really know you. Can't be sure of anything about you.' The old harshness had returned. 'If *Sunboro Beauty* is disqualified now there is nothing left for me. Not even the book. I'd be destroyed. I would have thought that was self-evident.'

She waited, watching his face in the dim light of the binnacle, hoping he would give her some encouragement but somehow knowing he wouldn't.

'You can trust me,' she pleaded. 'I promise I'll go below – keep out of sight – when we get to Port Castries. It's different, you see. I *was* afraid before, but not now. That's why I went swimming after we first made love.'

He said, 'You lied to me about that, didn't you? You may have told other lies. How do I know? Easy to promise not to show yourself at Port Castries, then break the promise. And I'd find that out too late, wouldn't I? You've only got to be seen for a couple of seconds and I'm finished. Even if they see movement through a portlight, or hear your voice, it's enough to finish me. I can't afford to take that sort of risk. You must be reasonable – try to understand.'

It was too important to give up, so she persisted. 'Don't these last few days mean anything to you? Our closeness to each other? Our love-making?'

'Not enough to change my mind about Port Castries.' There was not a grain of warmth in his voice. 'Anyway, what's so awful about being gagged and bound. You know I won't harm you. And it isn't for long.'

Above them the stars shimmered remotely and watching them she felt lonely and afraid. 'You're a non-caring person, Martin,' she said. 'You don't understand that humiliation is just as much a form of violence as a kick in the stomach.'

'Rubbish!' He put more venom into the word than it deserved. 'This argument is boring. You'd better go below.'

Of course she'll try to get away, he told himself when she'd gone. There's nothing in this for her. She's here by accident. Her own fault, but she's a prisoner and wants to escape. Simple as that. She knows that the tough time, the dirty weather, has still to come – that it'll be hard, bloody uncomfortable and dangerous. She's trying to make a thing of the sexual relationship. Why should that make a difference? A healthy man and woman, isolated together for weeks on end, at last having sex? What's so special about that? She says I'm a non-caring person, whatever that means; but of course I care – I feel things. Sometimes only anger and contempt because of what she's done. At others something quite different. I don't really know how to describe it – but I can't help liking her, even admiring her. She's good to look at, capable, sensible, and she's certainly got guts. Can't be easy for her here. Frightened, not knowing what lies ahead. Thing is, I mustn't get too involved emotionally. That can't do any good. The race is too important. Nothing else really matters.

At four-thirty that morning with Pointe du Cap broad on the port bow he picked up the lights marking the entrance to Port Castries. It was still dark but the lights of small craft were visible in the distance. Before long they would be close. He engaged the self-steering and went below, taking a coil of rope with him.

She was curled up on her bunk behind the lee-cloth. At first he thought she was asleep, but she called out, 'How far now?'

'About seven miles,' he said. 'Just sighted the lights at Port Castries. We'll have to get on with it.'

'Oh, God!' She sat up. 'Can't you leave the gag till later. It's awful having one's mouth plugged up. Especially in this hot weather.' She left the bunk and leant against the chart-table, her naked back to him.

Watching her in silence he wondered what he should do. At last he said, 'All right. We'll do the gag later. Unless somebody looks like coming close. There are several small craft around. May be more as we get further in.' He put a hand on her shoulder. 'If you don't mind, we'd better get on with the rest.'

She brushed his hand away. 'I *do* mind. And it's *you* not *we* doing it. I think the whole thing's despicable.' She slipped on a T-shirt and jeans, moved back to the chart-table and leant on it, head in hands.

He stared at her for a moment, his face expressionless;

then he pointed to the space between the saloon table and the starboard bunk. 'Come on,' he said. 'There isn't much time.'

Reluctant, frowning, she knelt, then lay down. Neither spoke while he bound her feet and arms until, towards the end, he said, 'I can imagine what you're thinking. I'd just like you to remember that I didn't ask you to come on board – I didn't want you here. You've yourself to blame for what's happened. No one else. As far as I'm concerned you're a complete disaster.'

'I feel that about you.' She turned on him with sudden spite. 'I certainly didn't want to be here. Wouldn't have come within a mile of this awful boat if I'd known what was going to happen.'

They watched each other uncertainly for a few hostile moments, after which he went to the chart-table and called Port Castries on VHF. The acknowledgement came through, he gave the ketch's name and race number, and amended the time of arrival to half past six.

He took a pillow from the navigator's bunk and put it under her head before he went back to the cockpit.

In the east the sky grew lighter behind the line of hills and mountain peaks, their ridges silhouetted against the rising sun as the ketch covered the last few miles into Port Castries, and he experienced that strange but special thrill of arrival which belongs to the end of a long voyage.

Two years earlier he had done a delivery trip to St Lucia and during a week at the Malabar Beach Hotel he'd fallen in love with the island. Now, sailing down the coast in the half-light of early morning, he was able to pick out familiar landmarks: Pigeon Island, Rodney Bay, Anse du Choc, and Rat Island, the small hump he'd so often seen from Malabar Beach. Lights still flickered along the coast in the dawn haze and the smell of the land drifted across the water: a heady odour of seashore, sugar cane, copra and spices and wood smoke, pungent and evocative, recalling native villages, beach parties, calypso dancing and steel bands, and breakfasts in the shade of tropical trees with humming birds hovering over sugar bowls, fragile creatures of exquisite beauty.

The wind had backed slightly to the nor-nor-east but coming down the coast he'd been keeping far enough out to avoid the lee formed by the mountains. The reporting point was a mile due west of Pointe d'Estrees and now that he had to close the land he feared losing the wind. The light was growing stronger and in the distance he could see small craft coming out from the harbour. He prayed they were not a welcoming party.

When the nearest boat was two miles away he engaged self-steering, went below and gagged the girl. She said nothing while this was being done but when he'd finished her eyes were wet with tears. Feeling wretched, he wiped them away with a tissue and said, 'I'm terribly sorry, Sarah. I hate doing this.' He looked at her sadly, wondering if she would ever understand what drove him.

The VHF speaker came alive. A rasping voice announced that the race launch was about to get under way and expected to be at the reporting point in fifteen minutes; the delay was regretted – there'd been a hitch. He acknowledged the message and was congratulating himself that the voice was not that of Billings when the VHF speaker crackled again. 'What cheer, old sport. Thought I'd collect the drama and pics in person – shake the maestro's hand – ha ha! Got some mail and goodies for you, old dear. We'll be alongside pronto pronto. Casting off now.'

## CHAPTER FIFTEEN

In the lee of the land off Port Castries the wind had all but dropped and by the time the race launch appeared the ketch was just making way through the water.

Despite shouted objections from *Sunboro Beauty* the

West Indian skipper tried to put his boat alongside to exchange mail and hand over Billings' 'goodies'; in the course of this manoeuvre the launch bumped the ketch's starboard quarter and an infuriated Martin Savage let loose a stream of invective: 'Keep your bloody boat away from my hull,' he roared. 'I haven't come four thousand fucking miles to be sunk by you.'

It was a pardonable exaggeration. But for the avoiding action he'd taken at the last moment the ketch's self-steering gear might have been damaged. The race launch maintained a respectful distance after that, a restrained exchange of information taking place while they moved away from the land. Even the effervescent Billings had been subdued by the near disaster. 'All the best, old soul. Sorry we gave you a spot of bother,' were his last shouted words as they parted company.

What Billings and those with him were not aware of was Martin Savage's fear that the girl might somehow draw attention to herself if the launch remained in close company for any length of time. Throughout what seemed to him an interminably long and unnecessary delay he was consumed by the desire to get away before she might work a hand free, loosen the gag and shout for help; or make a noise that could be heard across the still waters by banging her bound legs against the lockers. The longer the conversation with Billings and the race official went on, the greater this fear became, particularly as a number of local yachts and motor cruisers had arrived on the scene and were showing an interest in *Sunboro Beauty*, some circling her, their occupants calling out messages of congratulation and good cheer.

Faced with such unwelcome attention he lost no time in setting off on a long beat to windward; one which would take the ketch sufficiently far to the east to clear the island of Martinique.

The race launch was making its way back into Port Castries.

'Know him well?' inquired the yacht club man who represented the TRISTAR committee.

'Yes,' said Billings. 'We're members of the same club on the south coast.'

'I see.' There was a pause. 'Tell me, is he always like that?'

'Bit ratty, you mean? No. Not at all. It's the strain you know, old boy. He's been at sea on his own now for thirty-three days. Probably short on sleep. Sailed over four thousand miles in all sorts of weather, yet knows he's only half way. On top of that he was involved in the search for *Karamagee*. First to pick up the MAYDAY and relay it. All that adds up to a hell of a lot of tension, you know." He lowered his voice, jerked his head in the direction of the wheelhouse. "Boyo in there made a bit of a cockup didn't he? Certainly didn't help.'

The race official nodded understandingly. 'Must say I wonder why these single-handers do it? Incredibly long voyages alone. No one to talk to. Nobody on deck when you're asleep. Tackling all that bad weather, sail handling and navigation, cooking and radio and God-knows-what else alone. Not for me. I'd go round the ruddy bend.'

'I think some of them do,' said Billings cheerfully. 'You've got to be a bit of a wierdo in the first place. To want to do it, I mean.'

'How did you people come to sponsor him?'

'I fixed it actually. Knew his chum Tim Baxter, the bloke who helped with the fitting-out and tuning. He told me Martin Savage was hunting around for a sponsor. I didn't really know him well then, but his sailing record was common knowledge in the club. Tim and I both reckoned he'd put up a good show. So I put it to our people and they fell for it. Just like that.'

'I expect you're not sorry. He's doing pretty well considering the competition he's up against.'

'Doing bloody well, I'd say. Lying eighth now, but a lot can happen before the finish.'

In the wheelhouse the skipper throttled back the engine, spun the wheel and the launch headed for the jetty in the boat harbour.

Two hours later, the ketch then clear of the land, he went

113

below. He took off the girl's bindings and removed the gag; it was still too risky for her to come up so he made sure she wouldn't by laying her on the navigator's bunk and tying her wrists behind her.

Staring at him in sullen silence she said nothing while he did this. Which was just as well because he was in no mood for argument of any sort.

By four o'clock that afternoon they were fifteen miles nor-nor-east of Pointe-du-Cap.

The wind had freshened in the early afternoon and before long it was blowing strongly and heading the ketch. With the genoa, main and mizzen sheeted well in *Sunboro Beauty* plunged, gyrated and bumped into head seas, the needle of the automatic log hovering around the six knot mark. It had been a tiring day with frequent tacking and some sail changing; and to make matters worse a jib halyard had jammed. With the ketch on self-steering he'd gone up the mast to clear it; a difficult, time-consuming task which had in no way helped his dark mood. But once the halyard was cleared and the genoa hoisted and set again, the exhilaration of sailing returned, he forgot his problems and chuckled exultantly as douches of spray thrown up by the bows sluiced over the cockpit, wetting and refreshing his tired body.

Towards evening he went below and released the girl. By then the setting sun had washed the western sky with shades of gold and salmon and when it had finally gone, a brief tropical twilight followed which soon gave way to night. It was then that he set the wind vane, engaged the self-steering and went below to read the letters Billings had brought him.

Sitting on her bunk, feet against the passageway bulkhead, she was busy rubbing a soothing cream into the weals and abrasions left by the ropes which had bound her. While doing this she considered the events of the day. She'd heard his shouted exchanges with the race launch, felt the bump when the ketch heeled over, and heard him roar at someone in anger. For a wonderful moment, then, she had thought

114

that rescue was close at hand.

Although she was deeply resentful of the way he had treated her, she somehow could not muster the fear and outrage she'd experienced at Santa Maria. She had to admit that he was right—she would have shown herself, shouted out, done whatever she could to attract attention at Port Castries. Not to punish him, but because she was afraid something awful was going to happen to her if she remained on board. Had he really been her gorgeous man she'd have wanted to stay and see it through. But she couldn't trust him, he was too unpredictable; his obsession with the race had put him out of touch with reality. As far as the TRISTAR was concerned she really did think he was insane, even if he appeared to be normal about other things.

So what should I do? she asked herself. I suppose the most sensible thing is to humour him, to co-operate, to try to make more of the emotional side and hope that somehow—God knows how—things won't work out the way I fear they will. If only I knew what was *really* in his mind it would make such a difference. I wonder? Perhaps it would only make me more frightened?

He's so mixed up, she thought, remembering how, when he'd come to gag her, he'd wiped away her tears and apologized for what he was doing. Did that mean he did in some strange way care for her in spite of his harshness? At least it showed that he was capable of sympathy.

At that moment he came down the companion-ladder in his swimming trunks, his brown body and tousled hair shining wetly in the light of the pressure lamp. He watched her in silence for a moment before saying. 'Hi,' and smiling sympathetically. 'Those marks'll soon go.'

'I hope so.'

'Now for the mail,' he said, opening a locker and taking out a bundle of letters. 'Haven't had time to read it.' He went to the chart-table and began slitting the envelopes. She noticed that he put one aside—a blue envelope with an airmail tag. It was addressed in a small neat manuscript.

She wondered if it was from the Crystal Gayle girl? Later, when the conversation went the right way, she'd ask him about that. In the meantime there was supper to be got ready. She went to the stove and began preparing a one pot meal—a tin of stew and onions, with new potatoes from another tin. She was busy with this when she looked round and saw him put the opened mail back in the locker; all but one letter on blue paper which he held in his hand as he went up the companion-ladder.

'Want it here or up there?' she called after him but he didn't reply. The blue envelope was still on the chart-table. She went across and looked at it. Postmarked 'London', it was empty.

## CHAPTER SIXTEEN

While he steered a part of his mind was on the compass card, the set of the sails, the wind and the sea, but mostly it was taken up with Tessa's casual off-hand letter. She was sorry she hadn't written in time for Santa Maria: *We've been madly busy in the office.* Some inconsequential chat about friends and the weather, then the real news: *Just back from a fabulous time in Paris. VS has found an exciting new writer there – a young Frenchman – a sort of latter-day Sartre. Did the Bal Tabarin, dinner at Fouquet, etc etc etc. VS madly energetic as usual.*

She finished the letter with: *Hope you're fit and enjoying your single-handed odyssey. L-of-L, Tessa.*

L-of-L was, he knew, low in Tessa's loving message category. She used it for aunts, uncles and old school friends – rarely if ever in a love letter.

VS was the publisher's editor for whom she worked – Victor Sandelson: charming, intellectual and married, but not – if Tessa were to be believed – above making a pass. He recalled her stories of Victor's importuning after lunches in the West End. Tales coyly told in the days when she and

Martin tolerated each other's extra-mural adventures; and though she never admitted it he sometimes thought she might have slept with Victor, ascribing her lack of candour to a desire to protect him. He remembered one of their conversations:

'VS took me out to lunch today.'

'How very nice.'

'Why the sarcasm, Martin? You know it's not the first time.'

'But of course.'

'You should be flattered.'

'Really. Why?'

'That other men want me. Isn't it rather like, well, owning a high performance car' – she'd had the grace to snigger at that – 'which other men want to drive?'

'Funnily enough I'm not flattered. I imagine VS is the sort of chap who'd like to drive a lot of other people's cars.'

'That's a bitchy remark, Martin.'

So Victor Sandelson had taken her to Paris. Well, well. Something of an advance on lunches; certainly a heavier call on the expense account.

When he opened her letter and read it he'd been bitterly disappointed because it wasn't what he'd expected. A fit of jealous anger had been followed by self-pity; how could she be so callous and unfeeling when he was engaged on a hazardous undertaking aimed at improving their fortunes – at least that was how he liked to look at it – a time when he needed all the moral support he could get? Then, thinking about the letter and its implications, his mood changed and he enjoyed the irony of the situation: Tessa flaunting the Paris adventure to make him jealous, to underline what he was missing on his long lone voyage. But it wasn't a lone voyage; he had a girl with him, a rather attractive one who grew more so as the voyage lengthened.

What's that, Tessa ——?

Oh *that*. Yes. Of course we have ——

The sound of his sudden laughter rose above the noise of wind and sea.

\*

She was standing at the foot of the companion-ladder, a two-handled aluminium can in her hands, a spoon stuck into it, when she heard his laugh, high-pitched, out of tune with the deep voice.

'Hi,' she called. 'Your stew. It's ready. Come and get it.'

He left the wheel, came to the hatchway, leant down and took the can from her.

'What were you laughing at?' She eyed him curiously.

'Nothing really, just life.'

She went back to the sink to clean up. He really is mad, she thought. Laughing in that crazy way.

Later that night he came down to listen to the news and it was evident that he was in one of his gloomy, uncommunicative moods. Her instinct told her it was something to do with the letter in the blue envelope, but she said nothing. It was not the time to discuss that sort of thing. She was thinking about the Crystal Gayle girl, her mind shut to the voice of the newsreader, when something alerted her to what he was saying: . . . from St Lucia, West Indies, turning point for the third leg of the TRISTAR it is reported that the United States yacht *Tornado Four* has a substantial lead. She is followed by *Grande Rapide*, a French entry and *Mercedes Express*, a trimaran sailed by Kurt Grosse, current holder of the record for the fastest single-handed voyage around the world. The TRISTAR – a scratch race for production yachts of up to fifty feet in length – with one hundred thousand pounds of prize money – fifty thousand pounds to the winner – is the first British-controlled event to offer money prizes on this scale. There has been some opposition in yachting circles to what is seen as commercialization of a sport long regarded as the preserve of amateurs, but a spokesman for the consortium which put up the prize money has pointed out that . . .

He switched off.

'Good heavens,' she said, and her surprise was genuine. 'I'd no idea all *that* money was involved.'

'Perhaps you can now understand what you've done to me.' There was a sombre look on his face.

Without thinking she said, 'Aren't you assuming that *Sunboro Beauty* would have won the race? What about the six boats ahead of us?'

'Seven,' he corrected. 'But we're likely to do a lot better.'

She shrugged, looked away. 'What can I say? I've already apologized as best I can. If I could make amends, I would.'

He went to the companion-ladder, put his hands on the grab-rails. 'Like jumping over the side,' he said, staring at her for a moment before climbing the ladder.

When he'd gone she sat on the end of the bunk, her fingers tapping nervously on the chart-table. The callous way in which he'd said that, the cold stare, were frightening. It was almost as if he were telling her what she *should* do. As to the news about the prize money – well, it was devastating. Apart from the large sum for the winner, there was the £50,000 left for second and third places – perhaps even fourth, she'd no idea. Little wonder that he was so determined to do well. She had always thought it was the honour and glory of winning that drove him, but now she knew it was a lot more than that.

The longer she thought about it that night the more frightened she became until eventually she worked herself into a state of near panic in which she thought of all sorts of desperate remedies: like telling him the story of the letter to her solicitors; dropping a bottle with a message in it over the side at St John's, their next reporting point – and telling him she'd done it; jumping over the side if close to land, or near another ship; putting something in his food – ground Nembutals? – then tying him up; hiding somewhere in the boat, lying in wait for him and knocking him over the head with a spanner; pushing him over the side; calling for help by radio?

But she didn't know how to work the radio and she knew nothing of navigation beyond a little elementary chartwork. She wouldn't know what to do in a storm without him. He was far stronger than she was, and a violent man at that. Perhaps if they had another calm and he went swimming she could sail the ketch away from him. But how? In a calm? In the end she decided that her first idea was the only practical

119

one; she'd have to tell him she'd written to someone in London before coming on board. That would provoke a ghastly row but he wouldn't know whether it was true or false.

The awful thing was that there was no one to whom she could turn for advice. If only she could discuss it with Carlos, or Dinah Ferrars, or even her mother. Feeling alone and helpless she lay on the bunk and quietly cried herself to sleep.

## CHAPTER SEVENTEEN

The day after they left Port Castries the wind freshened, veering to east-south-east, and during the following night further to the south, so that the ketch was running with a fresh wind fine on the starboard quarter. The switch of wind, not unusual in the Variables, was a welcome bonus since he'd been prepared to beat up against the north-east Trades until well beyond the twenty-fifth parallel. As it was, aided by the current, *Sunboro Beauty* made excellent progress, recording runs of 181 miles on 11 December, and 187 on 12 December. But for heavy showers of rain the weather had remained fine.

His sailing plan was to head to the nor-nor-west to pass about a hundred miles to the west of Bermuda; there he hoped to pick up the Westerlies, whereafter he intended to make for Newfoundland on north and north-easterly headings.

At noon on 12 December he made the latitude 22°15′N, the longitude 62°40′W, and the nearest land the Virgin Islands, 260 miles to the sou-sou-west. The fine weather, combined with *Sunboro Beauty*'s good progress, had lifted his spirits and for the time being he pushed Tessa's letter to

120

the back of his mind.

On board, too, things were better. The girl appeared to have got over her mood of resentment and their relationship had improved, though it was no longer that of the halcyon days before St Lucia.

On the previous night he had listened as usual to TRISTAR competitors reporting their positions. The race order remained unchanged but for *Caspar's Folly* overtaking *Wilson's Savoury* which was now also losing ground to *Sunboro Beauty*. There was still no report from *Omega Challenger*; at Port Castries he had been told by Billings that her transmitter having packed up her skipper had asked for spares to be sent to St John's. Billings' shouted bulletin included the news that *Wilson's Savoury* had put into Port Castries with rudder trouble—'Makeshift welding job. Had to be done pronto pronto. Shore people not happy but skipper wouldn't wait. Hope it holds!' Even at thirty feet Billings grin belied the note of concern. 'You may soon be moving up in bed, old dear.' Then he'd told of *Tornado Four*'s troubles—a broken forestay repaired at sea, the delay lopping twelve hours off the sloop's large lead.

It was evident that Billings, the archetype extrovert, was relishing his job as sponsor's surrogate—jetting into Fayal, back to London, then out again to St Lucia; living it up in tourist paradises, dispensing bonhomie like a vicar at a church fête, all at the expense of Sunboro Beauty Products. But he liked Billings, was grateful to him, and though the man could be a pain in the neck he was nonetheless generous, warm hearted and never spoke ill of anyone. But for Billings he would probably not have found a sponsor. Without one he couldn't have competed in the TRISTAR.

The basket of 'goodies' taken on board at Port Castries had in it letters and press clippings besides its load of fruit, chocolates, after-dinner mints, cherries in Maraschino and a bottle of Hine Antique—'Liquid bullion from the directors' cellar, old sport.'

Reading the press clippings was a task he shared with the girl. Most of them bore the Billings imprint; they laughed at some of his extravaganzas and cringed at others: *Martin*

121

*Savage, first on the scene in response to* Karamagee's *MAYDAY call, altered course to race to the assistance of the burning trimaran knowing that this would cost his* Sunboro Beauty *many vital hours. A selfless act, but evidence if any were needed that the spirit of Nelson still lives in the hearts of British yachtsmen. . . .*

When she passed the clipping to him she said, 'What d'you think of that?'

He looked at it, shook his head. 'Makes me want to vomit.' He tore it into small pieces.

In the early hours of 13 December wind and sea moderated and by daylight *Sunboro Beauty* was almost becalmed. The sails flapped idly as he tried one heading after another, chasing the breezes which came fitfully from various quarters. By noon the wind had freshened and settled in the north-east, and he put her on a long beat to the nor-nor-west. The frustration of chasing winds that failed to materialize had made him tired and irritable, and though the girl worked hard and tried to be cheerful his mood got the better of him and his manner was churlish.

It happened soon after midday and she wondered after-wards if it had had anything to do with it being the thirteenth. She was down below preparing a snack lunch when the ketch went about suddenly, he shouted and she knew at once that something was wrong; dropping everything she scrambled up the companionway. He was not in the cockpit, nor could she see him anywhere else on deck. The fore and aft hatches were shut because of spray, and in the ten to fifteen seconds since he'd shouted there'd been no time for him to open either and go down. With awful conviction she realized he'd fallen overboard. Her heart racing, she stared astern. But she was looking into the sun and could see nothing but its glare reflected on the surface of the sea. For a moment she panicked—then, remembering what he'd taught her, she pulled the horseshoe buoy from its rack and threw it overboard with its strobe light. Shaking with anxiety, afraid that she could be doing the wrong thing,

122

she eased the sheets and brought the ketch round into the wind. Realizing that it would be difficult—and time consuming—to handle all the sails they were carrying she at once hove-to in the way he'd explained would be necessary in such a situation, and lowered the genoa and mizzen. That done she hoisted the jib and bore away before the wind until the heading was south-south-east, the reciprocal of the course steered when he'd gone overboard.

All this took a good deal longer than she'd expected and not until it was finished was she able to concentrate again on looking for him. There was a moderate sea running with a fair scattering of white horses, and while sail changing the lifebuoy and the yacht had drifted apart and she'd lost sight of the buoy. She searched the sea on that side but at first could see nothing. Later she saw the flutter of the little yellow flag on the strobe light and her heart quickened. I'm going to find him, she told herself, I'll have him back on board soon, I know I will.

But though the flag showed each time the buoy lifted to a sea there was no sign of him and her spirits began to sag. Sitting well to windward, one hand on the wheel, she watched with tense concentration. As the ketch moved downwind and the distance from the buoy increased she found it difficult to see the little flag, but she consoled herself with the knowledge that he was a strong swimmer and would surely reach the buoy once he'd seen it. When she judged the distance from the flag to be several hundred yards she brought the ketch round and began a series of short tacks upwind. It was a slow business with *Sunboro Beauty* close-hauled, but the buoy was drifting downwind and this helped narrow the gap.

Several tacks later she was within a hundred yards of the buoy when a wave lifted it but there was still no sign of him and once more the pit of her stomach shrank and she wondered if he'd been stunned as he went overboard. The thought made her sick with anxiety. Feeling miserably alone and frightened she wondered how she would ever be able to sail the ketch to the nearest land if she failed to find him. She had just decided that a lot would depend on the weather when the yellow buoy rose on the crest of another wave and—marvellously, as if it were a miracle—she saw him swimming towards it. She waved excitedly, shouted, 'Martin, Martin,' but then, realizing that her voice could not carry against the wind, she concentrated on getting the ketch to windward. Not long afterwards she saw him reach the buoy and slip into it—a shout came down on the wind and though she couldn't make out the words at least it told her he'd seen *Sunboro Beauty*.

On the next tack to windward she got within fifty feet of the buoy and heard him shout, 'Put a line over the stern.' She threw the end of the mizzen sheet over the side and let all sheets fly. The ketch lost way and began drifting down to where he was in the water until the wonderful, unbelievable, moment came when it bumped gently into him and she saw his hands reach up and grasp a guard-wire stanchion.

'I'm bloody tired,' he gasped. 'Give me a hand.'

The ketch was drifting beam-on to the seas, rolling noisily with sails and sheets flapping. She could see that he was exhausted but it was an opportunity which would not occur again and in the last few moments a plan, unpremeditated and hazy, had taken shape in her mind. 'I'll pass you a line first, then get you on board,' she told him as she began hauling in the sheet which was trailing astern.

'For Christ's sake,' he shouted hoarsely. 'What are you doing?'

Without attempting to reply she continued hauling until the end came home. Then, having made a bight in it, she knelt on the deck immediately above him. 'Here.' She passed it down. 'Put that over your shoulders and under your arms.'

'What are you playing at?' His bloodshot eyes stared accusingly.

'Trying to make sure you don't let go while I'm trying to get you back on board,' she said.

'Forget it. Unnecessary. Slacken off that rigging screw where the guard-wire's secured to the pushpit, and slip the pelican hook. If you help me I'll get aboard there.'

She shook her head. 'No, Martin. Let's first make sure you're safe. I don't want to lose you.'

'You're being absurd.' It was a hoarse growl of disapproval, but he gave in and holding the stanchion with one hand, he used the other to pass the bight over his head.

Switching hands he got it under his arms. 'Right,' he snapped. 'Now let's get on with it.'

She took in the slack and made the inboard end of the sheet fast to a cleat. Then she knelt once more and for a few moments watched him in silence feeling strangely self-assured and unsentimental. It was the first time she'd held the master card and she was enjoying the sensation of power. The way that card was played would, she believed, be important to her survival.

Leaning down so that her face was close to his she said, 'Martin, I want you to make a promise.'

'What's that?' The ketch rolled and the sea washed over his head. He held up a hand. 'Come on, Sarah, Get me out of this.'

'Not until you promise.'

'Promise what?' he spluttered, half choking. 'Are you mad?'

'No. But I'm afraid *you* may be. Listen. I'll help you back on board if you promise to get me safely back to England.'

'For Christ's sake stop playing the fool, Sarah. This is no time for that sort of thing.'

'Sorry but I must have your promise.'

The ketch rolled again, once more the sea surged over him, again he gasped and spluttered. 'Of course I'll get you back to England. You must be crazy to think I won't.'

'Promise me,' she persisted. 'On your word of honour.'

'Stop these childish games, Sarah.' There was a mixture of fear and anger in his eyes now, but she was unmoved. More water washed over him and at last he gasped, 'All right. On my word of honour. Now come on. Help me out.' Once more he thrust a hand towards her.

She ignored it. 'One last thing, Martin. In case you don't keep your promise – in case I don't get back safely to England –' she spoke very slowly and deliberately – 'you must understand that it will be known that I'm on board *Sunboro Beauty*.' She hesitated, watching his face to see if he was taking in what she was saying. 'Before we left Plymouth I sent a letter to a close friend.' She had decided that sounded more convincing than 'my solicitors'. 'In it there was a sealed envelope which she will open if I'm not back by the end of January.' Her manner was cool and audacious. 'Do you understand what I've just said, Martin?'

He closed his eyes. 'Yes. I'm not deaf. Now get me out of the bloody drink.'

It took some time and a great deal of effort to get him back on board, and at one stage she thought she'd never be able to do it. Indeed, but for helpful seas which from time to time lifted him to deck level, she would have failed. Once he was safely back in the cockpit she told him to go below and dry out. She set about recovering the make-shift man-overboard gear and securing the guard-wire. While doing this she saw that he'd made no effort to move, but was sitting hunched in a corner watching her in gloomy silence. His clothing was waterlogged and he was shivering.

'Don't sit there, Martin. You're shivering madly. Get below,' she commanded. 'Dry yourself. Put on warm things. There's some Bovril in the Thermos. I'll be down soon.'

Without answering he moved awkwardly, crabwise, to the hatchway, turned and went down. At no time since she'd got him back on board had he said a word.

'Remember,' she shouted down to him. 'I saved your life. You owe me mine.'

There was no reply.

# CHAPTER EIGHTEEN

'Good morning, Inspector.' Thorold rose to greet his visitor, pointed to a chair. 'Please sit down.'

They discussed briefly the weather and the fortunes of Plymouth Argyll in the FA Cup before the Detective Inspector came to the point. 'Thought I'd call in to let you know Scotland Yard haven't yet traced that missing girl – Victoria Brownson.'

'Good to see you, Inspector. Sorry to hear she's not turned up. Very worrying for her parents. So much violence these days, they can't be blamed for fearing the worst. I know I would if my daughter was involved.'

Mitchell tapped the underside of his moustache with a stubby forefinger. 'You've had no news I take it? In so far as the race aspect is concerned?'

'News of the race yes – but not of the girl. I think we can safely assume that her reference to the fun of being a stowaway in an ocean race was – as her girl friend suggested – a joke remark.'

The Inspector sighed. 'I suppose so.' He looked out of the window; rain spreading across the Sound had shut out Drake's Island and reduced to a shadowy outline the frigate moving slowly towards the Narrows. The scene was all greys – wet, cold and miserable – but for centuries it had been one of the great backdrops of English history and he felt for it an affection and respect he could not have expressed. The small dark eyes returned to the man behind the desk. 'And how *is* the TRISTAR going, Mr Thorold?'

'Very well, I'd say. The leading boats are putting up excellent times. Of course it's been a fair wind almost all the way. They've been reporting at St Lucia during the last few days – *Tornado Four* well ahead of the rest. She's a biggish sloop, you know, sailed by Gary Maddox. Tough American, experienced skipper, fine seaman. If the TRISTAR had been a handicap event he'd certainly have been scratch. Two multihulls were in second and third place at Port Castries – *Grande Rapide* and *Mercedes Express*, Fougeux's and Kurt Grosse's boats. Those three are well ahead. Nothing else threatening them just now.'

The Inspector fumbled in his pockets, produced a pipe and pouch. 'Mind if I do?'

'No. Not at all.'

He began loading his pipe with the slow ceremonial of the addict. 'If I recall the press reports correctly you've lost a few boats, haven't you?'

'Yes, we've had our share of troubles I'm afraid. Lost two boats with their skippers in the Biscay gale soon after the start. *Karamagee* caught fire last week – a few days' sail from St Lucia. They found Farran's life-raft but he was not in it. Very sad, losing these people. Ocean racing is like mountaineering. You take the risk and sometimes you pay the price. I've just heard of the latest disaster. Got the news an hour ago. *Wilson's Savoury* was sunk by a whale last night, two hundred miles south of Bermuda. It happened so suddenly that John Benn, her skipper, wasn't able to transmit a MAYDAY. The whale must have capsized the boat. Benn got into a life-raft and about two hours later sighted a ship, sent up flares and they picked him up. A Norwegian container ship on passage from Oslo to Jamaica. He's a lucky man.'

There was some further discussion about the joys and perils of ocean racing before the two men parted company with renewed assurances that they would keep each other informed.

It was not until noon the next day, when his mood appeared to have improved, that Sarah mustered enough courage to ask him how he'd fallen overboard. Until then he'd been morose and preoccupied. She imagined it was because for the first time on the voyage he'd had to play an inferior role, and he'd obviously not liked it. She was not surprised. The accident had involved him in loss of face. First the very fact of falling overboard, then having to be rescued by her and, finally, the way in which she'd exacted the promise. It must, she realized, have been terribly humiliating for a man like that.

Whatever it was, she had respected his mood and they'd got on with their separate tasks and for the most of the time ignored each other. When he wasn't at the wheel she'd seen him engrossed in charts and sailing directions, or writing up his voyage notes to which he devoted a good deal more time than she did. Soon after midday on the 14th he'd begun to thaw and when she went to the cockpit to take over the wheel at four o'clock that afternoon he was, she thought, in sufficiently good humour for the subject to be broached.

'Feeling all right now, Martin?' she asked.

'Yes. Fine.'

'You were in the water a long time, weren't you?'

'It wasn't that. It was the knock on my head. Didn't know where the hell I was in the beginning. Must have been semi-conscious when I went in.'

She looked at him with concern. 'You didn't tell me that. What knock on the head?'

'Here. It's a damn great lump.' He touched the back of his head. 'Feel it.'

Her fingers searched through the thick hair and found the lump. A large one, the size of a pigeon's egg. 'Good heavens! It must have been a nasty bang. Why didn't you say anything? Did you put something on it?'

'Yes. Some ointment. Doesn't help really.'

'Tell me,' she tried to sound casual. 'What actually happened?'

He put a hand to his face, pinched his nostrils between thumb and forefinger, looked up at the sails, breathed deeply. 'Nothing to tell really. I was just plain stupid. We were close-hauled on the port tack. I put her on self-steering. Went along the foredeck to take up slack on the main halyard. When I got back to the cockpit I saw that the wind vane was skew, vibrating badly. The holding bolt on the vane clamp had worked loose. I got a spanner, leant over the pushpit rail and tightened the bolt. As I straightened up from the rail she came into the wind, the bows dropped, the stern came up sharp and she went about. The mizzen boom hit the back of my head, I lost balance and went over the side.'

'Poor Martin.'

'Stupid twit,' he corrected, looking at the sails and turning the wheel. 'I was just bloody careless.'

'Lucky you had time to shout.'

He looked puzzled. 'I shouted? I don't remember that.'

'You did. I wouldn't have known you'd gone otherwise. Might have been some time before I came up from below.'

'Funny,' he said. 'Don't remember that at all. Must have been instinct.'

She was wondering if he was at last going to thank her for picking him up, or at least say something about her seamanship – critical or otherwise – but instead he said, 'Great drama for the book. Incidentally, how are you getting on with your notes?'

'Not very well.' She spoke quietly, feeling let down. 'I don't find it easy to write at sea. Too much motion and there's not much to say, is there?'

'Oh, come on.' He looked up from the binnacle, shot a quick glance at her. 'There's a lot to say. Not just the action – what you do and see and hear – but your thoughts. Your innermost thoughts about it all. My goodness. I'd love to know those. Must be *most* interesting.'

She regarded him thoughtfully, wondering what part of her thoughts would interest him most. 'I wonder,' she said.

'And talking of drama,' he went on. 'Tell me more about the not-to-be-opened letter you posted in Plymouth?'

His eyes were on the compass in the binnacle and she didn't know whether the half-smile indicated amusement or scepticism.

Looking very serious, lost for a moment in private thought, she came to and realized she'd have to tell the story she'd so often rehearsed. But first, playing for time, she said, 'I'm not sure what you mean?'

'I'm curious. You told me originally that you came on

board in Plymouth because you had nowhere to sleep that night. You said you had no idea *Sunboro Beauty* was sailing in the morning. Right?' His tone was friendly but she thought there was a flicker of antagonism in the blue eyes, so she didn't reply at once.

'You did tell me that?' he prodded.

'I can't remember exactly what I told you. It was quite long ago. But I do know I was very sick and frightened when you found me. I had to give some explanation, however feeble.'

The bows dipped into a short sea and a smother of spray swept the deck. It was cooler now but he was still in bathing trunks and his body, struck by the spray, glistened wetly. She found herself thinking what a fine body it was, muscular and bronzed like the statue of a Greek athlete.

His voice brought her back to reality. 'So what *was* the true story?' The pale blue eyes were quizzical.

'It's a long one,' she said. 'I'd better take the wheel. It's my watch. Tell you later.'

He shook his head. 'No. Tell me now, I'll carry on here till you finish.'

'Oh dear,' she sighed. 'It's rather embarrassing. You see, it involves you.'

'It certainly has done,' he said. 'But go on.'

'Well, actually I saw you twice down in the Millbay Docks a few days before the race began.' She glanced at him shyly. 'You looked very nice. I was terribly unhappy at the time. Then I saw you again the night before the start, in The Futtock and Shroud. You were with the Frenchman. I didn't know anything about the TRISTAR then. Didn't know you were in it or that you were sailing the next day. I just felt that I must see you. Get to know you. It was a very strong feeling. Difficult to explain it rationally now but – oh, I don't know. I suppose I was crazy. Haven't you ever fallen for a complete stranger? Someone you've seen but never met? Had fabulous fantasies about them? I did that about you. In my thoughts you were' she paused, embarrassed at the prospect of what she was about to say.

'Go on,' he prompted.

'In my thoughts you were my gorgeous man.' She managed a quick sideways glance to see how he was taking it; but his face was expressionless. 'That last night in The Futtock and Shroud I drank too much. Went mad, I suppose. Decided on the spur of the moment that the best way of getting to know you would be to spend the night in your boat. You'd find me there that night, or in the morning. Well – you know the rest. I mean what actually happened.'

'I certainly do.' He spoke with some feeling. 'And the letter?'

'Oh yes.' She had been so absorbed in telling her story, so carefully weaving fact and fiction into its texture, that she'd forgotten all about the letter. 'From the pub I went back to the hotel, got together my things, wrote the letter, posted it in the hotel box. Then I took a taxi to Millbay Docks.'

The sails began to flutter. He turned the wheel to correct the ketch's course.

'I see.' He nodded slowly and deliberately as if a great truth had been revealed. 'And who did you send it to?'

'Dinah Ferrars, my flatmate.'

More spray swept over them.

'If you didn't know about the TRISTAR, or that I was sailing the next morning, why was the letter necessary?' He turned to where she sat beside him in the weather corner and his eyes held hers in a deadpan stare.

'Can't you see?' she said wearily. 'You looked nice but I didn't know you. I was taking a risk. Going on board, spending the night in a yacht alone with a strange man. Anything might have happened.' She hoped it sounded convincing.

Neither spoke for a few minutes after that until he said, 'You're not a very good liar, are you?'

Her heart almost stopped beating, then it jumped and began racing. Where had she slipped up? 'What d'you mean by that?' she said.

'Nothing. Forget it. Now it's my turn to say something.'

'But I want. . . .'

'Pipe down,' he said. 'I've listened to you. Now you do some listening.'

132

She shrugged her shoulders. 'All right.'

'I can't understand why you don't trust me.' He narrowed his eyes. 'What makes you think it's necessary to get me to *promise* to take you back to England? If I'd wanted to get rid of you I could have pitched you over the side any time I liked. So why haven't I?'

'Because you're probably not sure if anyone else knows that I'm here.' She looked up at him, doubt in her eyes. 'And because I'm useful, I suppose. You get more sleep, you don't have to cook, more manual steering is possible, with two crew we go faster, and it's safer – you ought to know that,' she added meaningfully. He said nothing, so she went on. 'How do I know you won't ditch me towards the end? Especially if *Sunboro Beauty* is doing well. There's a lot of money and prestige at stake. I hate saying these things, Martin. But you asked me and I have to tell you what's in my mind.'

He shook his head. 'I've never heard such a load of rubbish. What you're saying is that murder would be no problem for me if I could profit from it. In other words, Martin Savage would murder for money. Not a very nice thought that, is it?'

She touched his bare arm with what she hoped was a reassuring gesture. 'Sorry. You put it in such a hard cold way. What I mean is that I'm an obstacle to your . . . your achieving something terribly important to you. Winning, or perhaps getting a place in the TRISTAR. Only I stand in your way.'

'I couldn't have put it better. You've ruined my chances. You're just about the most bloody awful disaster that's ever befallen me – if you really must know. But I'm not a murderer, and the only thing left for me after the mess you've made is the book. That just *might* hit the jackpot if your being on board is kept a secret – a *real* secret I mean – until THE VERY END.' He put heavy emphasis on those last words. 'That's why you have to be gagged and bound at times. That's why I won't even give you a chance to show yourself if there's anyone or anything around. It's *I* who can't trust *you*, you see. And with good reason. That's why I made you cut your hair, and why I shave – which I don't normally do at sea. Alone in the cockpit, you'd look like me if . . .'

'If what?' she interrupted.

He looked at her speculatively. 'If I was asleep below, for example, and a ship was passing close which you'd not reported. Like that cruise liner before St Lucia that nearly ran us down.'

'I see. I'd always wondered about the haircut and the shaving.'

He ducked to avoid a sheet of spray. 'D'you still think I might . . .' he grinned, '. . . get rid of you?'

'I don't know. I really don't know. It's terribly confusing. I'd much rather not believe something awful like that, but how do I know that you're not being – well, untruthful?' She frowned inquiringly.

'You can't know, can you? But what we both *do* know is that you are the proven liar around here. You couldn't swim, you remember? You came on board in Millbay Docks because your boy friend dropped you there late at night and cleared off, remember? You didn't see me that night in The Futtock and Shroud, remember that? So you're the liar, Sarah. It's very difficult for me to believe anything you say.'

There seemed no answer to that and, after a few moments of gazing sadly out to sea, she went below.


## CHAPTER NINETEEN


Three ships had been sighted during the day; two tankers northbound from the Caribbean and, early that morning, a south-bound container ship. One of the tankers had passed close and he'd locked the girl in the forward WC. It was her suggestion, made the day after Port Castries: 'Can't you lock me in a loo instead of always tying me up? Apart from the weals, the rope stops my circulation. It's very painful.' So he'd taken a bolt from the engine-housing and fitted it to the door of the WC.

Shortly before dusk the wind fell away to leave *Sunboro Beauty* becalmed on a smooth sea, rolling easily to the swell from the north-east, her sails flapping noisily.

On the following night Portishead called on schedule to inform him there was a private telephone call from London. While he waited for it to come through he tried to convince himself it was Tessa, but his hopes were soon dashed. It was Harry Billings to report that he was sending a video-camera and recorder to St John's. 'The race launch will hand them over. Give it a whirl, old sport, and come up with some man-against-the-elements drama. My BEEB connections will jump at good stormy-weather material. Won't be able to use it until after the race, but so much the better – keep old *Sunboro*'s name alive.'

Billings had embarked on his usual quick-fire exchange of news and information in the course of which he mentioned the destruction of *Wilson's Savoury* by a whale. 'So you've moved up in bed once again, old thing,' he chortled. 'Fabulous performance. Sorry for Johnny Benn but at least he's safe and sound. Only six ahead of you now. Keep up the pressure.' Billings had rambled on for a bit after that until he shut him off with a white lie: 'Sorry, Harry. Must go now. Awful noise. Something adrift on top.'

After hanging up he looked at the chart. Johnny Benn's disaster was news. It must have been very sudden. At the last round of position reporting *Wilson's Savoury* had been only thirty miles ahead of *Sunboro Beauty*. If there *had* been a MAYDAY he would surely have heard it.

A gibbous moon in the eastern sky shone through layers of cirro-cumulus, the sea in its path flecked with dancing points of light.

It was cool on deck after the heat of the day and she was glad that she'd be there until her watch ended at ten o'clock.

135

Without wind there was no need to steer so she sat on the cockpit coaming thinking, trying to recall their discussion that afternoon. His reaction to her explanation of the letter had been surprisingly mild. Either he didn't believe it, which was the impression he'd tried to convey, or he'd decided that it probably was true, in which case she supposed he had little option but to put up with her and make the best of things.

They had been having a low key discussion about life in general when he said he must go down to listen to Portishead. Most of that day he'd been in a good mood and when he came back she was hoping it had stayed that way. 'Guess what?' he asked, and she saw with relief that he was pleased.

'Miss United Kingdom's been raped?' she suggested.

'No. Billings has just told me that *Wilson's Savoury* was sunk by a whale early today. Johnny Benn was picked up soon afterwards by a container ship bound for Jamaica. May have been the one we saw.'

'You saw it, I didn't,' she said accusingly.

'Bad luck for Johnny but good for us. Bears out what I've always thought. It's not speed that necessarily wins these long distance voyages. It's often the hare and tortoise thing. Boats that plug along steadily and avoid trouble are just as likely to do well as the fast ones. Of course there's always a big element of luck. There's no way you can reason with a whale.'

When he spoke quickly like that, his deep voice more vibrant than usual, she knew that euphoria was taking over. 'So we're lying seventh, are we?'

He nodded. 'Yes. Only six boats ahead now. Great, isn't it?'

She didn't like the news or the affect it had on him, so she nodded in a noncommittal way.

'Which reminds me,' he said, 'I've left something below.' He went down and was soon back with the Sundowner Pack – the name he'd given to the basket in which they brought bottles and glasses on deck.

He produced the Hine. 'Harry B's liquid bullion,' he said.

'At last we've got the weather *and* the occasion for a celebration.'

While she held the plastic glasses he poured the Hine and she worried once more about the effect the race was having on him. At times like these he seemed to lose all sense of proportion. How else could he possibly celebrate Johnny Benn's disaster; it wasn't as if *Sunboro Beauty* had done something clever.

'Now,' he said, taking a glass from her. 'The toast.' She saw his face in the moonlight – he was smiling in a curiously private way, his eyes shining – and she thought, Oh God, how awful of him to feel like that about it.

'To Sarah, whose splendid seamanship saved my life,' he said, putting his glass to his lips. She was about to do the same when he stopped her. 'Hey! You can't drink to it. You're the toast. Here's one you *can* drink to.'

He raised his glass again in a ceremonious gesture: 'To *Sunboro Beauty* and our safe return.' When they had drunk that he took both glasses, threw them over the side, put an arm round her and kissed her. 'Thank you, Sarah.'

She said, 'Is that a prize for being a good girl?'

He laughed, kissed her again and took the basket below. Soon he was back with the transistor and a settee cushion which he laid out on the coachroof. Against a background of tiny wavelets lapping the side, the rustle of sails, and Crystal Gayle singing *I'll Get Over You*, they made love under the moonlit sky.

Towards midnight the wind freshened and blew again from the north-east, soon building up a moderate sea. With sails sheeted hard-in, the ketch set off on a beat to the nor-nor-west plunging and crashing, sails taut and wet, the rigging thrumming to the pressure of the wind.

During the next few days the barometer fell and the wind backed through north and north-west until it settled in the west. Wind and sea had been increasing since they passed the latitude of Bermuda on 16 December, and a day later he hoisted the smaller genoa in place of the large one. Since leaving the Leeward Islands he had taken *Sunboro Beauty* round in a wide sweep towards the North American coast, and later away from it, the nearest approach being on the 19th when they were some 300 miles east of Cape Cod and he altered course to the north-east for a landfall at Cape Race, Newfoundland, 670 miles ahead.

The glass continued to fall and the westerly winds to increase until on the morning of the 20th it was blowing at force seven with an indicated windspeed of thirty knots. Under single-reefed mainsail, mizzen and smaller genoa, the ketch ran with the wind broad on the quarter for several days, logging a steady seven to eight knots.

Lifting, plunging and surging through foam-marbled seas *Sunboro Beauty* made to the north-east, the temperature falling steadily as she reached higher latitudes until the full blast of northern winter was upon them. Though the hatches were shut and the cabin heater was on, life on board had become wetter and more uncomfortable than at any time since the gale in the Bay of Biscay. Now they spent most of the time in foul-weather gear, their yellow oilskins the only splash of colour against the monotonous greys of sea and sky.

For days the girl suffered from a recurrence of seasickness. He gave her seasick pills but little sympathy and insisted that she keep herself busy. In the end the treatment worked and she recovered. Since Bermuda he had made her wear her lifejacket and safety harness, and self-steering was engaged at night when she was on watch. Sleeping always with the 30-minute alarm switched on, he would come up at intervals during her watch to check that all was well.

Bad weather with its acute discomforts – and her seasickness – imposed a growing strain on their relationship and as the days passed tension mounted. Both were suffering from physical and mental fatigue, and his earlier resentment at her presence on board returned. Feeding on the harshness of their circumstances it grew until once more his mind was troubled by disturbing fantasies.

\*

Though he believed hot meals to be essential it had become increasingly difficult to provide them; instead they had to make do with hot Bovril, cold corned beef and biscuits. The weather brought other problems: wear and tear on rigging, sails and running gear added to his repair and maintenance load, and the need for frequent bilge pumping was time and energy consuming. There was also the difficulty of fixing the ketch's position with day after day of overcast skies and the land too far for radio bearings.

It was not until the 22nd, when Sable Island was less than 100 miles to the west, that he was able to get anything like a reliable position; he then made the latitude 44°00′N, the longitude 55°10′W. The Gulf Stream had pushed them a good deal further north and east than his dead reckoning allowed. He'd suspected that progress had been good but this confirmation delighted him.

That night he reported his position to Portishead and St John's and listened as always to others reporting. Though the race order remained the same the two multihulls, *Grande Rapide* and *Mercedes Express*, had lost ground to *Tornado Four*. This, he realized, was due to bad weather and the windward sailing involved at various times since leaving Port Castries. A significant change was the position of *Sweet Ribena*: she had fallen back until she was only 20 miles ahead of *Sunboro Beauty*.

When reporting his position her skipper had complained of severe stomach pains which he thought were due to the resurgence of an old ulcer. He told St John's that he would like to see a doctor on arrival if the pains continued.

Tired mentally and physically, Martin Savage switched off the radio, set the alarm, shed his oilskins and seaboots and lay on his bunk. He was deep in sleep when he heard the girl scream. Rushing up on deck he found the cockpit flooded and empty. After a wild search in total darkness he realized that she'd been swept overboard. He was struggling under an intolerable burden of guilt when the rattle of the alarm woke him. He got out of the bunk, steadying himself against the boisterous motion, groped his way up the companion-ladder and crawled into the cockpit. The girl was crouched beside the wheel.

'You all right?' He had to raise his voice against the noise of wind and sea.

'No problems,' she said. 'Nothing sighted. But it's terribly cold.' She had been on watch for just over half an hour.

It was a nightmare, he told himself, nothing to worry about. But its reality remained and pursued him through the night.


# CHAPTER TWENTY


During the early hours of 23 December the wind moderated somewhat and the motion became less violent, but later that day discomfort returned when the ketch reached the shallow waters of the Grand Banks where the seas were short, steep and dangerous. At midnight Cape Race, the southermost extremity of Newfoundland, bore 320° distant 41 miles by RDF fix which he checked against readings on the echo sounder. Soon afterwards he altered course to the north for the approach to St John's, then 81 miles away. With the wind blowing at fifteen knots from the north-west the ketch was once more beating to windward, a noisy, uncomfortable plunging and pounding.

There was a good deal of shipping about and, following a long winter's night with little sleep, he had to spend most of the morning of the 24th on watch. Shortly before noon he handed over the wheel to the girl and went below to fix the position and write up the log; by the time these tasks were completed it was twelve-thirty. Exhausted, he turned down the volume of the VHF receiver – it was crackling with voice messages to and from fishermen and other craft inshore – set the 30-minute alarm and lay on his bunk for a catnap.

A strange sound woke him soon afterwards. Unable to

place it, he scrambled from the bunk, wedged himself at the foot of the companion-ladder and listened. In the same moment that he recognized the familiar *flopaflopa* – *flopaflopa* of a helicopter, a voice came through faintly on the VHF speaker: 'Canadian Coastguard GYZ calling yacht below – what is your name? Over.'

He turned up the volume, took the handset from its rest and was about to reply when he thought of the girl. From its sound the helicoper was close – very close – and circling. The pilot would be looking at the figure in the cockpit. If the ketch answered by VHF while she was on deck it would mean there were two crew in *Sunboro Beauty*. Thank God, he thought, that in oilskins she could as easily be taken for a man as a woman with that short hair and sun-tanned face.

It was vital to get her down below immediately – but how? If he shouted up the hatchway she might not hear him, or just refuse to come. He had little doubt she'd not reported the helicopter because she saw in the incident a marvellous chance to show herself. It was an opportunity she was not likely to miss. The story would be out, he would have to land her at St John's and abandon the race. These thoughts chased through his mind in split seconds until, with sudden decision, he seized an empty Calor gas cylinder from the storage rack, moved across to the foot of the companion-ladder, held the cylinder aloft with both hands under the hatchway coaming, jumped to one side and let if fall. It crashed down the ladder and on to the sole and he screamed, following the scream with a hoarse, 'Sarah, Sarah – for God's sake – quick.' He fell on to his back and lay spread-eagled at the foot of the ladder. There was an anxious cry of, 'Coming, Martin,' followed by a brief delay during which he supposed she was engaging the self-steering. Moments later, through half-shut eyes, he saw her at the hatchway; then she had started down the ladder and was kneeling beside him, her breath warm on his face. 'My God, Martin. What's happened?' she cried.

Without answering he grabbed her with both arms and his pent-up anger exploded. 'You goddam slut. Determined to ruin my plans, aren't you?'

'Leave me,' she struggled fiercely. 'You're hurting.'

He interrupted: 'Too bad. Why didn't you report that helicopter?' Kneeling, crouching on all fours, he pulled her towards the heads while she continued to struggle and scream: 'Let me go ... you're hurting ... Oh, God! ... you bastard.'

Twisting her head round, she seized his wrist and bit into it. He wrenched the hand away, gripped her under the arms and dragged her forward. They reached the door of the heads, he opened it, bundled her in and shut and bolted the door. During the struggle blood from his wrist had smeared her face and for a moment he thought he'd injured her. It worried him. Angry though he was he hadn't wanted to do that. Breathless from his exertions he made for the VHF speaker where a gravelly voice was saying: 'Yacht below – I repeat – what is your name? – this is Canadian Coastguard helicopter GYZ – do you read me? Over.'

He lifted the handset, pressed the speak-button. 'I read you, GYZ. This is ketch *Sunboro Beauty* competing in the TRISTAR. Over.' The Calor gas cylinder was rolling and banging about the sole. He tried to stop it with his foot but failed.

'Okay,' replied the helicopter voice. 'Thought you might be *Sweet Ribena*. Her skipper radioed for medical help at ten-thirty this morning. Said he was hove-to, near to collapse. Went off the air while giving his position. Our medics reckon it may be a burst appendix. We're searching around the position he reported last night at twenty hundred. Have you any info?'

'I plotted his twenty hundred position. It put him twenty-three miles nor-nor-west of mine. It's not been possible to get an astro fix for several days. I fixed mine by RDF and soundings. He probably did the same. Easy enough to make an error that way. More so if he's in bad shape. Over.'

"kay. That's right. Can you give me your position at twenty hundred last night?'

He measured with dividers on the chart, gave the position. The helicopter pilot acknowledged, repeated it. 'Thank you, *Sunboro Beauty*. That's great. We'll have to expand the search area. Too bad he didn't use an emergency beacon. Guess the guy's real sick. Over and out.'

When the helicopter had gone he put the empty gas cylinder back in the rack, took the first aid outfit from a locker, applied antiseptic ointment to the bite on his wrist and covered it with a sterile dressing. 'Bloody bitch,' he murmured as he returned the outfit to its locker.

She sat wedged on the WC seat, feet against the door, her back to the side, elbows spread to counter the ketch's unceasing motion. Wet, cold and miserable, she sobbed intermittently like a tired child. He'd been brutal and her head and body ached from the rough handling, but it was the outrage to her emotions that hurt more than the bumps and bruises. She was innocent. The helicopter had come to them upwind; with the noise of wind and sea she'd not known it was there until the last moment. Nor had she had time to report it before the crashing noise and scream came from below. It was a mean trick to get her down there like that, and unnecessary because she was going down anyway, wasn't she? She couldn't remember. There hadn't really been time to consider what she would do. It had all happened so quickly.

His behaviour was the last straw. She couldn't face life on board with him any longer. She must get out of it somehow at St John's. It was her last chance. The cold wet misery of bad weather, his violent outbursts, his obsession with the race, the frightening prospect of gales all the way from St John's to Plymouth – and probably not enough food – were too much. Fears for her safety had returned with this latest assault, and they were now stronger than ever. She had heard his VHF reply to the helicopter: *This is ketch SUNBORO BEAUTY competing in the* TRISTAR. That was it – he really believed he *was* competing. It was impossible to trust him. The man was either demented or so close to it that it made no difference.

I can't face it, she kept saying to herself, I simply can't face it. It's got to end at St John's.

There wasn't much time left. Another twelve hours and

they'd be there. Whatever she was to do had to be done soon. But what could she do? Confronted with this insuperable problem she began to cry.

Through wind-driven spray he saw the distant light flash three times. He began to count slowly: *one-and, two-and, three-and* . . ., until at fifteen the three flashes came again. Cape Spear, he told himself, recalling the charted information: group-flashing 3 every 15 seconds, height 233 feet, visibility 17 miles. In that weather, beating to windward in a choppy sea, picking up the light at eight miles from a spray-smothered cockpit was, he decided, not bad.

They had passed Motion Bay and though he could not see the land he knew they were running parallel to the coast, about five miles offshore. He planned to beat up to a position several miles north-east of St John's, then go about and make for the harbour on a close reach. He had already informed the port authorities that the ketch should be at the reporting point round about midnight if the wind held.

The night was dark and cold with an overcast sky, the glass steady on a low reading, the north-westerly wind still blowing at force five though in the lee of the land the sting had been taken from the seas.

It was Christmas Eve. At midnight it would become the 25th of December. His heart warmed to the thought and pictures of other Christmases passed through his mind. On the last Christmas Eve he and Tessa had gone to a party in Hampstead, to the Sandelsons' whose Victorian house looked out under a full moon over frozen ponds to a snow-covered heath. It had been a jolly, noisy party which had gone on well into the early hours, ending in drama when some of the younger and wilder guests went down to the ponds and danced on the ice. Jack Robbins, youngest and wildest of them, had fallen through and only luck and foolhardy friends had got him back, frozen into sobriety.

Undressing at home that night Tessa had said, 'Fabulous party.'

'Not bad,' he admitted. 'Must say the food and drink were good.'

144

'Oh, much more than that, Martin.' The implied reproach meant she was ready to argue.

'Such as?'

'The whole thing. It was a rave-up. Super disco.' She looked at him archly. 'Marvellous dancing with VS. He puts everything into it.'

'And into other things, I imagine.'

'That's not funny, Martin.'

'Mrs VS didn't look as if she thought it was funny either.'

Tessa, on the edge of the bed removing her bra, the last of her garments, sat up and frowned. 'What exactly d'you mean by that?'

'I think,' he was choosing his words carefully, speaking thickly because he'd done himself rather well, 'that she may think VS puts everything into you.'

That had sparked an abrasive row.

He wondered what Tessa would be doing this Christmas Eve. A party at the Sandelsons'? Or would Mrs VS have persuaded VS that the party could do without Tessa? He rather hoped so.

His thoughts turned to Sarah. She had been locked in the heads that afternoon for more than three hours during which time she'd missed her midday meal. It would do her no harm to cool off, he'd decided, so he'd kept her down below until it was dark at four-thirty. That was a good thing because there were a fair number of ships and fishing craft about.

Early in the afternoon he had put the ketch on self-steering, set the 30-minute alarm and catnapped on and off until the light had gone, preparing himself for what promised to be a long night.

A few minutes after nine, with Cape Spear abeam five miles to port, he sheeted in the sails and brought *Sunboro Beauty* closer to the wind. The direct distance to St John's was less than eight miles, but it was to windward which added another four. The wind had held and the ETA of midnight still looked good.

At ten-thirty, when they would have about five or six miles

still to go, he would deal with the girl. Now that the heat of his anger had gone he was concerned about her. When he had let her out of the heads that afternoon her appearance had worried him. Eyes red and swollen, face blood-stained – his blood, he reflected sardonically – and she seemed to move with difficulty.

'Better wash your face,' he said. 'Get something to eat.'

She had refused to speak or even look at him, and hearing the catch in her breath he'd felt pangs of guilt. It was a miserable Christmas for her. He would have liked to have made it otherwise but that was not possible. So he fought back a desire to hold and comfort her, and went up to the cockpit. She had remained below ever since, lying on her bunk, back to the lee-cloth. He went down several times but she was always there in the same position.

Sulking, he decided, resentful, hating his guts. He could understand that, but he wondered if in her thoughts she accepted that it was her own fault, that she had brought it upon herself. And he wondered, too, if she ever thought about the damage she'd done to him.

At 2115 he called St John's on VHF and confirmed that he expected to reach the reporting close on midnight.

They were six miles north-east of St John's when he brought the ketch about. With the wind now to starboard he headed for the light at Fort Amherst on the southern side of the harbour entrance. The reporting point was a mile offshore; another hour and they would have completed the third leg of the race; over 6000 miles sailed in 48 days – still at least 2000 more to be sailed before they reached Plymouth.

With *Sweet Ribena* out of the race there were only five boats ahead of him; the sloops *Tornado Four* and *Omega Challenger*, and the multihulls *Grande Rapide, Mercedes Express* and *Caspar's Folly*.

If the Western Ocean lived up to its winter reputation for gales, high winds and big seas, the multihulls could be in trouble. Forty-seven yachts had crossed the starting line at Plymouth, twenty-one had already fallen out of the race for one reason or another and four had been lost. With two-

146

thirds of the race run *Sunboro Beauty*, a long odds outsider, was lying sixth. 'It's incredible,' he murmured to himself. 'Absolutely incredible.' His spirits climbed high.

In the light of the binnacle he saw that the time was close to eleven. The girl, he thought. Setting the wind vane and engaging self-steering, he went below.

## CHAPTER TWENTY-ONE

The navigator's bunk was empty and she was not in the saloon. He called her name several times, loudly, and when she did not answer he shouted, but there was still no reply. He went to the forward heads and opened the door. The compartment was empty. She must be in the after cabin or heads. He made his way back through the saloon. It was then that he saw the envelope stuck with Sellotape to the rack above the chart-table, 'Martin' scrawled across it in her untidy flourish.

The connection between her silence and the letter was something which he did not at first take in. It was only when he opened it and began reading that his stomach muscles tightened with the knowledge that something unpleasant was happening:

*I'm going, Martin, because I can't take any more. Better to have done with it than continue like this. It'll be the same in the end whatever I do – so what's the point in hanging on? You've resented me all along and wanted to get rid of me. Well, you've succeeded and I hope you're pleased. I'm too tired and frightened and worn out to go on worrying. I just want to end it all. You can do the worrying now – and carry on with your insane ambition. It's killed me and I think it may kill you.*
*Sarah.*

Panic seized him. The silly little fool! She wouldn't really do a thing like that, would she? It was a bluff to frighten him,

147

to dissuade him from binding and gagging her again. More in fear than anger he shouted her name again. The only reply was the sound of the sea against the hull and the muffled howl of the wind.

He began a hurried search. First back to the navigator's bunk. Her lifejacket was lying on it. Normally, in that sort of weather, she'd be wearing it. The safety harness was in its usual place on the hook at the foot of the bunk. He took a torch, went through to the after cabin and searched it – and the heads and lockers there – with furious energy. Most of the space was crowded with spare sails and other gear and there was no place to hide. There was still one compartment he hadn't tackled – the forward sail locker where the two cot berths were stacked high with sail bags and stores. He checked through it carefully, even removing sail bags to see if she'd somehow got under them. It was no use. Next he looked into the oilskin and clothes lockers on the starboard side immediately abaft the sail locker; but there too he drew a blank. There was nowhere else to look.

Wasting time, you bloody fool, he told himself, get on deck – she probably went up through the forward hatch as you came down the main hatch. He scrambled up the companionway, opened the hatch and climbed out, closing it behind him. The noise of wind and sea momentarily blanketed his thoughts. Then he searched along the upper deck, crouching, holding on grimly, the beam of his torch darting everywhere, piercing the cold wet darkness, douches of spray glistening in its light like liquid diamonds. Several times he shouted her name, but he soon realized it was futile. She was nowhere on the upper deck. The fore and aft emergency hatches were shut, the life-raft was in its canister, the lifebuoys in their racks. Whichever hatch she'd used, she couldn't have come on deck while he was in the cockpit without being seen. She must have waited until she'd heard him coming down, then gone up, probably through the forward hatch. Once up, she could have shut it immediately.

What had begun as a doubt grew into a nightmarish

148

certainty. The letter wasn't a bluff. She *had* thrown herself over the side. When? Say, five minutes ago? It couldn't have been much more. But on an almost freezing night in that sea and without a lifejacket she hadn't a hope.

With desperate resolve he took a horseshoe lifebuoy from its rack and threw it over the side with its strobe light and drogue. Easing the sheets he gybed the ketch round until she was heading downwind on the reciprocal of the course they'd been steering. The strobe light was showing each time it rode the seas – he decided to go half a mile downwind of it, then turn into the wind and carry out a zigzag search back to it. It was pretty hopeless, but he had to do something. The alternative was to report to St John's that he'd lost crew overboard. How the hell could he do that?

Half an hour later he had reached the strobe light and completed the search upwind. Though he had covered the sea to port and starboard every few minutes with the beam of an Aldis lamp, there had been nothing to see but an endless succession of foam-capped waves.

'Oh my God, Sarah, how could you?' he muttered in sudden and vehement despair. In a last effort he swung the beam full circle round the pall of darkness; but there was nothing but the running sea. Sick with anxiety, he set course for the light at Fort Amherst. What he would do and say when he got there was something he'd not yet sorted out from the chaos in his tired mind.

It was fifteen minutes to midnight. He looked astern for the last time, saw the strobe light flash briefly as it rode high on a sea. Setting the wind vane, he engaged self-steering and went below. He was about to call St John's on VHF to report an amended time of arrival when a wave of nausea overcame him and he felt he was going to vomit. Replacing the handset, he made for the forward heads.

As soon as she'd fastened the letter to the bookrack she went to the forward oilskin locker and wormed her way in between the foul-weather gear hanging there. It was not

149

easy. The depth of the locker was little more than the width of the coathangers, and so low that she had to crouch. Once in, with the door shut, it was a tight fit, dark and stuffy, and because the locker was near the bows the motion was severe. She wondered how long it would be before she gave way to seasickness. Unpleasant though the conditions were they would, she assured herself, be well worth putting up with if her plan succeeded. It was a simple one, by no means infallible, but at least it offered some hope. She had written the letter hours earlier, only fastening it to the bookrack when they were about eight miles from St John's, for she thought he would come down soon after that to lock her up. His rage over the helicopter incident convinced her that he wasn't going to take any chances.

She'd not been in the locker for long when she heard him calling her name; then the sound of the door of the heads opening and shutting a few feet from where she was hiding. After that he went back to the saloon. Later she heard him calling again, and the sound of the after-cabin door being opened and shut. Seizing the opportunity she moved into the heads, knowing that he'd already searched there. Another reason for moving was that she felt she might at any moment be sick.

She held her breath as the seconds ticked away until eventually she heard him go up on deck. Then, unaccountably, he came back and her heart beat faster – he was searching the lockers only a few feet from where she sat. She fought back the nausea, knowing that he'd hear her if she was sick.

The search was taking longer than she'd bargained for. The letter had been meant to convince him that she'd gone overboard, but it seemed he wasn't all *that* convinced. She was terrified that he might look into the heads again.

Just when she was most worried, she heard him go up on deck yet again. From the change in motion which followed she realized they'd turned and were running downwind. He must have accepted that she'd gone overboard and was now searching the sea. That he should trouble to do so surprised her, but she hadn't time to consider the implications. Instead her heart galloped and her spirits rose – the plan was working; before long he'd give up the search and make for St John's. When the race launch came alongside she would rush up on deck, they'd see her, and that would be the end of an awful experience. Well, it hadn't *all* been awful, she had to admit, but a lot of it had. She couldn't bear the thought of any more.

It was madness to have embarked on such a stupid adventure. She longed to get home, back to the comfort and security of life in London: to the apartment she shared with Dinah Ferrars, to the warm and friendly atmosphere of Flenterman McCallum's offices and – yes – even to Carlos. All those things that had made life interesting and worthwhile.

When he opened the door of the heads he was confronted by an apparition: a girl wearing the blue woollen cap and thick yellow sweater he'd lent to Sarah. She was wedged firmly on the WC seat and, because he couldn't believe his eyes, he stood in the doorway staring, the urgency of his nausea forgotten.

'It's not possible. I don't believe it,' he said, realizing that the girl *was* Sarah. 'Where the hell have you been? – why did you do it? – I've gone nearly crazy looking for you – why did you write that note? – I've searched everywhere for you.' The fragmented sentences followed each other in an unbroken stream.

She burst into tears, turned her head away from him, refused to speak. He took an arm, pulled her out – then, still wedged against the ketch's lunging motion, he put an arm round her, held her tight, his cheek against hers. 'Thank God you're safe,' he said. 'I thought you'd gone.'

'I was going to go, but you came down too soon,' she explained between sobs.

'For God's sake, you're crazy.' He held her even tighter. 'Can't you see what you mean to me?'

'No, I can't.' Tears streamed down her cheeks. 'You're awful to me. I'm frightened. I want to go home.'

'You'll be home soon, Sarah. I promise you. But we've got

to finish this race together. It's a joint venture. You know that. In a couple of hours we'll be starting out on the last leg. Before long the whole thing'll be over.'

'I know.' Her voice choked. 'That's what frightens me.'


# CHAPTER TWENTY-TWO

In the distance the lights of St John's shone mistily through rain and sleet as the ketch approached the reporting point a mile to seaward of the flashing red light at North Head; sheltered by cliffs north and south of the entrance, it offered a good lee.

When he saw the race launch coming out he turned *Sunboro Beauty* downwind and moved slowly away from the shore under jib and mizzen. Soon the launch – it was a large cabin cruiser – had come up from astern and taken station on the windward beam.

A check-capped, duffel-coated figure came out of the wheelhouse on to the small bridgewalk. 'Merry Christmas, old sport,' trumpeted the familiar voice, hugely amplified by a loud-hailer. 'And many of 'em.'

'Same to you, Harry,' he shouted back. 'What's the news?'

'The news, old dear, is that *Sunboro Beauty*'s lying sixth. Don't know how you do it.'

'Tell you some day, Harry. Got any mail for me?'

'But of course. *And* the video-camera and recorder, not to mention a few goodies.'

The race official who'd joined Billings on the bridgewalk broke in. 'Everything on board all right, Savage? Any problems with gear – stores – your health? Any urgent requirements?'

'No thanks. Everything's okay. All I need is friendly Westerlies to blow me home.'

'You'll get them all right. Bit of a lull just now. Rising

glass, wind veering northerly. Maybe some snow in the offing. Won't be long before the pattern changes.'

During the next few minutes the video gear, letters, telegrams, newspapers and 'goodies', packed into a watertight canister, were passed over by line, Billings announcing that he'd insisted on that method to avoid any repetition of the trouble at Port Castries. In between newspaper reporters taking flashlight pictures and shouting questions, Billings managed a staccato and often interrupted progress report. The helicopter had found *Sweet Ribena* and winched up her skipper who was in hospital with a burst appendix. 'Intensive care job,' remarked Billings cheerfully.

*Tornado Four* had, he said, reported at St John's four days previously, *Grande Rapide* a day later; then, two days behind the leader, had come *Mercedes Express* and *Caspar's Folly*, and a day behind them *Omega Challenger*.

For Martin Savage the only surprise was the news of *Omega Challenger*: because of her defective transmitter there had been no position reports to monitor and he'd had no idea where she was.

Billings said, 'They gave her a new transmitter yesterday. Had to go inside for it. Ken Hutchings went up the wall. Livid about the delay. Cost him three hours, poor old sod.'

Ken Hutchings at fifty-seven was the oldest man in the race.

'You'll find an instruction book with the video job,' explained Billings. 'Hope you get some great pics, old dear. BEEB very interested, you know.'

The cameramen's flashlights were popping, blinding his eyes. 'Can't guarantee I'll do any good with it, Harry. I'll try. Depends a lot on the weather. May not be possible.'

Over in the cabin cruiser everybody seemed to be talking and laughing at once, the spirit of Christmas evidently much in the air. This irritated him, for levity threatened delay and his only concern was to get away as quickly as possible. Working fast he put his letters and exposed films in the empty canister, secured the watertight lid, lowered the canister into the sea and it was hauled back on board the cabin cruiser.

As a concession to formality he shouted, "bye now,' and waved for the benefit of the cameras.

The cabin cruiser turned and made for the harbour and Billings' farewell drifted down on the wind. 'The best of British luck to you, old sport. And God bless. You deserve it.'

At last the time had come. He hoisted the mainsail, exchanged the jib for the smaller genoa and put the ketch on a course of 105°. With the wind broad on the port quarter *Sunboro Beauty* set off on the last leg of the TRISTAR.

The sleet had turned to snow.

She soon learnt that the solicitude he had shown when he found her, the way he'd held her, the things he had said, meant little. The look in his eyes – affection, sympathy, concern – had frozen suddenly. 'Come on.' He'd taken her by the arm. 'We haven't any time.' Then he'd hauled her through the saloon to the navigator's bunk, lifted her on to it and bound her legs and arms.

That was the only concession he'd made – leaving her trussed in her bunk instead of on the sole in the saloon. Half an hour later he came down, put the gag in her mouth and sealed it with plaster. When he'd finished he smoothed the hair from her eyes. 'Sorry about this, Sarah.' He secured the lee-cloth, climbed the companion-ladder and slid the hatch shut behind him.

While she lay on her bunk in semi-darkness – the oil lamp in the saloon turned well down – she thought about what had happened. The plan had failed, the last chance of escape had gone. She felt exhausted, emotionally and physically. It was no use fighting any more. She resigned herself to whatever was to come and fell asleep.

It seemed only minutes later that the change in motion woke her. Sounds from outside came down through the ventilator inlets in the coachroof: the throb of a powerful engine, followed by men's voices. She picked up odd sentences but before long it was all over. She heard Martin's 'bye now', and the sound of sail handling on deck.

The voice she had first heard, the one that shouted

'Merry Christmas, old sport', must, she thought, have been Billings.

Christmas? She couldn't believe it was Christmas! How incredibly different to the last one.

Dinah Ferrars had invited her down to Highfield, the family house on Bailey's Hill near Sevenoaks. It was a lovely old stone-walled house high on the Downs looking out over the Weald, a marvellous panorama of fields and woods and distant villages, of winding lanes and hedgerows and grey ribbons of road threading through a landscape spread like a great picture puzzle over hundreds of square miles.

They arrived in the afternoon of Christmas Eve to find the house bursting with family; sons and daughters and grandchildren, with the numbers swollen on Christmas Day when what Dinah called her mother's 'waifs and strays' arrived: two widows and a cheerful Blimpish major long retired, the relic of a wife who had run away with the regiment's colonel – 'Old boy friend of Mum's,' Dinah confided. It had all happened long ago, the principals were old, and it seemed to her very unimportant.

On Christmas Eve they had danced to hi-fi music, and Dinah's brother, Donald, had been very attentive. Next morning it was snowing and they went to church – ten of them – something she hadn't done for a long time; and though it all seemed rather strange, and she felt a bit of an impostor, it was a moving experience. Then back to Highfield to open presents after an enormous midday Christmas dinner at which she'd eaten like a pig but enjoyed herself enormously. Later they joined with the children in musical hats and chairs to a lively accompaniment of childish screams and laughter – and, of course, they listened to the Queen's Speech.

In the middle of these activities Donald had detached her for a walk through snow laden lanes on the slopes of Ide Hill. It was a crisp afternoon and she was glad to be alive; and though Donald at twenty-five seemed terribly young to her twenty-two, she had enjoyed his enthusiasm and zest for living.

That evening Carlos phoned her on some pretext to do with the office – 'Had to wish you a Happy Christmas,' he confided in a husky whisper. 'Can't wait for the New Year, darling. Got something rather special for you' – and she'd felt inhibited because members of the Ferrars family were near the phone and her attempts to respond to the office problem gambit hadn't sounded convincing. She ended with a limp, 'Happy Christmas to you – *and* a happy New Year,' and wished he'd not phoned her. It was the wrong time and place, and it struck the wrong chord. And, as it happened, it wasn't a very happy New Year for towards the end of it he ditched her.

Her thoughts were interrupted by the sound of Martin coming down the companion ladder. A moment later he was beside her bunk. 'Right,' he said. 'Let's get that out.' He peeled off the plaster, took the ball of cotton-wool from her mouth and patted her shoulder. When he'd finished untying the rope which bound her he said, 'There you are, Sarah. Thank God it's the last time I'll have to do that. I've hated it as much as you have.'

She sat up, avoided his eyes, rubbed the stiffness in her arms and legs. Her mouth felt horribly dry and she wanted a drink of water.

'. . . our relationship,' he was saying, 'reminds me of a hunter who's trapped a wild animal. He knows that at certain times it will smell the jungle and try to escape. Because he doesn't want to lose it he always locks it up when that happens.'

She watched him with ill-concealed contempt, deciding that anyone who could think like that was both idiotic and mad. 'And gags it no doubt,' she said.

He ignored that: 'With luck *Sunboro Beauty* should be home in twenty days.'

Why had he said *Sunboro Beauty* and not *we*?

She looked up, met the cold stare of the blue eyes, and shivered.

For two days after leaving St John's north-westerly winds

drove them to the east under overcast skies at a steady seven to eight knots. With the main, mizzen and big genoa set, the ketch surged and plunged on her way through endless processions of foam-crested seas. The snow had been left behind, but it was still intensely cold and rain and dashings of spray made life on board miserably uncomfortable.

Christmas Day had passed without celebration. The girl would not speak to him, ignored his 'Happy Christmas', refused a celebratory glass of Hine and others of Billings' Christmas goodies. In the late afternoon of 26 December he was below working on a fault in the bilge-pump when the ketch gybed while running hard before wind and sea. Rushing to the cockpit he found that one of the brackets securing the self-steering gear to the transom had worked loose. Disengaging the gear, he told the girl to take the wheel and get the ketch on course while he went below for tools.

Back on deck he lay above the transom, head and shoulders through the pushpit rails, and worked on the loose bracket where one of the holding bolts had sheared. Removing it would have been difficult at any time but under those conditions, the stern rising and falling like a roller coaster while big following seas lifted the transom and roared past only inches from his head, it was immensely difficult.

Soon after he'd begun work on the bracket she called out, 'You should be wearing your safety harness.'

'Gets in the way.'

'What happens if we're pooped?'

'We won't be with you at the wheel.'

'You should wear it, Martin.'

He realized from her tone that the gybe had broken the ice. She wasn't going to continue punishing him with silence. Later, with a note of anxiety, she asked, 'Think you'll be able to fix the Bosun?'

'Sure I will.'

'Good.'

It took the best part of an hour, but at last he got the broken bolt out, replaced it with a spare and tightened the bracket. That task completed, he set the wind vane and re-engaged self-steering. He put a hand on her arm, squeezed it affectionately. 'Well done, Sarah. I'd have had to heave-to if I'd been alone. Would've taken a lot longer.'

An icy burst of spray swept over them.

He said, 'Let's go down and have that snort.'

They went below and drank the Hine, and although she was quiet and a little subdued she smiled at times and was friendly and for that he was grateful. Her state of mind was something he'd spent a lot of time worrying about since the fright she'd given him off St John's, and he had resolved to be kinder and more considerate.

On the 27th the wind veered to the north and moderated, later veering again to north-north-east, the last shift accompanied by clearing skies so that he was able to get a sunsight for longitude. He found they had made good 472 miles since leaving St John's – an average, with the aid of the Gulf Stream, of just on eight knots, the best run over a 60 hour period since the voyage had begun. His delight, however, was tempered by a falling barometer. At 2200 he switched on the transmitter for the Halifax weather report. It was gloomy – a low was moving to the east over northern Canada and shipping was warned of a severe gale imminent in the area east of Newfoundland and Nova Scotia.

For some time after that he and the girl busied themselves securing things on deck and below, and generally making ready for the gale. Among other precautions he made sure that storm sails were easily accessible, that the life-raft canister, spinnaker poles and other movable gear were securely lashed, and that warps were ready in the after cabin for streaming if needed. The girl filled three large Thermos flasks, two with hot Bovril and one with coffee, and put various snacks – oatmeal cakes, corned beef, cheese lumps, dates and chocolate slabs – in the ready-use basket. By way of prevention she swallowed more seasick pills.

'Well, that's that,' he said, when they decided they had done all they could. 'Now we wait for it.' She didn't return his smile.

# CHAPTER TWENTY-THREE

At two o'clock that morning, having handed over the watch, she was making ready to go below when he said, 'Get as much sleep as you can, Sarah – while the going's good.'

'I will. I'm flat out after all that bloody sail changing.'

'Watch it. Your language . . . as bad as mine.'

'Catching, isn't it,' she said cheerfully. ''bye. Enjoy yourself.'

During the later part of her watch the wind had begun to back from the north-east and was now abeam, the noisy pounding and crashing to windward having given way to a less violent motion. But it was no more than comparative, for with a boisterous sea superimposed on the long westerly swell the motion remained sudden and unpredictable.

Waiting in the cockpit in darkness and discomfort for a gale known to be approaching at considerable speed was not, he decided, the nicest way of passing the time. He concentrated his mind on other things.

One of these was an assessment of his condition. The long voyage had drained a good deal of energy – he tired more easily now and suffered increasingly from tension and depression. These were signals of mental and physical deterioration caused by an accumulation of stress and fatigue; while he understood and accepted them as inevitable, he worried about their effect on the girl.

She had complained recently of strange experiences while on watch at night: on one occasion she thought she had seen two men on the foredeck; on another a ship had, she said, appeared close on the bow – within a hundred yards, she thought – but before she could take avoiding action it had disappeared.

He explained that hallucinations brought on by exhaustion were not abnormal. Having given her that assurance he resolved privately that she must get more sleep, so he reduced the length of her night watches at the expense of his own. She argued but he brushed her objections aside. He also increased their food ration; the economies he had insisted on from the beginning, the generous provisioning of the boat in the first place, and the good progress made, meant that they could afford to do this.

Though the approaching gale was much in his mind it did not cause him undue concern. They had taken the precautions he considered necessary, and from the start he'd bargained for gales in the Western Ocean; the important thing was to make the most of them. He was determined to keep *Sunboro Beauty* running before the gale as long as possible, only streaming warps, heaving-to or lying a-hull, if forced to do so. He had long been impressed by the views of Moitessier and Dumas that a yacht running in heavy weather was more likely to go out of control through carrying too little sail than too much. It was a view he intended to put to the test.

There had been a letter from Tessa at St John's – a fairly brief affair containing news of mutual friends, of two West End plays she'd seen with VS, and a blow by blow account of Derek Blandford's recent achievements. He was now, she wrote, chairman as well as managing-director of the insurance broking firm, his father having at last retired: *They've celebrated Derek's success by buying a villa in the Algarve. Near Albufeira. Looks absolute heaven in the photos Isabella showed me. He really has done well, hasn't he?*

Strangely enough he found himself more bored by the letter than annoyed; perhaps because her only reference to the TRISTAR came at its end ... *we hear that* Sunboro Beauty *is doing rather well, though VS says* Tornado Four *and two multihulls are days ahead of you. Bad luck! Perhaps it's wiser to confine one's ambitions to more ordinary things like the*

*Blandfords have done – sons at Harrow, Isabella's Mercedes, Derek's new Daimler, and now the Algarve villa. Or am I being unkind?*

'You are,' he muttered as he tore up the letter and threw it over the side. The gesture did him a power of good. One way and another he wasn't missing Tessa too much; possibly because he had on a number of occasions in recent weeks found himself comparing her with Sarah, and Sarah had come out of it rather well.

Tired though she was after handing over the wheel at two that morning she did not fall asleep. Instead she lay in the sleeping bag thinking, her back to the lee-cloth, knees and hands against the side, body wedged through long practice in such a way that it countered the ketch's motion.

The decision she had made to give up the fight, to accept her lot, was working better than she had hoped. He was being more considerate and that cushioned the strain of life on board in the wet cold days of a North Atlantic winter. It was a relief not to have one's mind in a constant turmoil about what was going to happen, to be able to accept the days as they came with some sort of fatalism.

*This hour, this day, this air we breathe is more important than all eternity . . .* Carlos used to misquote, knowing that he failed miserably to live up to that philosophy – poor Carlos.

Since he'd dropped her she had tended to dwell on his faults, perhaps to magnify them, but she was well aware of his good qualities. Basically he was a kind and generous man, even if he did lack moral fibre. His conceit was, she was sure, a defence mechanism, a means of reassuring himself. On rare occasions he would drop his guard and become engagingly honest. She remembered one of them, in a hotel bedroom near Piccadilly Circus after lunch; he had rolled away from her to lie half propped up, chin in hand, his eyes on the grey sky beyond the double glazing. 'Wish I were a different sort of man,' he said.

'What sort is that?'

'The lawn mowing type. Faithful husband, adoring father, dedicated home lover. No divided loyalties.'

161

She raised her head to look at him in surprise. 'Anything else?'

'Yes. A different sort of job.'

'I thought you adored yours?'

'That's a front. I have to convince myself I'm doing something worthwhile, something creative, or I'd go round the bend. But every now and than I stop and see myself as I really am, and the work I do for what it really is – and neither is flattering. After all, what is it I do so industriously? Preside over a bunch of nitwits working like beavers at brainwashing people into believing they want things they don't need. All those eye-catching ads in the glossies – know why they work? Because they appeal to the basest of human emotions: acquisitiveness, envy, keeping up with the Joneses – all that sort of nastiness.'

'Isn't that a harsh judgement, Carlos? Surely advertising has other functions, like letting consumers know what's available and where. And – well, I've heard you say it's the keen edge of the market place, polices prices, etcetera.'

'I've been brainwashed too.'

'What *is* worthwhile work?'

He sighed deeply. 'Something genuinely creative. Architects, design engineers, painters, composers, writers – at the end of the day they've created something tangible, something that endures if they're any good. Not pieces of paper, budgets, market surveys and sales curves.'

'You're a strange man,' she said, thinking that this was the nice Carlos, the one she really cared about.

In the early hours of morning the few clear patches of sky darkened and with a falling barometer the wind freshened and backed in stages. As the wind and sea increased he reduced sail, exchanged the genoa for a smaller foresail and put two reefs in the main. Determined to make the most of the weather he disengaged self-steering and took the wheel, forgetting his tiredness in the challenge of the weather.

At five in the morning the wind backed again – this time to the west – and blew at the bottom of force eight, driving before it grey seas which rolled unceasingly eastwards. With the wind on the quarter registering between thirty and thirty-five knots *Sunboro Beauty* surged forward on the big seas until they passed her by and she settled in their troughs, only to climb again as those that followed lifted her high on their advancing slopes.

When the girl went below at two o'clock that morning he had told her to stay there until she was called. At seven he heard the main hatch slide open, her head and shoulders appeared and she shouted, 'God, isn't it awful! You must be freezing. Come down and get something hot. I'll take over.'

It was a tempting offer. But for a few thirty-minute snatches he'd had a sleepless night and was not only tired but wet and very cold. Ahead in the eastern sky the first pale light of day was unfolding a panorama of windswept sea, enormous foam-streaked waves racing from astern, the wind shrieking as it flattened their crests and tore from them streamers of spindrift. Would she be able to manage on her own in that weather? He decided that she would – but not for long.

'Right. You take over,' he said. 'I'll put another reef in the mainsail before I go down. Look out how you come aft. It's dodgy.'

She clambered out of the hatchway, shut the hatch behind her, crawled and slid to the after end of the cockpit, secured her lifeline to a strong point and took the wheel. He stayed with her until he was satisfied she'd got the feel of things. That didn't take long and he wasn't surprised. She'd had more experience in the last seven weeks than many a yachtsman would have had in years. He went forward and put the last reef in the mainsail. When he got back to the cockpit he asked her how she was getting on.

'Fine,' she said. 'I'd rather be here than rattling about down there.'

'Good. I won't be long.'

There was more daylight now. He took a last look at the bleak scene, the slopes and valleys of the big seas blown to a chalklike white by the gale. Happy to leave it, he went below.

It was warm in the saloon and snug, and despite the

violent motion the scream of the wind was distant and muted, though he could hear only too distinctly the hiss and wash of sea against the hull. Wedged beside the chart-table he had a meal of corned beef and oatcakes and hot coffee from a Thermos while he listened to the news from Boston. After the meal, energy restored, he checked the bilge. There was less water than he'd expected, but he pumped it out and then checked the batteries. They could, he decided, do without charging, which was just as well under those conditions. Next he advanced the DR position on the chart and wrote up the logbook. When he'd done these things and found a moment to relax he realized how tired he was. He went back to the cockpit and spoke to the girl. She was managing well. Finally reassured, he gave in to his exhaustion and her insistence that he should go below and sleep. Shedding safety harness, oilskins and seaboots, he climbed on to his bunk and stayed there until ten o'clock.

At midday the barometer began to rise, the wind veered in stages to the north-east, its velocity dropping to twenty knots, the sea moderating with it though still confused and lumpy as it quarrelled with the westerly swell. There were occasional clearings in the sky but the sun remained obstinately behind clouds and a sunsight was not possible. He plotted the DR position at noon before going up on deck to help the girl with sail changing. After that he went below for more sleep. At 1430 the alarm woke him. He looked at the barometer, put on his foul-weather gear, seaboots and safety harness, made his way to the cockpit and took the wheel from her. 'You've been a marvellous help,' he said. 'Really got my head down that time.'

She looked tired and bedraggled, her woollen cap and yellow oilskins encrusted with salt spray, but her eyes shone and she smiled. 'It's been quite an experience.'

He glanced at the sky. 'It's a lull, I reckon. Glass falling again. Must be a cold front passing over with a low behind it. Better get some sleep while you can.'

His prediction was soon borne out for during the next few

hours the wind backed to the south-west briefly before settling once more in the west. As the barometer fell wind and sea increased and by ten o'clock that night *Sunboro Beauty* was running before a gale under deep reefed main and a small jib. At times there were heavy showers of rain and these combined with spray and spindrift to lay an opaque screen round the ketch.

The wind was now blowing at forty to forty-five knots, reaching fifty and fifty-five in the gusts. Determined not to take in sail until it was absolutely necessary, he kept the wind slightly on the port quarter, having found that the ketch responded well to that treatment. The motion was an exhilarating one, *Sunboro Beauty* lifting to seas which roared up from astern, then with sudden energy surfing forward on their crests until they drew ahead and she sank back into the troughs as if abandoning the unequal struggle. The seas were so high that she would lose the wind in the troughs until a following sea lifted her, the sails filled again with a loud slap and she would surge ahead. For much of the time the automatic log was recording eight to nine knots, the needle touching twelve when she surfed.

At midnight he estimated the wind to be blowing at force ten – it was screaming through the rigging, wailing banshee-like, whipping the crests from the seas and blowing them into stinging spray, the needle on the windspeed indicator at times coming up against the 60 stop. It was time to further reduce sail. He set the wind vane, engaged self-steering and struggled forward, crouching and crawling, clipping and unclipping his lifeline as he went; securing it to the mainmast, he took the turns off the halyard cleats and set about lowering the mainsail. The only way in which he could do that safely was to wait for a trough; then, with most of the wind out of the sail, he was able to hand it. Not only was the motion violent but when they were on the crests the wind tore at the sail and he had to hold on for dear life while waiting for the next trough. When at last he got the mainsail down and lashed to the boom he struggled back to the cockpit, secured his lifeline to the binnacle, unlatched the self-steering and took the wheel again. Without the mainsail the ketch's downwind speed was reduced and he felt he had her under more positive control.

As the night wore on the storm grew fiercer. By three o'clock in the morning the seas were mountainous, the windspeed indicator hovering between fifty-five and the sixty-knot stop. But for the race he would have taken in all sail and either run under bare poles or let her lie a-hull as he'd done in the Biscay gale. Then, however, there'd been two months ahead in which to make up time. Now, nearing the race's end, with *Sunboro Beauty* well placed and still sailing fast under the storm jib, there was every reason to press on. She would, he felt, be making better progress than the multihulls in these exceptionally high winds and seas; it was time to use the solid advantage of her weight, draught and seaworthiness. He had thought of streaming warps but decided against it.

The screen of flying foam and spindrift which blanketed the night shut visibility down to nothing, but he could feel the big seas picking up *Sunboro Beauty* and hurling her forward on their crests. It was an eerie sensation, like riding a huge waterborne roller-coaster, the violence of the motion, the powerful forces involved, demanding quick reaction at the wheel if broaching was to be avoided.

It was a combination of his exhaustion, of a rogue wave, a great gust of wind, and the mizzen's boom lashings carrying away – the sail then blowing part way up the mast track – it was the simultaneous occurrence of these things which, shortly after four that morning, caused the ketch stern to lift high on a great sea which slewed it to starboard, thrusting the bow deep into the water and rolling *Sunboro Beauty* over on to her starboard side. He was on the windward side of the wheel, spinning it in a last-minute attempt to avert the broach, when the sudden lurch catapulted him head first on to the leeward coaming.

His last thought before he lost consciousness was that the ketch had been knocked flat and might turn over if she failed to right herself before another sea struck.

166

# CHAPTER TWENTY-FOUR

It was impossible to sleep under those conditions, the ketch lifting and plunging, the hull shuddering from the impact of massive seas, the sound of water surging past the side only inches from where she lay. At four in the morning she gave up. In the dim light of the saloon's oil lamp she put on seaboots, oilskins and safety harness and then, for want of anything better to do, wedged herself between the end of the bunk and the chart-table. That seemed marginally safer, for she was at least ready now to go on deck at a moment's notice.

Earlier when he took over the wheel she had said, 'Why don't we lie a-hull under bare poles like we did in the Bay of Biscay?'

'This is a race,' was his stolid reply. 'Not a pleasure cruise.'

She saw his face in the binnacle light – tight-mouthed, determined – and knew there was nothing to be gained by argument. So she went below, cold, miserable and very frightened. For some time she had sat at the chart-table holding on grimly, gazing apprehensively at the windspeed indicator and barometer; then, realizing that what she saw only increased her fear, she took off the foul-weather gear, got back into her bunk and tried to sleep. That hadn't worked either, so here she was back at the chart-table, holding on as tightly as ever, wondering if the muffled scream of the wind and the distant rumble of breaking waves would ever cease – and wishing above all that she'd never embarked on such a crazy adventure.

'You stupid idiot,' she scolded herself. '*You* put yourself here. You could have been safe and warm in London.' As if to emphasize her misgivings, a sea broke on the coachroof with a dull thud and the hull shook in protest. Her sniffle of

167

sorrow was drowned by the thunderous noise of a big sea which lifted the stern high and slewed it to starboard. The next moment she was catapulted across the saloon and slammed against the stove, a multitude of loose objects cascading around her. She lay breathless, bruised and terrified, believing the ketch had turned over. The oil lamp had gone out and agonizing seconds passed as she waited in the dark for the inrush of icy water. It didn't come. Instead, unbelievably, *Sunboro Beauty* came upright and lurched back to port, all the loose things crashing across to that side with a shattering noise.

Her one thought now was to get up on deck while it was still possible. She found a torch, clambered up the companionway, slid the hatch open and was momentarily taken aback by the furious buffeting of the wind and stinging spray. She shouted, 'Martin,' but got no reply.

Wedged in the hatchway, she shone the torch aft and saw him lying behind the wheel in the starboard corner of the cockpit, his arms over the coaming. She called his name again, louder this time, her voice more frightened, but he didn't move. Dead? Her heart all but stopped beating. Then came a moment of relief when she saw that his lifeline was still made fast to the binnacle pedestal; at least he wouldn't be washed over the side by the next wave that swept the cockpit. She aimed the torch at the mizzen mast. Its boom and much of the sail were hanging over the side, trailing in the sea, most of the luff having torn away from the slides in the mast track. The wind vane on the self-steering had gone and what was left of the gear was banging against the transom as the stern rose and fell. There was not time to examine the damage more closely but she was relieved to see that both masts were standing, their shrouds and stays apparently intact. Looking forward again she saw that the storm jib had filled and was pulling the ketch's bows downwind. That meant running again before those huge following seas. She wasn't going to have that. *Sunboro Beauty* had weathered one gale lying a-hull and she was jolly well going to weather another. The storm jib would have to come down. She put the wheel amidships before setting off on a slow and desperate crawl along the foredeck, clipping and unclipping her lifeline as she went.

After a long struggle, and taking advantage of the slackening of the wind in the troughs, she got the storm jib down and lashed to the guard-rail stanchions at deck level. Back in the cockpit she began to work on the mizzen. The metal bracket on the heel of the boom had broken away from its gooseneck and the boom was in the sea, smashing against the hull. With the serrated blade of a sheath-knife she cut the mizzen sheet, unclipped the halyard and kicking strap and with a great effort forced the luff slides out of the mast track. Working frantically she had succeeded before long, and boom and sail blew over the side. All this took a lot out of her, she was very tired so she decided to tackle the self-steering later.

With the jib down and the wheel hard a-port the ketch slewed across the seas and lay a-hull with the port quarter slightly into wind. In this attitude she rode the seas well, giving to them without shipping water.

Now to see to him. She shone the torch on the prone body. His eyes were closed and blood trickled from a gash on his forehead. She knelt beside him. 'Martin. For God's sake. Can't you hear me?'

There was no reply.

Shivering with apprehension she tried to feel his heart but soon gave up. It couldn't be done through all that foul-weather gear. She put her ear to his mouth, listening for breathing, but the noise of the storm drowned all other sounds. His face and hands were ice cold.

'I must get him below,' she kept repeating to herself. 'I can't leave him here.' Before long she found that it was one thing to say, but quite another to do in those appalling conditions.

It took time and every ounce of her strength to drag him from the after corner of the cockpit, past the wheel and along to the foot of the hatchway. The problem then was to get him into it and down the companionway. She looped a jibsheet round his chest and under his arms and turned its end up on a self-tailing winch. That done she slid open the hatch and, starting with his legs, pulled and pushed him in stages over the washboards, making what use she could of the ketch's pitching. When the jibsheet took the weight she went back to the winch and paid it out until it went slack and she knew he must have landed on the sole. Her constant fear was that a sea might break aboard and flood down the open hatchway before she'd got him below; but though spray found its way there, solid water didn't. With a last look round she went below, shutting the hatch behind her.

Once she'd got the oil lamp lighted and back into its gimbals she cleaned his wound with cotton-wool soaked in hot water from a Thermos and put an antiseptic dressing on it. She was bandaging his head when he came to. 'What's going on?' he asked in a hoarse voice, his bloodshot eyes staring.

'You got a nasty bang on your forehead when we were knocked flat. I'm bandaging it.'

He tried to move.

'Keep still,' she said. 'It's difficult enough with all this movement and banging about.'

Each time the ketch rolled, everything which was loose clattered from one side of the saloon to the other.

He put a hand to his forehead. She pushed it away. 'No. Leave it alone. I haven't finished.'

'Knocked flat? When?'

'About an hour ago. Around four o'clock.'

'Christ! I don't remember that. All that time. How did I get here?'

'I dragged you down.'

'You!' He closed his eyes. 'God, my head's bursting!'

'When I've done the bandage I'll give you some Disprin.'

There was a thud against the hull on the starboard side. The ketch lurched.

'What's that?'

'A sea pounding us. Nothing to worry about.'

'Still blowing?'

'Yes. Can't you hear it? A full gale.'

'What sail are we carrying?'

'None. We're lying a-hull.'

'I see.' He opened his eyes. 'I must go up.'

'No. Not yet. First we'll get you into your bunk for a rest. Don't worry. I'll look after things on top.'

He stared at her. 'You?' His voice was thick. 'What do you know?'

'Enough,' she said.

When she'd finished the bandaging she dissolved three tablets in a mug. 'The Disprin,' she explained.

He looked at her doubtfully, hesitated, swallowed the mixture, passed the mug back. She filled it with hot Bovril. When he'd drunk that she helped him into his bunk, put a rug over him and secured the lee-cloth.

'What's the time?' he asked.

'Ten past six.'

'Have you set the alarm?'

She nodded reassuringly. For the next hour she was busy putting away the bits and pieces which lay around the saloon in hopeless confusion, mopping up the sole and dealing generally with the mess the weather had made.

There was nothing more she could do below or on deck, the ketch was riding the seas well, it had been a long and exhausting struggle and she was near the end of her resources, so she got into her bunk. She did not set the alarm. As far as she was concerned they were going to sleep for hours and hours.

In early afternoon, waking from deep sleep, he lay in his bunk wondering where he was and what had happened. Slowly his mind cleared: he remembered the girl bandaging his head, helping him into the bunk. They had been knocked flat, she'd told him. He couldn't remember that happening. He fingered the bandage. The headache was still there but nothing like it had been.

The movement, the sounds of wind and sea, told him that they were still lying a-hull though the gale seemed to have lost some of its fury. 'Must go on deck,' he muttered, and dragged himself out of the bunk. The chart-table clock showed 1.33. The girl was in the navigator's bunk. He peeped over the lee-cloth. She was asleep, breathing deeply. She needs it, he thought. How on earth had she managed on her own in that weather to take in sail and get the ketch lying a-hull? More incredible still, she had got him out of the cockpit and down to the saloon. It was a marvellous effort.

He was putting on his foul-weather gear when she woke up.

'What are you doing?' she challenged.

'Why didn't you set the alarm?'

'I did. Didn't you hear it?'

'No. If *you* heard it why didn't you call me?'

'I thought you must have heard it. I was dead-beat. Anyway you shouldn't get up.' She began to move out of her bunk. 'You're still concussed.'

'Not any longer.' He was fastening the lifejacket and harness. 'Head's as clear as a bell. Must see if everything's shipshape on top.'

'I'll do that. You need more rest.'

He shook his head. 'We should have been running under a storm jib – or even bare poles. You should have streamed the warps and run after the knockdown. Nobody wins a race lying a-hull.'

'Oh, forget the bloody race.' She said it with sudden vehemence. 'We're not in it. And for your information, we've not got a mizzen any longer – nor any self-steering.'

He stared open mouthed. 'What d'you mean?.

She told him what had happened, what she'd done about it. He shook his head in disbelief. 'You're quite a girl, Sarah.'

'I'm not a girl.'

'I suppose not.' He looked at her speculatively. 'I'm going on deck.'

'I wish you wouldn't.'

He started up the companion-ladder with heavy uncertain movements, clutching the handrails to steady himself against the rolling.

'Wait for me,' she called after him as she struggled into her oilskins and seaboots.

Before dark they had rigged a jury mizzen boom using a

172

bearing out spar and hoisted the storm jib and the spare mizzen reefed. They lashed the head of the damaged self-steering gear to the pushpit stanchions and streamed warps. 'I'll tackle The Bosun when the weather improves,' he said.

Though the wind was blowing at force eight and the seas were still big, there was less gusting and the valleys between the crests had lengthened so that *Sunboro Beauty* was able to ride them more comfortably. It took time to get her properly balanced but eventually she was running well with the helm slightly to starboard, the wind ten to fifteen degrees on the port quarter. It was not safe to leave the wheel unattended so they decided to split the night into two-hour watches. The girl wanted to do the first spell so that he could get more sleep but he wouldn't have it. 'No. Hot food is more important. See what you can do about that.'

So she went below and with some difficulty and after several minor disasters warmed up a tinned stew and vegetables. It was the first hot meal they'd had since leaving St John's.

At 2000 she took over the wheel and he worked on the chart, up-dating the DR position. It was largely guesswork. All he had to work on was the automatic log reading of distance run since the last DR position. But log readings took no account of direction current and drift in a gale and until the skies cleared and sights were possible – or a ship passed to which he could speak – there was no way of knowing where they were.

Later that night he switched on the transmitter and called Portishead but there was so much static interference that he couldn't get through, nor could he hear other TRISTAR competitors reporting.

By daylight the gale had blown itself out. Its place was taken by a breeze from the south-west and a heavy swell left by the big seas. During the night he'd replaced the storm jib with a bigger headsail and soon after dawn on the 30th he hoisted the mainsail. Before long *Sunboro Beauty* was running well, logging near to seven knots. The sky had cleared in places and at ten o'clock – not without difficulty because it was something of a challenge to find a horizon in that big swell – he got a sunsight for longitude. He ran the position line on to noon when he managed to get a meridian altitude. These gave a position of 45°30′N: 33°10′W. They had made good 800 miles since St John's, averaging over 5 knots. Progress in the gale had been better than he'd expected, something he put down to drift and the current.

During the rest of the day he was busy checking running gear and standing rigging, pumping the bilge, charging batteries and dealing with storm damage as best he could.

The girl had occupied herself cleaning up below, hanging out wet clothing and bedding to dry, helping him on deck at times and preparing food.

The self-steering gear had been a problem. After several abortive attempts he decided that repairs were not possible. Enormous forces had twisted the wind vane clamp and its axis in such a way that he couldn't fit a spare vane without straightening the metal. That required heat treatment which was beyond his resources. The voyage would have to be completed with manual steering only. He could have managed that alone, but with two of them to steer it would be easier – and they would make better progress.

What he badly wanted to know was how other yachts had fared in the storm, especially the multihulls which had been two and three days ahead of him at St John's. They might still be in the gale, for it would have reached them later than it had *Sunboro Beauty*. Atmospheric conditions had improved and he looked forward to the Portishead schedule that night when he hoped to be able to give his position, tell them of the gale, and ask for news of other competitors.

# CHAPTER TWENTY-FIVE

Fearing that he had a duplicate key to her locker Sarah had, since St John's, hidden her voyage notes under the mattress beneath the temporary sail bin in the after cabin. It was not that there was anything to suggest that he'd ever read her notes – but how could she be sure?

What had really persuaded her to hide them, however, was the belief that the notes now had a very much more important purpose than simply providing material for a book. If she did not reach England they might be found by whoever cleaned out the cabin after the race. There was always a chance it might be someone other than Martin – in which case her story of the voyage would be out.

On several occasions he had stressed the importance of making the narrative an honest one. 'We must feel free to write an uninhibited account of the voyage,' he'd said early on. 'The incidents as we see them, our reactions to them, our beliefs and innermost feelings. I couldn't do that if I thought you were reading my notes. I'm sure the same applies to you.'

In spite of this she had recorded little of what she really thought and felt. Since St John's, however, things had changed and though she made no entry until the 30th, when she described the gale and its consequences, what she wrote on the following night was certainly not inhibited:

*31/12 – New Year's Eve!* Wind westerly, force 5, long swell, moderate sea, *SB* running comfortably under mizzen, main and No. 2 genoa.

Last night M came up and told me the Portishead news. No reports from *Mercedes Express* and *Caspar's Folly* – Portishead worried that they don't reply.

*Grande Rapide* had to heave-to for 48 hours – storm damage – forestay carried away and rudder trouble – now only two days ahead of us.

M tried to sound calm but I know him and that voice so well. Even in the dark I knew he was excited – thinking, I'm sure, that *SB* could be lying 4th if John Caspar and Kurt Grosse were in real trouble. The hoarse voice trembles and goes higher in key when he's like that. I hope and pray those two aren't in serious trouble. If M really begins to think *SB* can win the TRISTAR, God help me. There's some comfort in what the others are doing. *Tornado Four* now only a few days from Plymouth, and we're unlikely to overtake *Omega Challenger* – she's bigger than we are and M says Ken Hutchings is a marvellous skipper – *Grande Rapide* evidently going well again and should stay ahead with the following winds.

This afternoon I asked M about the cameras – when was he going to take pictures?

'What pictures?' He looked at me sideways, spoke quickly.

'You know. For the book. Pictures of me, the stowaway. Me at the wheel. Me hauling on a sheet. Me and you together – skipper and stowaway.' I managed a mildly theatrical laugh, hoping it sounded as if I was joking.

He was at the wheel, head bent forward, eyes on the binnacle – his concentrating posture. 'Oh those – well – any time now. Let's say tomorrow or the next day.'

'Are you going to use the video camera?'

'Depends. Sounds very complicated. See what happens in a day or so.'

He did a quick switch of subject then. Had I done anything about the chafing on No. 2 genoa? Typical Martin. Work, bloody work. Hates to see me idle for a moment.

*Later – 2.35 p.m.* I'd been below for about ten minutes when I heard him talking. At first I thought he was calling me, but I listened at the foot of the ladder

176

and it wasn't that. He was talking to himself. Incredible! He hasn't done that before. I couldn't make out what he was saying, even with a following wind. Something about majesty and purity – and he rambled on about Breton fishermen praying – *O God, be good!* – that I heard distinctly.

It was unnerving listening to such gibberish. Quite eerie! He really is insane. It's terrifying.

He wondered what had happened to the multihulls. John Caspar and Kurt Grosse holding their cards close to their chests? They'd done that before. Both probably sailing on great circle courses instead of the rhumb line. They might have missed the worst of the gale. If their weather hadn't been too desperate they could be overtaking *Tornado Four*. She was only a day or so ahead of them at St John's. All depended on how they'd fared in the gale. Perhaps they really were in trouble ... A tremor ran through his body and his stomach churned.

How bad was *Grande Rapide*'s storm damage? Broken forestay – inner or outer? – and rudder trouble. What sort of rudder trouble? Hove-to for forty-eight hours? Was that due to the weather or storm damage, or both? Pierre Fougeux was a first-rate seaman. He'd make a good job of whatever could be done. How marvellous to beat him. Of all the TRISTAR competitors Pierre was the man he knew best and admired most. He recalled their conversation in Plymouth about single-handed racing.

They had been discussing the risks, the taking of chances. Pierre said, 'Some we must take – we have to sleep, *n'est-ce pas?* – but we should take them only where there is no logical alternative. You know, *mon vieux*, the character of the sea. It has purity and majesty, but it is restless, relentless, ruthless. So it has always been. It does not change. Treat it with respect, be logical always, and it will carry you safely on your way. But take liberties – then, *mon vieux*, it will cruelly destroy you. You know the prayer of the Breton fishermen – *"O God, be good to me. Thy sea is so wide and my ship is so small"*. You see they understand these things. And

177

we who sail alone must understand them also. If we affront the purity and majesty of the sea we destroy ourselves.'

What would Pierre Fougeux think if he knew what was going on in *Sunboro Beauty*? Wasn't that an affront to the purity and majesty of the sea?

The girl had forced him to turn what should have been the greatest and most exciting adventure of his life into its biggest lie: a deceit maintained, ostensibly, for a book which might never see the light of day. The tragedy was that *Sunboro Beauty*'s chances of finishing well were beginning to look better than ever.

How would it all end? He made no attempt to answer the question. He was too tired, his head ached infernally and his mind was confused.

*9.30 a.m. – New Year's Day!* Wind veered to NNW during the night, force 4/5, *SB* going well with wind on beam. Same sails. It's cold, grey, wet – lots of rain – and miserable. Like me.

Soon after five this morning I'd just come off watch when the Marconi alarm began warbling. I knew from our *Karamagee* experience that that meant a call on 2182 kiloHertz, the international distress frequency. M has never shown me how to work the Marconi Falcon or the VHF – deliberately of course. Thinks I might shout for help. Suppose I might if I knew how to – but what would I say? 'Help! I'm on board *Sunboro Beauty* and fear for my life.' They'd think it was a joke – trouble is, I don't know about wave-lengths. When he's finished with either set he turns the various knobs back to zero and locks away the card which gives the wave-lengths. Perhaps I'll try the VHF when next we see a ship – it's a much simpler looking set. Or when we sight the English coast I may have a shot at it. Call Land's End Radio – if I'm still on board.

When he came back he said, 'That was a Belgian coaster. She collided with an unidentified vessel at 4.50 this morning, 98 miles south of the Fastnet. It sank immediately. They picked up one survivor. Unconscious. He requires urgent medical treatment. The coaster is still searching for survivors.'

'Where's the Fastnet?'

'Ireland. Off Cape Clear, the southernmost point. Nearly eight hundred miles ahead of us.'

'Why did the coaster call us?'

'She didn't. It was a MAYDAY. I heard various ships and shore stations acknowledging. The RNAS at Culdrose are sending out a helicopter to lift off the casualty.'

M took over the wheel then – sent me below.

When I went up after breakfast I said, 'Happy New Year.'

He stared at me with a glazed look, said, 'Is it?' He looks awful, the blue woollen cap pulled down over the dirty bandage – he won't let me change it – his face covered in stubble (hasn't shaved for days), dark hollows under staring eyes. They're more red than blue now – he gets far less sleep than I do. Always comes up several times during his watch below to check on me. I think that tension (me?), fatigue, and the bang on his forehead have taken a lot out of him. Though he doesn't complain – and I *never* see him taking them – a lot of Disprin are missing.

*1/1 – 4.15 p.m.* M got a fix at noon. 45°50′N, 23°20′W. He'd been gloomy all morning but after the fix his mood switched and he was cheerful.

'Know what?' He was grinning.

'What?'

'We passed the halfway mark early this morning.'

'Super. What's the weather going to do?'

'Glass still rising. Expect the wind'll go round to the east.'

'Pouf! More threshing to windward.'

'Not for long. BBC forecast for shipping reports another low coming down from Greenland.'

'God! Not that again.'

'I don't mind,' he said. 'It'll blow me home.'

179

Why did he say 'me' and not 'us', or even *SB*? – these Freudian slips scare me.

*Later – 10.15 p.m.* The worst has happened. I was on the wheel when he spoke to Portishead and reported *SB*'s position. He came back to the cockpit – told me the news in a sort of stifled voice, trying hard to sound calm. It was dark and I couldn't see his face but I think he was in an almost manic state – hoarse voice lifting into that high key.

'Gary Maddox is all right,' he said.

'How d'you mean he's all right?'

'He's in hospital recovering.'

My heart stopped beating then. 'Why? What's happened?'

'It was *Tornado Four* that was sunk by the Belgian coaster. That's why they couldn't find any other survivors. There weren't any, of course.' He was bubbling with repressed excitement.

I didn't say anything – I was too upset – it was the most ghastly news.

But there was more to come.

'Poor old Pierre's still having trouble with his steering gear. He's only about sixty miles ahead of us.'

'So we're catching up,' I said, hoping he'd deny it.

M switched on the masthead light to look at the burgee – one of his ploys when the conversation gets dodgy – and I saw that sinister private smile.

*Poor old Pierre* my foot! – M was obviously delighted – that was what the sneaky smirk was all about.

'The field's folding up,' he grinned. 'We're lying fifth, maybe better.'

I knew what that meant, so I said, 'Any news of Kurt Grosse and John Caspar?'

He lost interest in the burgee, snapped his head round – gave me a sharp look. 'No,' he said. 'Nothing yet. I hope they're all right.'

What an appalling hypocrite! I'm sure he hopes nothing of the sort. If anything dreadful has happened to those two, only *Omega Challenger* and *Grande*

180

*Rapide* will be ahead of us – and M, who is well out of touch with reality, will be thinking of the £50,000 and the honour and glory etcetera . . .

I am very, very scared – please God, don't let anything awful happen to me.

*Later – 11 p.m.* Glass falling and wind backing. Why, oh why, did I ever do this mad thing?

## CHAPTER TWENTY-SIX

*2/1 – 9.30 a.m.* The gale didn't materialize. Passed south of us M says – thank God! Wind variable during early hours – from SE now, force 4, *SB* close-hauled starboard, sails sheeted hard in. Sea moderate but confused.

Last night I heard him talking to himself again. I couldn't make sense of it except once when he cackled with laughter and said 'Ten little nigger boys' – mad, mad, mad!

Yesterday morning he congratulated me on the breakfast. Boiled eggs, ham, baked beans and coffee – good beginning to the day but it didn't last. I was on the wheel about 11 a.m. – wind gusting all over the place – I dozed off and we went about. M came rushing up – What the hell was I playing at? I knew the mood – the cold fury one – so didn't argue. Just said I was sorry but conditions were difficult.

'Couldn't have happened,' he said, 'if you'd been watching the wind and the sails.'

I said 'sorry' again in my deadpan voice. This must have annoyed him – he flared up. 'Your being sorry won't mend a broken sextant.'

Seems he was taking it out of its box on the chart-table when we went about – he lurched sideways, slipped

181

and the sextant banged into something. There was nothing I could say so just shook my head. He gave me one of his eerie stares – eyes like blue chips of ice – 'Wouldn't be surprised if that wasn't deliberate,' he said.

I asked him what he meant.

'Work it out for yourself.'

'That's a dreadful thing to say,' I told him. 'Take it back.'

But he wouldn't – just went on looking at me in that cold calculating way, then went below.

*3/1 – 1.20 p.m.* It was only a sun-shade that broke on the sextant, not a mirror. There are two other shades he can use.

Wind has gone back to the west and freshened, force 5/6. Lively seas – lots of white crests – *SB* bounding and lurching along under full sail, big genoa set. This good progress does wonders to M's mood.

When he'd fixed the noon position he said, 'Six-nine-five miles to Plymouth. We're logging over seven knots. With the current, we're making good eight. If that keeps up, the day's run could be close on two hundred.' The muscles in his face were flexing!

It gives me cold shivers when that happens because I know what's in his mind – *SB* winning the TRISTAR. It's crazy of course – how can he get away with it? Unless he ditches me? – quite! – I don't think my fears are exaggerated.

*Later – 5 p.m.* This afternoon the sun came out and we had a camera session. He said conditions were 'just right'. Took lots of me doing various things, and I took some of him. M says they'll be marvellous material for The Book. I wonder? He's probably done it – photographs I mean – to reassure me. He can always throw away the film once he's ditched me. He wouldn't use the video-camera – said it was too complicated – he was too busy and too tired to bother with it.

My rationing of paper panties about right! Who says

they won't wash? – three left and a week to go, plus or minus, to Plymouth. Or will I go sooner? I'm frightened. Much more than I can explain on paper.

*Later – 11.50 p.m.* M spoke to me about his latest Portishead session, voice grave: Kurt Grosse picked up by freighter yesterday from life-raft – it was still made fast to dismasted waterlogged *Mercedes Express* which the freighter later sank by ramming – danger to navigation.

He said, 'Marvellous. Old Kurt's safe' – his voice was hoarse, raspy – 'Our gale must have caught up with him. No news of *Caspar's Folly*. Hope John's all right.'

I got rigid with fright while he was telling me the news. When he finished I just said, 'Oh.' But what I was thinking was that only *Grande Rapide* and *Omega Challenger* were ahead of us now. So *SB* is lying third unless *Caspar's Folly* is okay and ahead – please God let her be.

*4/1 – 9.20 a.m.* Wind SW, force 5/6, sea rough. The Falcon's alarm warbled again this morning about six-thirty when I was on watch. M came up soon afterwards – spoke with phoney calm – 'That was Pierre Fougeux calling Portishead on 2182 kHz. Having more rudder trouble. Gudgeon carried away. Reckons he can fix it if the weather improves. Won't accept assistance.'

I asked if Pierre had given a position? He said, 'Yes – he's about 90 to 100 miles ahead of us. Hove-to. Can't steer.'

Wondering what his reply would be – I suppose I was testing him – I blurted out, 'You must be very happy with *SB* so much in the running?' He looked away, pinched his nose, said 'I wouldn't say very happy – but I'm pleased that *SB*'s doing well' – he glared at me – 'even though she's not single-handed.'

Then – like an idiot and without thinking – I said, 'But the TRISTAR Committee and a lot of other people think she *is*.'

His face took on that curious speculative look, and his mouth twitched as if he was about to say something.

183

Whatever it was didn't come out and he went below.

*5/1 – 11.20 a.m.* Weather unchanged – *SB* still going strong – sadly! My resolve at St John's to relax, stop worrying and accept what's to come, isn't working. The whole thing's really too ghastly. I'm completely shattered. All these casualties to other competitors – everything's going in *SB*'s favour – it's as if somebody up there loves M. I used to think I did, or could. I certainly don't now.

I'm not sleeping well – most unlike me – too worried. This morning Billings spoke to M via Portishead. M came up from the call looking very grim and pre-occupied. I know him so well now – his moods show like railway signals. In his face – his mouth – his gestures. I said, 'What was all that?'

'Harry Billings.' He was looking up at the burgee – bad sign.

'Anything interesting?' I felt that with *Sunboro Beauty* likely to finish at least in the first three it was terribly important that I should know what they'd been discussing.

'No. Usual Billings. Full of bull.'

I was determined to get something from him so I said, 'Is he pleased with *SB*'s performance?'

'Wouldn't you be?' His face was all dark and tense. 'I mean if you were in his shoes. He's getting marvellous publicity for his Sunboro outfit – and he'll get a lot more before the end.'

'How do you mean?'

'Wait and see.' He gave me a horrible creepy look and went below.

*Later – 4.15 p.m.* I took the bandage and dressing off his wound after lunch – I'd forgotten what a gash it was – still red and angry. I asked him if the headaches had gone – he said they hadn't but he could cope. A strange man. He doesn't like sympathy – probably thinks it's a sign of weakness.

His manner towards me now is mostly formal, non-committal, but occasionally if he's pleased he pats my shoulder or squeezes my arm – then, a moment later, we can be having a furious row. If anything goes wrong on deck or below – and it often does on a voyage like this – he gets in a frenzy. Like when I had an accident with the stove last night. He went berserk – said I'd 'set the bloody boat ablaze' if I wasn't careful. In that sort of mood his face gets ugly and he looks at me as if he hates me – which I'm sure he does! We are both suffering from exhaustion, I think – madly tensed up and worried – at least I am.

I wonder if I'll ever again have the ordinary things I long for like a gorgeous hot bath full of perfumed foam – my own room with its lovely bed, duvet and soft pillows – a long night of deep sleep – to wake to the sound of birds and distant traffic – and dress in decent, clean clothes. Oh dear, I never thought I'd be so utterly miserable.

What was in M's mind yesterday when all he would tell me of his chat with Billings was, 'wait and see' – I'm sure they were discussing the finish – 'Do you realize, old sport, that *Sunboro Beauty* may win the TRISTAR – the great single-handed epic – £100,000 prize money – whacko, old sport!'

*Single-handed*? That's why M came up after the phone call looking so grim and preoccupied.

Please God, help me. Sorry I've been such a miserable sinner.

*8/1 – 9.20 a.m.* The weather was much too bad for note-making from 6th until today. Barometer dropped suddenly late on 5th, wind backed through SW to SSE and by morning blew a full gale from the south – our course was E by N so huge foam-lathered seas came in on the starboard beam – indescribably beastly. Determined to win his bloody race M pressed on with too much sail – mizzen, deep-reefed main and No. 1 jib. Just asking for trouble. Soon after dawn on the 7th the jury mizzen boom carried away, the jib blew out and we had to heave-to. It took most of daylight and some hours of darkness to fix things – a really awful, freezing wet, banging-about time sorting out thrashing mizzen, jurg boom (the metal spar!), torn and tattered jib, sheets and halyards in a hideous tangle. Then furling the main, hoisting a mizzen staysail and exchanging the busted No. 1 jib for a headsail. When we'd finished M eased *SB* off the wind, put her on ENE after which she managed the high wind and seas rather well. First time we've used this mizzen stormsail (96 sq. ft). M very bucked. He had it made as a heavy-weather sail for just such an emergency and it's worked. Heavy rain showers during the gale – miserably wet and cold but not nearly as bad as our big storm last week. Forty-eight hours after it began this one blew itself out. During it the most extraordinary, terrifying thing happened. When we were battling with the mizzen *SB* lurched and I was thrown over the pushpit rail and hung half in the sea suspended by the lifeline on my safety harness. I really thought I'd had it. But M heaved me back – gave me hell for being careless – then kissed me (!) – said, don't do that again and sent me down to change.

*Later – 2 p.m.* M very peculiar today – he's exhausted, having been on the wheel most of the 6th, 7th and 8th. I don't think he trusts me after my doze! He looks dreadful – gaunt, haggard, sunken inflamed eyes, stubbled face.

My hands are terribly rough and chapped – all the freezing wet sail handling since St John's – and my face is a disaster area in spite of lashings of Sunboro Beauty Cream. I smell like a junk shop! So does M!

*Later – 6.30 p.m.* Wind from SE force 5/6 – *SB* close-hauled to starboard, banging into head seas, but still a westerly swell. Motion absolute hell – we pound, lurch, buffet, plunge – not enough words to describe it. I was on the wheel most of the afternoon – M slept for hours with only the course alarm on, *not* the time alarm. Can't remember that happening before – he *must* be feeling the strain! Lots of dark clouds about still and heavy rain showers. He made our position at noon – RDF/DR 49°40'N: 8°53'W – distance covered since noon, 5th,

251 miles, average 62.8 per day. M terribly disappointed – says gale and current have pushed us too far north. I thought progress not bad in that weather, especially as *SB* was hove-to for eight or nine hours.

At noon we were 130 miles south of the Fastnet and 165 miles west of Land's End. M says if wind remains in SE we've another two days before we turn the corner off the Lizard for the final run into Plymouth.

For no real reason I'm not as depressed as I was. Firstly, this gale wasn't nearly as frightening as last week's; secondly, I felt safe with M at the wheel through the worst of it – he's a marvellous sailor; thirdly, and *most importantly*, his hauling me back when I went over the stern rail, and his reaction to that little drama, seemed good omens! Or am I being naive?

I expect it's because we're so close to England that I feel less terrified. And because a plan, still hazy, is taking shape in my mind. It needs his co-operation. Will he agree?

*9.37 p.m.* First real hot meal for days – same old stew and veg but how good it was. Even M smiled after it – something he hasn't done for a long time.

## CHAPTER TWENTY-SEVEN

Thorold put the phone down and considered for a moment the curtain of rain and mist being drawn slowly across the Sound from Mountbatten Point over Drake's Island towards Mount Edgecombe. He and Inspector Mitchell had been discussing the checks to be carried out at the finish of the TRISTAR. For the purposes of the race, he'd told Mitchell, only the first six yachts in would be subject to inspection. Mitchell, doggedly pursuing his slender clue to the missing girl, said he had arranged with Customs and

Immigration to give all competing yachts a thorough going-over no matter when they came in.

Towards the end of the conversation the Inspector had asked how things were going with the race, and what news if any there was of *Caspar's Folly*? Thorold told him there was still no news of the missing multihull, but he took the opportunity of mentioning his phone conversation that morning with the naval attaché at the US Embassy in Grosvenor Square.

'He said he was posting me a sealed package received from the Navy Department in the Pentagon. I asked him what it contained. Said he'd no idea – it was marked "Confidential". The message from Washington instructed him to forward it to the authorities controlling the TRISTAR, unopened and without delay. Presumably it has to do with casualties. Report on wreckage or something of the sort. Might throw light on what's happened to *Caspar's Folly*. We've been hoping her trouble was no more than radio failure but I'm afraid that's now wearing rather thin.'

The Inspector agreed. Soon after that their conversation had ended.

Thorold looked at the carriage clock on his desk – ten-fifteen. Within the next forty-eight hours the TRISTAR should have been decided. At midnight *Omega Challenger* had been leading by a margin of nine hours, with *Grande Rapide* in second place. Lying third, five hours behind the French yacht, was *Sunboro Beauty*. It was an amazingly close finish to an eight-thousand-mile ocean race. He knew Ken Hutchings and Pierre Fougeux well – they were among ocean racing's superstars – but Martin Savage was a comparative newcomer. Thorold had met him a couple of times at yachting functions: a big rugged man, reserved, almost shy, but reputed to be a good seaman. He was certainly showing he was that, even if he had started out as a long odds outsider. Fascinating thing ocean racing, reflected Thorold; one needed not only skill and experience to do well but also a fair share of luck.

Turning to the letters on his desk he sighed deeply. The TRISTAR was taking a lot of his time.

*10/1 – 7.20 a.m.* Wind SE, force 4/5, confused sea, westerly swell. I got a terrible fright early this morning – pitch dark – *SB* close-hauled to starboard, splashing and plunging into wind and sea – I was steering and very tired. Suddenly an immense rocky cliff loomed from nowhere on the starboard bow – only about 100 yards away. I shouted (screamed?), spun the wheel to port, brought *SB* round – untidily because I was scared stiff. M came rushing up with his usual 'What the bloody hell?' I pointed astern. 'We nearly hit a huge cliff.'

He said, 'Which cliff? – you're crazy,' and shot below. When he came back he said he'd got an RDF fix and echo soundings. 'We're about thirty-five miles sou'-west of the Scillies. You couldn't have seen a cliff – there's nothing ahead and to starboard but miles of ocean.'

He brought *SB* round into wind and when she was sorted out and back on course, sails trimmed, he said, 'There was no cliff, Sarah. Just another of your hallucinations' – surprisingly calm and understanding for him! He was due on watch at five-thirty anyway, so he didn't lose much sleep. For me it was a shattering experience – the horror of it is still in my mind.

*Later – 9 a.m.* M has ordered me below until further notice – too many ships, coasters, fishing craft about, he says. I hate this incarceration. Marvellously fresh and invigorating on deck. There were lots of seabirds about at dawn. I thought I could smell England – M said wind was the wrong way for that, so it must be in my mind. Now I'm stuck below writing up notes and wondering what's going to happen to me. He has locked away the transistor we use for BBC news – says it'll get smashed if it's left out. When he listens I'm on deck – so I'm not allowed to hear the BBC – why, why, why?

This morning he told me that both transmitters had packed up. I said wasn't it extraordinary that both should do that at the same time? He looked blank – said he'd told Portishead his batteries were low, and the charger unserviceable. Both untrue – why is he lying? He told Portishead he wasn't sorry – too tired and busy to talk to media and others who want to chat him up. That includes Harry Billings, of course. Apparently the chap at Portishead was understanding – said radio breakdowns were sometimes convenient. M won't acknowledge any calls now – VHF included. 'About time I held my cards close to my chest,' he said with a non-funny laugh – it didn't amuse me. Fancy shutting down on communications at this of all times.

*Later – 2.20 p.m.* Soon after two o'clock he shouted down that Bishop's Rock was abeam to port, distance sixteen miles, and he altered course to east-by-north for the run-in to the Lizard. There's no land in sight he says, 'but it's comforting to think we're so close to England' – wish I felt comforted.

Glass rose throughout the forenoon, wind veered to SSE, force 4, wind freer and *SB* going better, logging 6 knots against west going tide – M euphoric about improved progress.

At 2.15 p.m. he locked me in loo when a helicopter approached and flew round us – taking photos, he said. It called us on VHF but M wouldn't answer – thought Harry Billings was in it. M's behaviour is too sinister for words.

He let me out of loo at 3 p.m. – I've been below ever since – I'm to be allowed on deck after dark (4.30 p.m.). If I come up without his permission he'll bind, gag and lock me up indefinitely he says – why gag? Bizarre!

*Later – 5.20 p.m.* He handed over the wheel at 4.30 p.m. and went down to plot position etc. – back twenty minutes later. 'Been listening to the BBC news,' he said – hoarse voice, trembling as always when he does the phoney calm bit – 'At 1400 today *Omega Challenger* was found drifting with sails set – no one on deck –

190

heading for the Wolf Rock. Trawler fishing there thought she was behaving strangely – went alongside and put a man on board. No one below. Last entry in the logbook 0400 – Ken Hutchings must have gone overboard some time after that. Trawler took the yacht in tow.'

I said, Oh God, how awful. M said yes, isn't it. I think he thought my 'awful' was for Ken Hutchings (who I don't know) but of course it was my reaction to a situation which is becoming increasingly dangerous for me.

After that I managed to mumble, 'So only *Grande Rapide*'s ahead now?'

'That's right,' he said. 'But according to the BBC she's hove-to eighteen miles sou'west of the Lizard. Rudder trouble again. Unless Pierre gets her under way before then we should have overtaken him by midnight.'

'So we could be leading the field?'

'Right.' His haggard face looked scary in the weak binnacle light. 'Seems I may win this bloody race yet.'

It must have been the *I* instead of *we* that tipped me over the edge. 'My God, Martin you *are* mad,' I said and my voice sounded hysterical even to me. 'You really think *SB*'s still in the race, don't you?'

He stared at me, looked baffled. 'She is, isn't she?' The way he said it – so obviously believing it was true – was totally shattering.

'How can she be? I'm still on board!' I shouted – or shrilled – definitely hysterical by then.

'I'm well aware of that.' He switched on the masthead light, looked up at the burgee, stared at me as if I were a stranger.

'So what are you going to do?' My body and voice were shaking.

'There *is* a solution.' The forbidding way in which he said that, the wild look in his eyes, made me shiver. He *is* mad. It was the moment to tell him about my plan, so I blurted it out. 'We'll be off the Lizard tonight. If you'll go in close, say half a mile, I'll swim ashore. I'm a strong swimmer. With the wind from the south-east it won't be difficult. When I get there I'll tell them the French yacht I was on was run down by a tanker during the night – the tanker didn't stop and the two Frenchmen who'd picked me up in Cherbourg a few days back were both drowned.'

'Their names?'

'Jean and François.'

After he'd thought about that he said, 'Name of the yacht?'

'I'll say I've forgotten it – it was something in French. I was only on board for three days and still in a shocked condition when I got ashore.'

'Most ingenious,' he said. 'So you will swim ashore? What happens if you don't make it – or they don't swallow the French yacht story?'

I said, 'If I don't make it what matter? Nobody but you knows I'm in *Sunboro Beauty*. The same thing applies if they don't believe my story – you arrive single-handed and you've won your race.'

It was some time before he said, 'So nobody knows except me? I find that most interesting.'

My insides jumped, then shrivelled – idiot! I'd thrown away my last defence. The Plymouth letter!

At that his mood changed, he turned suddenly nasty, said my plan was simply a ruse to escape – of course he wouldn't close the coast in order to make it possible. I wouldn't last for ten minutes in that icy water or survive landing on a rocky lee shore – but why, he asked, this obsession with escape throughout the voyage?

I said, 'I'm a prisoner, aren't I? Have been ever since I came on board. You treat me like one. Bind me, gag me, lock me up.'

'You know perfectly well why I've had to do that,' he said.

I said, 'I've no freedom – no say about what is to happen to me.' I looked away from his staring eyes because they frightened me. 'You talk of my obsession –

it's nothing compared with yours, Martin. You're determined to win the TRISTAR – and I stand in your way. Of course that terrifies me. Makes me want to escape.'

He frowned, looked very grave, his tongue teasing his lower lip. 'It's like your hallucinations,' he said. 'You think up dangers that don't exist, just as you see things that are not there. You're not a prisoner. You came on this voyage uninvited and you ruined my chances in the TRISTAR. It was a bloody awful thing to do. I wonder if you ever stop to think about that? If not I suggest you do – and stop accusing me of making you a prisoner, and seeing yourself as the innocent victim of a wretched situation. You happen to be the guilty party.' He shot another of those frosty looks at me. 'Guilt invites retribution you know.'

That frightened me even more, but he was getting pretty steamed up so I said nothing. Then I decided I couldn't leave it like that, so eventually I asked him, 'What *is* going to happen to me?'

He did his masthead burgee act again. 'Perhaps you'd better wait and see.'

He really is a sadist.


## CHAPTER TWENTY-EIGHT


Thorold passed the wallet of coloured photographs across the desk to Detective Inspector Mitchell. 'They arrived from the US Embassy about an hour ago.'

The Inspector gave him a sharp look of inquiry, opened the wallet and took out the prints.

There were three of them; all taken close to the surface of a white-capped, ruffled blue sea. From the deck of another yacht, decided the Inspector as he began his examination.

The first print, taken from a position on its port bow – a long shot – showed a yacht under sail with two men on deck: one at the wheel in the cockpit, the other sitting on the coachroof. Naked but for bathing slips, both were suntanned. The man on the coachroof had his back to the camera.

The second shot, again taken from the port bow but a good deal closer, showed more detail.

The third shot, very much closer, had been taken from directly astern. The man at the wheel had his back to the camera but his companion on the coachroof, now facing the camera, had the full, slightly upturned breasts of a young woman.

On the yacht's weather-stained transom which filled the foreground appeared the name *Sunboro Beauty*, beneath it in smaller letters, 'Lymington'.

The Inspector looked up, his dark eyes incredulous. 'What's the story behind these?'

'Taken through the attack periscope of the US submarine *Skippack* on the sixteenth of December, one hundred and eighty miles sou-sou-west of Bermuda. The submarine was on passage to the US Naval base at Guantanamo, Cuba. She was apparently using *Sunboro Beauty* as a target for an intercept and attack exercise. Took the periscope photos as part of the routine. They were processed on board. Handed in with various other addenda to the Captain's voyage report on arrival at Guantanamo. Some time later a junior officer in the Pentagon processing the report saw the prints and recalled having heard on the news that *Sunboro Beauty* was among the leaders in a single-handed ocean race, the TRISTAR. The Pentagon sent the prints to the naval attaché in Grosvenor Square and they came to me this morning.' Thorold paused, rubbed his chin. 'Incredible, isn't it? A competitor in a *single-handed* race doing a thing like that.'

'Who owns *Sunboro Beauty*?'

'Martin Savage. The man at the wheel in those photos.'

'Know him?'

'Not well.'

'What's his reputation?'

'Good as far as I know. An insurance broker by occupation. Apart from that, an experienced and capable yachtsman with some ocean racing experience.' Thorold pointed to the prints. 'The girl? Think she's your Victoria Brownson?'

The Inspector looked up from the photos. 'Probably. Difficult to tell from these.'

'You realize that with *Omega Challenger* now out of it, and *Grande Rapide* having steering trouble, *Sunboro Beauty* may well win this race – or at least take second place?'

'Not surprised,' said the Inspector phlegmatically. 'Quite an advantage to have a spare hand in a single-handed race, I'd say.'

'So what do we do?' Thorold's face bore the classical imprint of a worried man.

'Quite a lot,' suggested Mitchell. 'There's fraud, conspiracy, maybe abduction and a few other things involved.'

A long discussion followed before they agreed on what was to be done. Thorold's view was coloured by the need to protect the good name of ocean racing in general, and the sponsors and organizers of the TRISTAR in particular. Inspector Mitchell, on the other hand, was more concerned with ensuring that if there had been a fraud its perpetrator should be brought to justice. For this reason he was insistent that no action should be taken until *Sunboro Beauty* had crossed the finishing line.

'Wouldn't it be better to intercept the ketch and get Savage out of the race before the finish? Avoid all the unpleasant publicity, sensational stuff – that sort of thing.'

'No. I'm afraid not,' said Mitchell. 'The unpleasant publicity's there whatever we do. The millions who've been following the race on radio and TV know that *Sunboro Beauty* is likely to win – there'll be just as big a sensation if she's hauled out of it shortly before the finish. No – I'm quite sure the thing to do is to wait until she's crossed the line. That is the act which will confirm the fraud. After that we can deal with her skipper.'

Thorold drew a hand across his forehead, pursed his lips.

'Well, I daresay you're right. Hopefully *Grande Rapide* will win, or at least be close to *Sunboro Beauty* at the finish. That means we won't keep a huge crowd, a fleet of spectator boats, the Lord Mayor and other VIPs waiting for hours to greet the winner.'

'Right. Might even have *Caspar's Folly* in the picture at the end. Who knows?'

'A bit late for that, I'm afraid. She'd have been sighted by now if she was to be placed at the finish.'

At 2210 he eased the sheets, brought the wind abaft the beam and steadied *Sunboro Beauty* on the north-easterly heading which would take her across the tanker lanes to a position south of the Lizard. Broad-reaching in a fresh south-easterly wind under mainsail, mizzen staysail and the big genoa, the ketch surged and plunged through the frosty cold of a January night.

Fine on the port bow a distant speck of light blinked every three seconds. It was the Lizard. Once off it he would alter course for the final run into Plymouth. Based on the ketch's position at 2200, and providing the wind held and his tidal allowances were right, he estimated they would arrive at the finishing line between 1400 and 1500 on the following day.

The loom of lights along the Cornish coast, the steaming lights of ships, and occasionally those of low-flying aircraft, relieved the pall of darkness which hung over the night.

From time to time the girl would come up, bringing with her snacks and hot coffee or Bovril. They seldom spoke; he supposed because they were both very tired. He sensed, too, that she was preoccupied and worried and that being his own state of mind he made no effort to break the silence.

During the previous night he had slept for no more than two hours and that had by no means been unbroken sleep. He'd been on deck continuously since five o'clock that morning and the strain – coming on top of too little sleep since St John's – was taking its toll. Close to exhaustion physically, his mind confused, he was in no condition to deal with the problems which confronted him. For this reason, and because he did not want things to be complicated by questions from the shore, he had long since switched off the Marconi Falcon and VHF receivers. No doubt efforts were being made to contact him: personal messages from family and friends, messages from his sponsor, instructions from race officials about arrangements at the finish. Too bad. He couldn't be bothered with all that now. His only remaining link with the shore was the transistor he used for the BBC news – and that he used sparingly.

Problems came flooding through his mind. Where was *Grande Rapide*? Ahead or astern? If he felt tired what must Pierre be feeling? But at least the Frenchman's self-steering would be working once the rudder was fixed. He'd heard him reporting that a day or so earlier. The girl? God, what a problem she'd been. He'd have to see to her before daylight, before the spectator boats arrived. If the wind held the ketch would be twenty miles off the coast then. What a God-awful mess she'd landed him in – and herself. He was sorry for her in a detached sort of way, but he felt she deserved all she got.

Tessa would most certainly be somewhere around at the finish. What was he going to say to her? No sooner had he banished her from his mind than Harry Billings strode into it. How did one handle a man like Harry when one was exhausted? And Thorold and the others, the TRISTAR officials, the media boys – newspapers, BBC and ITV – the press conference, peering eyes and quizzing tongues. There would be nothing but confrontation and interrogation when all he would be good for was sleep. The very thought of what lay ahead was enough to drive a man up the wall. The only people he looked forward to seeing were his mother and Tim Baxter. Hopefully they'd come out in the same boat, somewhere among the many hundreds? The BBC news that night had forecast a mammoth welcome, notwithstanding the wintry weather. An armada of small craft, an official reception in the yacht club where the Lord Mayor, the Flag Officer Plymouth, the TRISTAR sponsors and other VIPs would be doing their stuff. Fifty thousand quid! What couldn't a man do with that? Certainly solve the worst of one's financial problems. Not to mention the prestige! No difficulty in setting up on the business side of yachting with the TRISTAR under one's belt.

Where the devil was John Caspar: dead or playing a deep game near the finish? Surely the media sleuths with their helicopters would have picked him up by now in those close waters?

More likely to be *Sunboro Beauty* and *Grande Rapide* – he and Pierre Fougeux fighting it out. They hadn't thought of that one in The Futtock and Shroud the night before the start.

The barometer was falling. If the wind backed as it should there would be head winds on the last lap into Plymouth, and head winds would suit *Sunboro Beauty* a lot better than they would *Grande Rapide*.

His head ached. He rubbed his eyes, tried to concentrate on the dimly-lit compass card, the lights of ships nearby, the winking light on the Lizard and the set of the sails. In spite of the bitterly cold wind and driving spray which pricked into his face he found it difficult to keep awake. He had been on the wheel all day. No self-steering. Hellish handicap. Fine when he could use the girl, but there'd been too much traffic for that. Once they cleared the Lizard and its busy shipping lanes and were drawing away from the land again he would hand over to her. He would have preferred not to do that, but he had to get his head down for a couple of hours. It wouldn't be unbroken sleep but it would make all the difference over the last lap and at the finish. He was going to need a clear head then if ever he did. The Lizard to Plymouth, fifty miles – say ten to twelve hours' sailing, allowing for the tides.

Towards midnight the wind backed to east-south-east and not long afterwards *Sunboro Beauty* was four miles south of the Lizard having crossed the tanker lanes. He altered course to the north-east, sheeted the sails hard in, and the ketch began what he hoped would be her last long beat to windward.

Almost three hours later they were five miles south of The

Manacles. In that time they'd made good only nine miles against the adverse wind and west-going tide.

With the distance from the land opening steadily as the ketch beat up towards Plymouth, he decided the time had come to go below. He called the girl and she took over the wheel. For some minutes he stayed with her, pointing out the lights at The Manacles and St Anthony's Head and those of ships in the vicinity which required watching; then, having told her to call him at a quarter past five, he went down. He plotted the ketch's position, wrote up the log, noted that the barometer was still falling, set the course and time alarms, climbed into his bunk and was soon asleep.

The strident buzzing of the alarm woke him. He switched on a torch, saw that the glass was rising and that the time was 0335. Only twenty-five minutes since he'd left the cockpit. The course and wind tell-tales, the noisy slatting of the sails, told him the ketch was in irons. What the devil was the girl up to?

He pulled on his woollen cap, took a torch and clambered up the companion-ladder. There was no one at the wheel. He shone the torch fore and aft, saw that the life-raft canister was open and empty. The raft had gone.

Was it a repetition of the St John's scare? Instinctively he felt it was not. He got the ketch back on course, set the wheel and carried out a hurried search below. She was not there but her note was – stuck on the inside of the door to the after heads. She must have put it there before taking over the wheel. He went to the chart-table, switched on the light and began reading: *Martin, I'm sorry. Must do this whatever the risk. I suppose I'm half out of my mind but you terrify me and I don't trust you. You're determined to win this race and I'm in the way – my own fault. The last thing you wanted was a stowaway. I know I've been incredibly selfish. Now, perhaps, I can make amends – funny, I believe I care for you in spite of everything. It's been a fantastic experience – awful at times – marvellous at others. Don't worry. If I get ashore I won't give you away. It'll be the French yacht story. Goodbye – Sarah.*

In a sudden fit of rage he threw the letter at the rack over the chart-table. 'You selfish bloody bitch,' he shouted hoarsely. 'You've ruined everything. For Christ's sake, why do you have to do a crazy thing like that? Don't you ever think of anyone but yourself?'

What was he to do, he asked himself desperately? She must have dropped the life-raft over the side and waited for it to self-inflate before lowering herself into the sea. Then she would have climbed aboard and cast off the line securing the raft to the ketch. Although she was a strong swimmer she must have been wearing her life-jacket. It was nowhere on board.

But when had she gone? Some time in the twenty-five minutes since he'd gone below after handing her the wheel. With sails properly balanced – something the girl was good at now – the ketch could have kept on course most of that time. She had probably launched the life-raft once she was satisfied he was asleep. In twenty-five minutes *Sunboro Beauty* could under these conditions have made good up to two miles. With these factors in mind he measured off and marked on the chart a two mile section along the yacht's track. At its nearest point the land would have been five and a half to six miles distant. He estimated that the fresh south-easterly wind would carry the life-raft towards the shore at around two to three knots. Allowing for the tide – it was on the turn – the raft should fetch up somewhere between The Manacles and Helford River two to three hours after launching. But would she ever make it? Even under the raft's canopy she would be feeling the effects of the bitterly cold night; as if that were not enough, she would be landing on a lee shore on a rocky coast. Must be out of her mind, he muttered.

It was a dark night, the sky heavily overcast. To search for her under those conditions, not knowing at what time she had gone, was a hopeless undertaking. He switched on the VHF, picked up the handset. 'MAYDAY-MAYDAY-MAYDAY,' he said, speaking slowly in broken, heavily-accented English. 'Please to look urgently for life-raft with survivors drifting to the land between Manacles and Helford

River. Can be only few miles from shore at this moment.' He repeated the message several times. There was a good deal of shipping about and among many acknowledgements – none of which he answered – were Land's End Radio, an RN minesweeper, and the Falmouth Coastguard station. All of these asked for further details, but he did not reply. Between them, the minesweeper and the coastguard service, would, he was sure, organize a search without delay. There was nothing more he could do that would be of practical help. He switched off the VHF, went back to the cockpit, trimmed the sails and got *Sunboro Beauty* back on the course from which she'd wandered.

He was so tired, his mind so confused, his judgement so irrational that he had little comprehension of the significance of what he was doing. All that he was conscious of was resentment at what she'd done, and determination that neither she nor anyone else was going to stop him reaching the finishing line.

He'd started single-handed and he was going to finish single-handed. She'd come and gone of her own accord. It was nothing to do with him. None of it had been his decision. Perhaps it was all fantasy? Maybe she'd never been on board? How could one really know?


## CHAPTER TWENTY-NINE


Daylight came with rain and sleet shutting down visibility to under a mile. From *Sunboro Beauty*'s cockpit the view was a desolate one of leaden sky beneath which frothing seas pursued each other endlessly, thumping and pounding on the ketch's beam, the wind blowing spray back across the deck.

At seven o'clock he got an RDF fix which put them 9.3 miles 263° from the Eddystone Light – seventeen or eighteen miles from the finishing line in Plymouth Sound; another three and a half to four hours' sailing if conditions remained as they were. He knew that somewhere ahead Pierre Fougeux's catamaran was banging and buffeting its way towards the finish; at six that morning the BBC had reported that *Grande Rapide,* her rudder repaired, had passed the Lizard at about eleven o'clock on the previous night. That put the catamaran at least an hour ahead of *Sunboro Beauty.* The news had come as a blow. He'd believed that the Frenchman's rudder trouble would not be easily dealt with in that weather; but he was wrong and Fougeux was leading. The BBC newsreader had said there was no word from *Sunboro Beauty*'s skipper who'd reported radio trouble two days earlier; but the ketch had been sighted by a helicopter south of the Scillies the day before and was believed to be not far astern of *Grande Rapide.*

The barometer was rising and by eight o'clock the wind veered to blow boisterously from the south-south-east. Cursing his luck, for he wanted head winds not stern winds, he considered hoisting the spinnaker but decided against it. The ketch was now sailing well on a broad reach, but with the wind abaft the beam he could not hope to outsail *Grande Rapide,* spinnaker or otherwise.

The sky cleared and out on the starboard bow he saw the Eddystone Lighthouse poking into the sky like a huge index finger. Soon afterwards the sails of the early-comers of the welcome fleet appeared ahead, to be overtaken moments later by a black and yellow helicopter. It circled *Sunboro Beauty,* one of its occupants busy with a camera, another waving. He waved back. There were three men in it. One of them might have been Harry Billings. He couldn't be sure

At nine o'clock he switched on the transistor for BBC West's news service. He listened with half attention as the newsreader ran through the main headings – the TRISTAR item came sooner than he'd expected ... *Grande Rapide* was still in the lead from *Sunboro Beauty,* said the newsreader, but it had just been reported by her skipper, Pierre Fougeux, that he was hove-to a few miles west of the Eddystone Light with recurrence of the rudder trouble which had dogged him over the last leg of the race. *Sunboro Beauty* had been sighted shortly before nine o'clock. The British yacht, went on the newsreader with a note of chauvinism, was now less than two miles astern of *Grande Rapide* and was closing the distance steadily.

My God, he thought, I've still a chance to pull it off. His tired spirits soared and he scarcely heard the disembodied voice go on to say, '. . . Mark Frensham's *Applegay Fancy*, another British entry, reported a hundred miles west of the Scillies at eight o'clock this morning, is lying third. An armada of small craft – yachts, sailing dinghies, cabin cruisers and motor launches – has for some time been making its way out across Plymouth Sound to welcome the TRISTAR leaders. Around the Sound crowds of spectators are gathering . . . on the Hoe at Jennycliff Bay, on Staddon Heights, at Rame Head and other vantage points . . . to see the finish of this eight-thousand-mile epic . . . a finish which seems likely to go down as one of the most stirring in the annals of ocean racing . . .'

Minutes later, less than a mile away to starboard, he sighted *Grande Rapide*. She was lying head to wind, presumably with a sea anchor streamed. It was more than two months since he'd last seen the tricoloured hull at the start in Plymouth Sound.

With binoculars he could see the Frenchman leaning over the stern where some sort of contraption had been rigged on either side of the wind vane. Bless you, Pierre, he thought, I don't quite know what you're doing but I hope to God you don't get that flaming rudder fixed just yet. A knot of anxiety tied itself in his stomach and despite the biting wind he began to sweat under his foul-weather gear.

Before long he had passed within half a mile of the catamaran. With an immense feeling of relief – and scarcely believing that it had happened – he realized that *Sunboro Beauty* was leading the TRISTAR. Heavy rain began to fall and before long *Grande Rapide* had dropped out of sight astern. All he could see now were the two yachts to leeward which had turned on to the same heading to sail in company. Setting the wheel he went below, poured himself a mug of hot coffee, took three tablets from a small brown bottle and swallowed them with the coffee. It was the first time since leaving Plymouth that he'd used the amphetamines Tim Baxter had given him. He mistrusted stimulants of that sort but with the finish now so close, his physical state so perilously low, he had put his prejudice aside.

While returning the Thermos to its rack he noticed that one of the three normally kept there was missing. He remembered then that the girl had come up with a flask when she took over the wheel early that morning. 'Saves me coming down and disturbing you,' she'd explained. At least she'd had the good sense to take it with her in the life-raft. It could be important in the fight against hypothermia.

The glass continued to rise and the wind to veer further to the south. Running with it fine on her quarter *Sunboro Beauty* was logging seven knots as she headed towards Plymouth Sound still hidden in the rain ahead. Things were happening so fast – or so it seemed to his weary mind – that later he was to have little more than a jumbled recollection of the events of that morning.

The number of yachts and other small craft accompanying him had grown steadily and now formed a ragged crescent, its base astern, its horns to port and starboard, leaving him clear water ahead. Some came closer – mostly the power boats – their occupants waving, photographing, shouting greetings and encouragement. Vaguely conscious of what he was doing, thinking of other things, he waved back. The rain came and went intermittently, the ketch drew closer to the land, and more and more spectator boats joined the escorting armada. A large cabin cruiser came bustling up, turned and closed on the starboard side. It was flying a pink flag with some sort of emblem. He waved it away 'Keep clear,' he shouted. 'You're stealing my wind.'

A man in oilskins and sou'wester hailed him. 'Welcome back, Martin. You're leading the field. Magnificent performance, old sport. But watch out for *Grande Rapide*. She's coming up fast.'

He waved to Harry Billings, the cabin cruiser dropped astern and took station on the ketch's quarter. Billings continued to bellow, but he ignored him. There was no time for that sort of thing now, and he wasn't in the mood.

So Pierre had got going again? He looked astern but couldn't see the catamaran. It must have been hidden by the rain and the sails of the spectator boats.

Two fast motorboats with media men arrived on the scene. They came in close, fired questions. He waved them away. 'Not yet. See you later,' he shouted.

There were now only two things in his mind: an obsessive resolve to get *Sunboro Beauty* to the finishing line, and a nagging fear that Sarah might have drowned. It was a fear which had displaced his earlier resentment. The shift of wind at five-thirty that morning meant that she would not reach the land where he'd expected. The life-raft would drift further in towards Falmouth, be that much longer afloat. She had been in his thoughts constantly since her disappearance; desperate thoughts, gloomy thoughts, guilty thoughts and occasionally positive ones – like his intention to hand *Sunboro Beauty* over to Tim Baxter as soon as the finishing line was reached. That done he would go straight ashore and begin his inquiries. How he would set about them he wasn't sure, but of one thing he was certain – tired though he was he wouldn't rest until he'd found out what had happened to her. There had been nothing in the radio news bulletins about a survivor from a yacht coming ashore. Perhaps the incident wasn't regarded as sufficiently important? He found no comfort in contemplating the answer to that question.

At half past ten *Sunboro Beauty* was a mile south of Rame Head. Easing the sheets he altered course to 043°, bringing the wind finer on the starboard quarter. Still sailing under the big genoa, full main and mizzen staysail, the ketch surged ahead on the new course. It seemed to him that having scented home she was responding to the pull of her sails with an urgency as great as his own.

As the land drew closer he saw crowds of people on the cliffs between Rame Head and Penlee Point. For a moment he wondered dully what had brought them there in all that rain. Then it dawned on him that *Sunboro Beauty* was the attraction and he warmed to the tiny distant shapes, waving to them and feeling embarrassed that they should have gone to all that trouble for him. If only they knew! Off Penlee Point he altered course to 020° for the final run-in to the line a mile and a half ahead. In the cabin cruiser Billings was shouting, gesturing wildly astern.

He looked back and saw that the escort of spectator boats had cleared the way to let *Grande Rapide* through. Her tricolor spinnaker was bellying full in the fresh wind, little white waves rising and falling at her bows and floats as she surfed forward on the crests of following seas. The conditions were ideal for multihulls – a twenty-knot wind blowing from astern. The French catamaran would be travelling through the water at close to twice the speed of *Sunboro Beauty*.

Penlee Point was falling astern – less than a mile to the finish! He could see the light tower at the western end of the breakwater; the line ran from it across the Western Channel to the jetty at Picklecombe Point. Could *Sunboro Beauty* make it before *Grande Rapide* overtook her? She must, he told himself, straining forward as if that would in some way help her along.

In the wheelhouse of a cabin cruiser which lay bows to wind near the light tower at the end of the breakwater, its engines just turning, the TRISTAR burgee fluttering, Inspector Mitchell and Bob Thorold were watching the finish through binoculars.

To seaward of the breakwater a minesweeper and two naval motorboats were patrolling Cawsand Bay, keeping the area between Penlee Point and the finish clear of spectator boats. On the western end of the breakwater, race officials were standing by to check the crossing of the line. In its lee, from a position where they could watch the finish, lay a number of VIP boats: the barge of the Flag Officer Plymouth, the Queen's Harbourmaster's launch, two police launches – and others including those of HM Customs and Immigration.

As if to celebrate the occasion the rain stopped and a wintry sun shone down fleetingly through a break in the clouds, its light catching the sails and weather-stained hulls of *Sunboro Beauty* and *Grande Rapide* as they raced down the last half-mile. Behind them the two fleets of spectator boats had merged into one, their lively movements, the bright colours of their sails, providing a regatta-like backdrop to the finish. Overhead two helicopters circled and hovered, cameramen and broadcasters busy inside the Perspex domes.

'It's going to be a fantastic finish.' Thorold's eyes were pressed to binoculars. 'I'd never have believed it. The same thing happened last year at the end of the Route du Rhum. But that was a four-thousand-mile race. The TRISTAR's twice that. And a much tougher course. It's really remarkable.'

'In more ways than one,' observed the Inspector dryly.

Thorold lowered the binoculars for a moment. 'How on earth does he imagine he can get away with it?'

The Inspector gave him a sharp look. 'He'll have got it all worked out, won't he? Maybe he plans to slip her across into another boat as they go in. Or claim she joined him from a spectator boat on the way to the docks after the finish. He has no means of knowing what we know – or that we're watching him.'

'Your people ready to pounce, Inspector?'

'Not necessarily pounce. But he's been under surveillance since Rame Head and it's going to continue. He won't get away with anything.'

Thorold raised his binoculars. 'A most extraordinary business I must say. We've always disliked the idea of these big money prizes. They're foreign to ocean racing. It'll become like Formula One if we don't stop it. Not that we thought they'd ever result in anything like this. But I suppose fifty thousand quid can . . .' He broke off in mid-sentence. 'I say – look at that catamaran. She really *is* moving.'

'Right. But *Sunboro Beauty*'s going to win,' said the Inspector grimly. 'Only a hundred yards to go. The Frenchman can't catch him in that distance.'

'My God!' interrupted Thorold. 'What on earth is he up to now?'

In *Sunboro Beauty*'s cockpit Martin Savage could be seen spinning the wheel to port, the ketch's bows paying off rapidly until she had described a complete U-turn short of the finishing line, to end up head to wind, her shivering sails sheeted hard amidships.

'He's disqualified himself,' said Thorold with a mixture of dismay and relief. 'He's not finished.'

Moments later *Grande Rapide* scooted across the line, the finishing gun sounded, and the air over Plymouth Sound throbbed to the orchestrated blast of hundreds of sirens and foghorns.

The Inspector looked thoughtful. 'Seems as if he's deliberately abandoned the race. So *that* aspect is settled. But there's a lot that isn't. He's still got some explaining to do.'

# CHAPTER THIRTY

When he judged the distance from the line to be no more than a hundred yards he spun the wheel to port and gybed the ketch sharply into wind, sheeting the sails hard in as she turned. Seconds later *Grande Rapide* shot past his starboard side and he saw the look of incredulity on Fougeux's bearded face. He was about to ease sheets and bring *Sunboro Beauty* off the wind when a fast motorboat came racing towards him, its bows throwing up sheets of spray as it bumped the seas. Soon afterwards it stopped alongside; he recognized one of the men in it as a member of the race committee.

'You've failed to cross the line,' the committee man called to him. 'Better cross it now or you won't even qualify for second place.'

Savage shook his head. 'Thanks. I know that but I don't intend to finish. I've withdrawn from the race.'

'Good heavens, man! You were leading. You can't do that.'

'Can't I? Why not?'

The committee man stared at him in disbelief. 'Gone round the bend, have you?'

'Could have, I suppose. I'm not sure.'

The other man shook his head. 'I don't begin to understand. Great pity. You've sailed a magnificent race. However – it's your funeral.' He turned away, nodded to the man at the wheel, the powerful engine roared and the boat shot away, a churning wake behind it.

While waiting for a tow he set about taking in sail. No sooner had he begun than the pink-flagged cabin cruiser arrived. With a glum and silent Harry Billings looking on, a line was passed and the cabin cruiser set off towards the docks with the ketch in tow. Once in the lee of the breakwater they stopped, Harry Billings was transferred to the ketch in an inflatable dinghy, it returned to the cabin cruiser and the tow was passed.

'What on earth . . .?' Billings gulped as he climbed aboard *Sunboro Beauty*. 'I mean . . . for God's sake what's happening, old sport . . .? What was it? Steering gear? Mistake the finishing line? I mean . . . old chap. All that money we sank in you. My people . . . What am I to say to them?'

'Don't worry, Harry. It's going to mean a lot more publicity for Sunboro Beauty Products than if I'd won. There's a fabulous story to be told. Just one loose end to tie up – a bloody important one – and I'm off to see to it now. Call a press conference for this time tomorrow. You won't be disappointed.' Soberly, he added, 'At least I hope you won't.'

A perplexed Billings pulled at the drooping ends of his moustache, his eyebrows knitting in a monumental frown. 'Don't know what you're talking about, old soul. Perhaps you ought to see a doctor . . .' He was interrupted by the arrival alongside of a motorboat with Tim Baxter at its wheel. There were two young men with him. Baxter clambered aboard, delivered a crushing handshake. 'Marvellous effort, Martin. But I don't begin to understand. Nor does anyone else. What happened?'

'Tell you later, Tim. Had no option. You don't think I enjoyed doing that, do you? Those my letters you've got there?'

Baxter handed over the bundle of mail. Martin Savage looked round. 'My mother?'

'She's ashore,' said Baxter. 'At the Mayflower waiting for you. Terribly disappointed she couldn't come out but she has a roaring cold.'

'Poor mother. Tessa?'

'She couldn't make it. Told me her letter will explain.'

'I see.' For a moment he looked at Baxter with puzzled eyes. 'Harry's going to take *Sunboro Beauty* into Millbay

Docks,' he said. 'I must get ashore as quickly as possible. Frightfully urgent. Can you run me in?'

'Of course.' Baxter nodded in an offhand way. 'How the hell could you, Martin? Fifty thousand quid chucked away like that. Christ! It doesn't make sense, man.'

'Funnily enough, Tim, it does. Now I must go.'

'What, looking like that?'

'Yes.' His sunken red-rimmed eyes managed a smile. 'Like this.' He ran worn and calloused hands over his five-day beard, tousled hair and salt encrusted oilskins. "bye now, Harry.' He patted Billings on the shoulder, stepped over the guard-rail and got down into Baxter's motorboat.

The throttle was opened, they waved feebly to Billings, and made off across the Sound. They had not gone far when he looked back and saw two launches making for *Sunboro Beauty*. Their markings left him in no doubt. Customs and Immigration. He'd forgotten about those formalities. Billings would have to see to them.

On board the TRISTAR cabin cruiser, Inspector Mitchell was speaking to a police launch by radio telephone. 'You saw that did you, Baker? He's transferred.'

'Yes, sir. We'll follow at a distance.'

'Good. Keep the shore party informed. Point of landing and so forth. He's to be tailed until further notice. I want to know where he goes and what he does. I'm shifting over to Coles' boat now. I'll get back to my office as soon as we're ashore.'

'Very good, sir. If anything comes up in the meantime I'll contact you in Sergeant Coles' boat.'

On the way to Millbay Docks he had shed his oilskins and foul-weather gear and managed a hurried clean-up of his face with a battery shaver.

The motorboat went alongside at the northern end of the docks. With Baxter he climbed on to the quay, moved anonymously through the waiting crowd, his legs unsteady after the long time at sea.

They had not gone far when he was recognized by a local

211

newspaper reporter, a young man who'd interviewed him shortly before the start. The reporter said he'd heard the broadcast account of the finish – what, he wanted to know, was the reason for the U-turn short of the line? Savage handed him off with, 'Sorry old chap. News conference tomorrow. You'll get it all then.' Leaving the reporter gaping, they reached Tim Baxter's car, climbed in and drove out of the docks.

All that he had with him apart from the heavy sweater, faded jeans and plimsolls he was wearing, was the shaver, the girl's crumpled letter and his wallet and cheque book.

Inspector Mitchell sat at the desk, hands clasped behind his head, chair tilted back, thinking. He'd been given a running account by two-way radio of Martin Savage's movements: the landing in Millbay Docks with the bearded man, the two of them picking up a car, the bearded man driving. The visit to the Westminster Bank in Royal Parade, the return to the waiting car, then on to the Post Office at St Andrew's Cross where Savage had been seen to consult telephone directories before entering a telephone booth. He had then dialled two numbers, had two separate conversations. The first brief, the second lasting for just on a minute. There had not been time to have the calls monitored. He had then returned to the car which proceeded to the Plymouth railway station. There he bought a ticket to Falmouth . . .

At that stage, recalled the Inspector, he had instructed the CID sergeant in charge of shadowing to bring Savage in for questioning. He was awaiting his arrival with more than ordinary interest. It was a most unusual case; nothing quite like it had come his way before. Earlier he'd been puzzled by a report from the CID officer accompanying the Customs and Immigration men who had searched *Sunboro Beauty*. There was no woman on board, the CID man reported, but he had found a few small items of female clothing lying about and a rough diary dealing with events since the ketch had left St John's. It had been hidden beneath a mattress below a sail bin in the after cabin and appeared to have been kept by a woman. A very frightened woman, it seemed. The yacht's life-raft was missing from its canister.

By the time the policeman in the outer office rang through to announce Savage's arrival, the Inspector had formulated an explanation of these developments.

Savage was no fool, he decided, but it would be interesting to see his response to the surprises they had in store for him.

The CID man opened the door and ushered him into an austere office which had about it the PWD smell of officialdom. A heavily-built man, dark, with eyes like black diamonds, sat behind a desk on which a nameplate identified him as 'Detective Inspector Mitchell.' The CID man said nothing, the Inspector pointed to chairs on the far side of the desk, they sat down and he was warned that he did not have to answer the questions put to him but, should he do so, anything he might say could be used in evidence against him.

'We would like to question you about a missing person,' the Inspector went on. 'A young woman named Victoria Brownson, believed to have been in the Plymouth area during the first week of November last.' The dark eyes bored into him like gimlets. 'Do you know anything about this person?'

Cheerfully and with conviction he said, 'Never heard of her.'

The Inspector took a paper wallet from a drawer, opened it and removed three coloured photographs. 'These may refresh your memory.' He passed them across the desk.

Martin Savage examined the photographs, looked up. 'Marvellous! Where did you get them?'

'Thought you might be interested. They were taken through the attack periscope of the USS *Skippack*, sixteenth of December last, one hundred and eighty miles sou-souwest of Bermuda.'

'Peeping Toms, aren't they – these submariners.' He grinned.

The Inspector was not amused; his mouth tightened in a hard line. 'Recognize the woman?'

'Of course. Know her well.'

'A moment ago,' said the Inspector severely, 'you said you'd never heard of her.'

'I said I'd never heard of Victoria Brownson. The girl in those photographs happens to be Sarah Thompson.'

The Inspector paused, glowered disapproval at him. 'How did she come to be on board *Sunboro Beauty*?'

'Stowaway.' He released the deep breath of a tired man. 'Didn't find her until the third night at sea.'

The Inspector shook his head. 'That story won't wash, Savage. It will speed things up if you tell us the truth.'

'That is the truth.'

The Inspector smiled at the CID man in a dry, unamused way. 'You say she was a stowaway. You made no signals to that effect at any time in the voyage. You called at Santa Maria, Port Castries and St John's. At each place you were in touch with race officials. At no stage did you say you'd withdrawn from the race. You never mentioned the woman, nor was she ever seen. She was not on board on your arrival here today. What have you done with her?' The Inspector leant forward menacingly.

Martin Savage took the girl's letter from his pocket, straightened it out on the desk, passed it across. 'I think that answers your questions.'

The Inspector looked at him, read it, grunted, passed it to the CID man. 'We don't know that she wrote it, do we? But even if she did it could have been under duress.'

Savage smiled indulgently. 'Why don't you ask her?'

The Inspector looked up from the pad on which he was making notes. 'I imagine you have made sure she won't be available . . . dark night at sea, weights on the feet, that sort of thing. Then, to support her letter, early this morning you launch the life-raft, leave some of her clothes lying about below where they can be seen. If the life-raft's found and she's not in it, fair enough. She could have failed to make it. That's not unusual.' The Inspector paused, looked at the CID man with a scarcely concealed smile of triumph. 'Better tell us what really happened, Savage. Save a lot of time and aggravation, you know.'

'My God, you have a devious mind, Inspector. Not your

fault. Too much contact with the seamy side of life, I daresay.'

The Inspector straightened up in the chair and his voice took on a hard note. 'Better just answer the questions. Do you more good in the long run. Impertinence won't help, you know.'

He looked at the Inspector with tired, expressionless eyes. 'The girl is in Falmouth Hospital. I suggest you get your people to check *that* right away. Then get them to ask her how she came to be there. And for good measure, check with her the rest of what I've told you.'

The Inspector stared at him in disbelief. 'How do you know where she is?'

'I used a telephone.'

'It would have saved a lot of time if you'd told us that in the beginning,' said the Inspector.

'You didn't give me much chance, did you?'

The dark eyes considered him for a moment with the sort of regard a ferret has for a rabbit. Turning to the CID man, he said, 'Take him along to your office, Brooks. I'll talk to Falmouth.'

The CID man got up, opened the door. 'Come along then.'

When Savage reached the door he turned to the Inspector. 'I'd be grateful if your people in Falmouth could let Sarah – Victoria to you – know that I hope to be with her later today.'

The Inspector concentrated hard on whatever it was he was writing. 'We'll see about that,' he said with a distinct lack of warmth.

# CHAPTER THIRTY-ONE

The train began to slow down. Wakened by the change in motion, he looked through the windows into the gathering darkness. On the road which ran beside the line cars had already switched on their lights, and as fields and hedgerows gave way to the outskirts of a town other lights flashed by. His tactics in buying a first class ticket had paid off. Since leaving Plymouth he'd managed to sleep for an hour and a half in the compartment which he had to himself. In addition, he had slept sitting on a hard chair in Sergeant Brook's office for the best part of an hour. Now, mildly refreshed, he was able to think clearly about what had happened and what lay ahead.

Inspector Mitchell had been quite reasonable, really, once the police at Falmouth had seen her and checked his story. Shortly before daylight that morning the life-raft had been found off the Helford River by a local fishing boat. They had, said the Inspector, taken the girl into Helford that morning where a doctor examined her. Later she'd been taken by car to Falmouth Hospital where she was being treated for exposure. Not serious, said the Inspector, getting up and going to a window through which he looked with bored familiarity at the buildings opposite. She would probably be discharged in a day or so. He turned, came back, eyed Martin Savage enigmatically. 'Her first story was that she'd been hitch-hiking and living rough in France. Said she'd thumbed a lift in a French yacht which left Cherbourg for Falmouth a few days ago. According to her it was run down by a tanker which didn't stop. Said she was the only survivor. Couldn't remember the name of the yacht or its crew. Said there were two of them. Jacques and François.'

At that Martin Savage had grinned. 'She's a pretty fluent liar but her memory's not all that good.'

'We know that now.' The Inspector examined his fingernails with casual interest. 'When they'd broken down that story she confirmed what you told us.'

The Inspector had wanted to know certain things: why had he continued in the TRISTAR after finding the girl on board, and why had he failed to make known her presence then and afterwards? And how had the French yacht story originated?

His answers to these questions seemed to satisfy the Inspector who conceded with some reluctance that no criminal offence appeared to have been committed. He proceeded then to deliver a lecture on the importance of honesty, how in the long run it always paid – and he'd thrown in a lot of stuff about sportsmanship, the trouble to which the police, the race committee and other authorities had been put, the gravity of the deception practised on the sponsors, the other competitors and the media – the incredible and unnecessary worry caused to the young woman's parents, and so on and so forth.

Anxious to get down to Falmouth to see the girl, fearful of prolonging the proceedings, unhappily aware that most of what the Inspector was saying was true, he had expressed his sincere regret and asked if he might go.

The Inspector said he could but he was to keep the police informed of his whereabouts on a daily basis as he might be required for further questioning. 'In the meantime you'd better get along to Falmouth.' For the first time the dark eyes were friendly. 'It seems the young lady wants to see you. Can't think why after what they tell me she's written in her diary.'

'What's that?'

'You'd better ask the lady. It's confidential. We'll be returning it to her.'

A strange sound woke him. The train was crossing a bridge; below it the winding course of the river shone brightly in the darkness. He couldn't understand why until he realized that it was reflecting moonlight. Beyond it, in the distance, he could see the lights of a town. He looked at his watch: five minutes past nine – another fifteen minutes and they'd be there. Would the hospital let him see her now or would he have to wait until morning? It didn't really matter. Either way they would be together soon.

He wondered how she would look, what they would say to each other when they met? The prospect filled him with exciting tingles of expectation, something he couldn't really define. The sort of feeling, perhaps, that he'd experienced in boyhood when looking forward to something very special.

His thoughts switched to Tessa's letter. So VS was going to get a divorce. Well, well . . . poor Mrs VS. Or *was* it poor Mrs VS? Perhaps she was pleased. It might have been her idea. Whatever it was he hoped for Tessa's sake that things would work out all right, that she'd be happy. At least that no one would be unhappy. He hoped that very much because he felt a little guilty about the large slice of happiness which seemed to be coming his way.

The future? More delivery voyages, more free-lancing. The book? He'd given that little thought in the last few days, yet it had been an important factor behind his decision to continue in the race. It was the book which had enabled him to convince himself that he had a valid reason for carrying on. Not that he'd ever thought *Sunboro Beauty* would lead the field, but now that she had the book would be enormously helped and Billings' press conference should give it the most fantastic advance publicity.

The notes would make writing that much easier – add a touch of realism. He thought of the Inspector's remark and wondered what it was she'd written. Evidently un-complimentary. He'd often been tempted to use the duplicate key and read her notes. He was glad now that he hadn't. She would never have forgiven him if he'd done that.

He thought of all they had been through together on the long voyage. What a super girl she'd proved to be. A splendid seaman and a marvellous person. He'd got used to having her around. Couldn't really imagine life without her. He thought of the letter: *You terrify me and I don't trust you.*

Didn't trust him? Why, for God's sake? He had never lied to her. Fancy doing a mad thing like taking to the life-raft. She must have been out of her mind. Of course he'd been beastly to her at times. Initially it had been sheer gut reaction, but looking back he realised that as the voyage went on it had become more than that. He had suffered enormous damage at her hands – it would have been absurd if she'd got away with that scot-free – so he'd exacted retribution and, as it turned out, rather more than he'd intended. He supposed that had in part been due to resentment, to extreme exhaustion, to the tension that went with it and the fantasies it induced in a tired mind.

Would she – or Tessa for that matter – ever understand what had driven him? A man was sometimes forced by circumstance and his nature to do things of which he profoundly disapproved. It was easy to say he had freedom of choice, but had he? Surely at the end of the day one's make-up was such that alternatives were illusions, the choice selecting itself, a process beyond control?

With a sense of guilt he recalled how he had kept her in ignorance of his plans for the finish. That had all been part of the retribution. He could so easily have told her of his intention to get her up on deck shortly before doing the U-turn – a startling revelation at the finish, meaty drama for the book.

After what had happened between them, all they had endured together, she must have known his feelings? Or was she so insensitive that he had to spell them out in black and white? How could she have doubted his promise to get her safely home?

In the letter she'd said: *Funny, I believe I care for you in spite of everything.*

Well, that was what really mattered; their feeling like that about each other. Nothing else equalled that in importance.

The future? There would be time to discuss that on the voyage to Martinique – the delivery trip which Tim Baxter had arranged for him. He would ask her to come along as crew. She'd like that – the Azores and West Indies again, down through the Trades and Tropics, fair winds and sunshine. A few days relaxing in Martinique, then fly home. It would be marvellous, absolutely marvellous.

It never occurred to him that she might refuse.